WHO'S YOUR DADDY?

Edited By

ERIC SUMMERS

Herndon, VA

Published in the United States by STARbooks Press
PO Box 711612, Herndon, VA 20171

Many thanks to graphic artist John Nail for the cover design. Mr. Nail may be reached at: tojonail@bellsouth.net.

Printed in the United States

Herndon, VA

STARbooks Press Titles by Eric Summers

CONTENTS

DADDY DEAREST
By R. W. Clinger

"Oh, Daddy," I moan, feeling Tanner's blond-gray stubble against my youthful rump as he slides his tongue into my core, removes it, and slides it back in. I pull my ass cheeks apart for his further exploration of my pink-tight inside and let him rock my world again. I become dizzy, lost under his spell, perhaps overexcited with his man-play, hungry and zealous for his skin.

He gently pulls off and away from me, but just for a second, and he says along the splay of my back, "You make me feel twenty years younger, Bobby."

"Thank you, Daddy. I'm glad I do something hot for you," escapes my grinding teeth as I prepare myself for more of his tongue, or whatever else he wants to shove inside my bottom, pleasuring the both of us, fully.

A light spanking alarms me. Tanner gently scolds me for being a naughty boy. How dare I use metal hangers in my closet! How dare I hide his Scotch! How dare I accidentally douse his screenplay with lighter fluid, so he can't study his lines for his new movie! Shame on me. Such a bad, bad Bobby.

"Oh, Daddy ... forgive me," I whisper, role playing again, caught up in the moment. While leaning over his leather sofa in his office, I rub my ass against his chin's scruff, overwhelmed with pleasure. My hairless balls thwap against his chin, driving both of us mad. I beg, "Put your cock inside me, Daddy ... Bang my bottom. You know bad Bobby wants it."

Academy Award winner Tanner Lewis teases me, a mature and skilled lover at fifty-five. His tongue darts into my tight hole, pulls out, and darts in again. Two groans escape his mouth as his fingers pull my ass apart. A third moan is heard as he toys with the hairless swinging

1

balls between my muscular legs, licking and lapping at the two in a feisty manner. Again, he provides me with a light spanking. This time he whispers, "How could you ruin my Brooks Brothers shirt? ... How could you wreck your Mercedes after I just bought it for you?"

I see myself in the narrow mirror on the opposite side of the room: twenty-two years old, military looks, a fresh Gulf veteran, Pacific-blue eyes, clean shaven, onyx-black hair, muscled shoulders, a zigzag-scar through my right eyebrow, dog tags swinging from my neck. Officer B. Sheldon is hot. No, steamy-sweet looking. Rough around the edges. Sexy as hell. A spitfire who likes older men, particularly ones who look and act just like Tanner Lewis.

The A-list actor reaches between my legs and begins to milk my eight inches of solid cock, which hangs down to the floor, ready to shoot its creamy load. Daddy's palm strokes the udder in a quick and steady up and down motion, attempting to get me off. Again, he licks my center with his outstretched tongue, driving me wild. And again, he spanks me with his free hand, scolding me for being a bad, bad Bobby, threatening to send me back into the Army, if I don't start behaving myself.

My role playing continues, just the way he wants it. I call over my right shoulder, "I'm sorry, Daddy ... Forgive me, Daddy Dearest," and ride his fingers with my cock, building up the finest orgasm, willing to spray sticky juice all over the back of his leather sofa.

"I'm going to make you shoot, Bobby," he warns, continuing the north and south movement on my tool, prepared to drain it all over his Berber carpet.

Consecutive strokes to my throbbing joint and his speedy licks to my pink hub catapult me into a position of no return. Limitless vibrations begin to ski throughout my core, and I gasp for oxygen, having the wind knocked out of me.

Behind me, busy with his diligent work, Daddy spanks me again. He shoves his tongue into my system as far it will go, drills my insides, pulls out, and demands, "Shoot it on my face, Bobby ... Let your gunk fly."

As if on cue, feeling fervent and on fire, I spin around, stand erect, and face my current caretaker. One final ripple cascades through my torso and prompts me to murmur, "Creaming ... Just for you."

White jiz spirals out of my untouched hose and decorates his handsome face. The stuff splashes against his Hollywood features, painting his five-o'clock stubble and wrinkleless neck. Becoming spent, I stand over him and growl with satisfaction.

Daddy reaches around me and spanks my bottom, calls me his sex-toy and American hero, and instructs, "Lick it up now."

His command is not demeaning; in fact, I get off on it. Cordially, I lean over and take in his middle-aged good looks: sexy crow's feet around his eyes, narrow pink lips, dull-blue eyes, a three-hundred-dollar haircut for his bottled-blond coif, broad shoulders and a corded neck. Hungry for my own spunk, I lick up the sticky goods from his right cheek, mouth and neck. Every drop of the ooze is consumed, leaving his flesh spotless.

Sadly, we are interrupted by Josh Martin, Tanner's pesky little weasel agent. Josh has a key and finds his way into the city apartment, witnesses our naked twosome, and chortles, "Am I too late for lunch, gentlemen?"

Josh even looks like a weasel: thin face, sharp little teeth, sunken and ominous eyes. His unannounced arrival is no surprise. Weasel is always invading our lives. He says to Daddy, "Tanner, we need to talk about your current role in the thriller *Whiplash* and ..."

Daddy and I bolt to his bedroom for cover: dicks swing between our legs, and the stink of male sex wafts behind our naked bodies. Both of us giggle like little boys during our escape.

Once behind the closed door, he takes me into his arms, plants a kiss on my right nipple, pulls away, and praises me with: "Bobby was a very good boy."

"You weren't so bad yourself."

He touches two fingers to my lips, provides an endearing smile of maturity, and promises, "Later, we can find the time to finish what we started."

Daddy and I have an agreement in our lives. I use his money, houses, fast cars, and take trips around the world. In return, he has every square inch of my tasty skin, anytime he wants it. Toss in a little dose of Hollywood, the paparazzi, visits by Lady GaGa, Rupert Everett, Neil Patrick Harris, and Christopher Rice, and I have a pretty good life. Of course, I can live without all the bullshit that goes with it, too: the fame, Josh the Weasel, no privacy, and Daddy's busy schedule. But hey, I have to take the good with the bad. Just like everyone else in the world.

This is the life. The bomb. My meal ticket for the time being that off-ers all the sex I want, alcohol, drugs, clothes, cars, and trips around the world. The actor is a great supplier of my needs. My boyfriend for now. Someone I appreciate and devour and hope that he keeps me around for a very long time.

Daddy has rules, though: Don't steal from me. Don't embarrass me in the Hollywood scene. Don't fuck around on me.

And, he warns me, "If you don't follow these simple rules, your ass is out on the street. There are a thousand other queers like you who would die to be in your position."

He's right. All the young gay guys (and a number of straight ones) in this uppity region of the world want a sliver of Daddy's life. So, I'm fortunate, and I win. Everyone has fifteen minutes of fame; this just happens to be my time.

Two days later, I honestly don't know where Daddy and I are. Somewhere in the Caribbean. On location for a scene in *Whiplash*. Daddy has a break from his three scenes, and we're on his private beach, relaxing in a shaded cabana. The temperature rocks at ninety-two degrees with some heavy duty humidity. A light wind blows off the blue-green ocean, attempting to cool our hot and sticky bodies.

Daddy's thinking is so one-dimensional most of the time: sex, food, alcohol, limited drugs, and bad acting. Standing to my right, he peels out of his tropical shirt and drops it to the white sand beneath us. He exposes his solid chest covered in a grey-blond pelt, hard nipples, rounded pecs and firm looking abs. Truth is he still looks good for his age. Marco Sandella, his physical trainer and dietician, deserves a medal. Goes to show you, no matter how old you are, you can still look sexy as hell. Daddy slips out of his Nautica trunk, pushing it down to the white sand, and says, "Duty calls, Bobby."

I rise to the occasion from my beach chair, drop my own Rufskin trunk to the sand, step between the actor's sun-baked legs, and fall to my knees. In a matter of seconds, I find it appropriate to open my mouth up like a little bird and consume his erect beef, swallowing all nine inches of it down the back of my throat. It glides smoothly into my center, falling and falling inside, offering pleasure for the both of us.

Daddy plants his palms on my shoulders, bolts his hips toward my mouth, and plugs my throat with his swollen throbber. All nine inches of his inflated tube slides down the back of my throat, pulls out, and slides down again. Above me, the older gentleman huffs and puffs, excited with his blowjob. He mutters, "Eat it all up. Be the bad little Bobby you are."

No, he is not porn quality, even if he has millions of dollars in the bank. Daddy is alluringly handsome. His face is wise looking with its dull-blue eyes, flared nostrils and semi-parted lips. Two grunts escape the man as I blow him. Three more grunts surface as my fingers play with the salt-and-pepper colored hairy balls between his thighs. Conditioned by my touch, he becomes chaotic with his movement above me. He thrusts his hips into my face, slaps his balls off of my chin, and holds onto my shoulders for dear life. Continuing to lodge his tool into the back of my head, he attempts to choke me, busy at work.

What transpires during the next few minutes on his private beach is something that I'm used to. When I was in the Gulf, military fuck buddies knew I would blow them for mediocre payments. I had a list of older closeted men, mostly higher ranking individuals such as commanders, corporals, and sergeants who liked to have their skin kissed, licked and sucked by a just-out-of-high-school pretty boy like me. These older men in the desert used me for my blowing services, among other sexual favors. In return, I had the best novels to read, the finest cigarettes to smoke, booze to drink, money in my chamo, and any kind of drug or other accommodations I wished. My experience with daddies has inevitably landed me everything I've always wanted, and Tanner Lewis is no exception, falling under my mouth spell.

Daddy Dearest mumbles, "You have to stop ... If you don't stop, I'm going to explode in your mouth."

Like a good little Army brat, I retreat from his dog, wipe my mouth off with the back of my right hand, and look up and along his hairy chest. I meet my naïve stare with his experienced one and simply ask, "Are you going to fuck me, Daddy?"

A striking smile surfaces on his face, and he replies, "Hard and fast ... I hope you're up for it. Now, get on your knees."

Skilled meat slides into my rump with a quick bolt, shocking me with pleasure. Daddy hangs onto my hips and says over my back, "Be a man and take all nine inches of it, Bobby. No holding back today. And don't cry this time, even if it hurts."

I consume what he has to offer: two inches ... six inches ... eight inches ... all nine inches of his hard stick jab into my bottom. Tears swell at the corners of my eyes with desired pain. The blanket covering the sand leaves nothing to grip for balance. One steady thrust pushes me forward, then a second, and a third. A rush of bliss waves through my torso as I ride his pole. Delight is found as our combined friction builds. I whimper with satisfaction and murmur, "Daddy ... don't stop. Please, Daddy Dearest, don't stop."

Another speedy and tempest-like bolt occurs to my center. I moan with deep fulfillment. Thump after sturdy thump corkscrews my insides and causes definitive enjoyment. The blasts continue for the next eight minutes. His fingertips dig brusquely into my hips. Tears drip down and along my boyish cheeks because of blissful pain.

Spanks ensue on my bottom: light and airy strokes with just a tinge of agreeable sting. I yelp from his vociferous palm-slaps and yell over my right shoulder, "Again, Daddy! ... Spank me again!"

As requested, he listens. One gentle spank turns into three, and he calls over the splay of my muscled and sweaty back, "You're such a bad little Bobby."

Continuous bolts gratify my bottom. His steady motion is a thrill ride for me, robust with elation. Like any good man consuming another man, he reaches his apex of erotic joy and murmurs, "Creaming."

Quickly, his junk is removed from my bottom and the plastic covering his nine inches is lost on the beach. I imagine Daddy behind me with his right palm and fingers wrapped around his upright buoy, stroking it from base to cap in a lively manner. I feel his hot sweat fly off his gliding torso and sting my flesh. I hear a grunt and groan and ... ooze arcs out of his cock in three long strings, decorating my back, left shoulder, and spinal column, sizzling against my skin.

Unexpectedly, our connection does not conclude. Following his spray-session, Daddy explains, "Let's get you off." He pulls me up against his hairy chest, sticking my cream-covered back to his abs and pecs, and reaches around me with his right hand. My eight inches of flag is genially manhandled and stroked with bountiful gratification. He whispers into my right ear, "Blow it, Bobby ... Don't hold back."

Mercilessly, I rock my beef into his palm, making myself believe it's his rump. As his left hand reaches around my core and discovers my chest, his fingers fondle a nipple. Light twisting and pinching progresses, and I feel an unstoppable orgasm whip throughout my chiseled core. Hot goose bumps dance along my skin's surface and ... scorching sap ejaculates from my extension of pulsing rod. The goo twists and turns through the air in acrobatic grace, ornamenting the beach blanket and the white sand beyond its edge.

Once euphoria is discovered between us, Daddy pulls me up and off the blanket, spins me around, congeals me against his chest, lathers my mouth with his tongue and lips, pulls away, and confesses, "You took it like a man."

I longingly caress his whiskered cheek and add, "You gave it to me like one."

Again, Daddy plunges his tongue into my mouth, melting my world.

# # # # #

My relationship continues with Daddy Dearest. I have a stack of black-and-whites to prove that we're intimate: Bobby pinned over the kitchen table in Santa Barbara; Bobby pressed against the bathroom floor with the superstar's mouth nestled against his bulbous ass; Bobby being sprayed down with the A-list's man-juice in the New York City apartment; Bobby being blown by Daddy in the Aspen château while on a skiing trip; and others, twenty-seven prints in all and …

Daddy ends up in my three-person shower one morning. He soaps up my ripped torso, stands behind me under the warm spray, and lathers my skin and pores. His right hand finds the throbber between my legs and toys with my balls. He applies kisses to the length of my neck while he strokes me off. Eventually, he pulls his lips up to my earlobe, and now my ear, and inquires, "Bobby, do you know what I'm doing back here?"

"As I matter of fact I do."

"I'm teasing you. Maybe someday you can do this to me."

I'm game. Someday can't come soon enough. I really want to position myself behind him, straddle his legs, and push everything I have into his hole. Whether it be in my shower, over a sofa, or while he kneels on his bed, I really don't care. As long as the opportunity arises and I get to fuck him.

Once our sexcapade in the shower ends (Daddy stroking me off while gently biting my neck) he asks, "What are you doing today?"

"Gym stuff. A workout. Maybe a run. You want to come along?"

He says he has things to do, which I get. And he adds, "We'll hook-up later. I'm going to need some more sex from you."

Indeed he will, and I will, too.

Approximately two hours later, I'm at a swanky gym lifting weights. While sweating and bulging, some guy who looks exactly like Anderson Cooper saunters up to my bench and stands over me. The man is handsome and the perfect age for me; another daddy ready to eat up my skin and take care of me. Again, I go over Daddy's rules inside my head and decide that I'm ready to tell the stranger I'm involved, to stop looking at me in a sexual manner, and go away.

The guy says, "You know who I am?"

"Anderson Cooper from CNN."

"I'm flattered. Thanks for the lift in my day."

I use a towel to remove sweat from my chest and ask, "Who are you then?"

"Ash Daily ... from *Gossip*."

A dirty rag in Hollywood that gives away stars' secrets. I frown and say, "Go away. I don't have time for you."

"It's not that easy to get rid of me," he confesses.

What is it about older men that I find so damn appealing? How come I melt in their presence and obey their thirsts? What exactly comes over me, prompting me to feel easy, windblown ... sexually needy?

Helplessly, I eye Ash up and down: sharp nose, tiny mouth, the slightest aging around his eyes. A navy-colored Rufskin hugs his hips and a mound of delicious looking cock hides underneath. I study his bare chest: curly cues of grey-white hair lining his navel, strawberry-pink nipples, and thin, almost unnoticeable wrinkles at the base of his neck.

Ash winks at me, comprehending my attraction to him. How easily we can discreetly slip away from the gym and share some man-with-man action back at his Hills home. This doesn't happen, though. I'm a very good Bobby and keep my composure together. No matter what creamy explosion occurs within my own gym shorts, I will not follow Ash home and have my way with his desirable skin.

He interviews me in a rather casual manner, attempting to seduce me with his kind appearance. "Do you live with Tanner Lewis?"

I nod my head.

Ash takes mental notes, a skilled journalist, clever at his trade. "Are you his houseboy?"

"Of course not. I'm his assistant."

"Are you Tanner's boyfriend?"

I roll my eyes, disgusted with the man.

Ash gets my drift. He leans into me, gently collides his fingers with the mound of Nike-covered protein between my legs, and asks, "You won't break, will you?"

"Never."

"Adorable and faithful to the end, aren't you?"

"Always," I whisper, standing. In a matter of seconds, I vanish from Ash's side and head to the showers; fortunately, he doesn't follow me.

Daddy Dearest meets me at a posh café for lunch in Beverly Hills. We have salads and vodka-heavy drinks for our meal. He is all smiles, glowing from ear to ear. He looks younger by ten years, freshly sexed ... something. Dull-blue eyes stare across the two-person table at me, taking in my young skin. Obviously Daddy wants to tell me something important.

I ask, "What?" like any twenty-two-year-old smartass, feeling uncomfortable.

"You had an interview with one of those disgusting rags yesterday, didn't you?"

I'm an honest guy, always willing to tell the truth. I nod my head and reply, "I did."

"I appreciate it that you didn't out me." He is so proud of me, beaming with a smile. He adds, "You could have thrown me under the bus if you wanted. The person interviewing you is a friend of mine ... and he was testing you."

"I never want to hurt you, Daddy. I like you too much ... And, I think you like me."

He nods his head in an appropriate manner. "I do, Bobby ... Now, guess what your payment is for good behavior?"

I have no idea. Honestly, I don't.

Daddy pushes a Tiffany box across the table. "Open it."

As instructed, I open the light blue box. Inside is a new condom. I pull the square out and hold it. "What's this?"

"Just a part of your gift."

"What's the other part?" I ask, fully intrigued.

He leans across the table and whispers, "You've always wanted to fuck me, haven't you?"

The temptation has always been present. Just the thought of my youthful dick in his experienced ass makes the joint between my legs firm up with newfound excitement. I admit, "I have ... Always. But you've never let me."

He points to the condom and beams a greedy smile. "Tonight is your lucky night, Bobby. I want you to bang my ass for as long and hard as you want."

Fingering the unopened plastic, I'm blown away with his decision. Thoughts of my palms pressed against his hips cause a few bubbles of pre-ooze to leak into my chinos. A heartfelt smile takes over my face, and I confess, "I'm going to make it hurt."

He grins from ear to ear, and retorts, "I was hoping you would say that."

Good boys always finish first; this is my motto. And good behavior always promotes good things, like having Daddy's rear pressed against my pelvis, riding my extension of horny beef inside his ...

Approximately eight hours after our lunch, I have Daddy right where I want him: on his back inside his bedroom with his legs spread wide open and his hairy hole ready for a freshman pounding. I grasp his knobby ankles with my hands, separate his legs, and say down to him, "Last chance to stop this."

Daddy glows on the bed, shakes his head, and responds, "Give it to me. Make me howl."

The instruction causes him to sound like he's begging for my timber to be jammed inside his rump. Like a good Bobby, I do as I'm told, release my left hand from his right ankle, wrap its palm around my swollen rod and direct the hard flesh inside his system.

When three of the eight inches of my cock enter his hub, a murmuring groan escapes his mouth. The actor closes his eyes, grits his teeth, and clenches his fists into the bed's expensive sheets.

Another three inches of my pole poke into him, which are immediately followed by the last two inches. I let my firm stick lie still inside his core, eventually provide a gentle twist against his hairy opening, and promptly pull out of his hub.

Daddy lets out a whimper. Tears roll out of the corners of his eyes. He gasps from my work and begs, "More, Bobby ... Be bad with me ... Please."

I don't know what comes over me and rush my weight into him again ... and again ... and again, pulverizing his ass. Sweat builds on my chest and thighs. My head begins to spin with enamored lust, and I become dizzy, lost in the moment. I ask, "Who's the Daddy now?"

"You are," he groans. "You're Daddy now."

My strength and movement heightens. Passion is found, and I keep banging his bottom with everything I've got to give him: prosaically, vigorously, without being timid. I ride his hole in a masculine manner, clinging my body to his, pulling away, and clinging to him again. My motion continues to drive him into a state of oblivion, and he becomes breathless, almost unconscious, but evidently enjoying my ride.

"Tell me again who I am," I whisper over his sweat-slicked chest, rushing my weight into him, pulling out, and rushing into his insides again.

"Daddy," he moans in pleasure. "You're my Daddy."

I reach down between his legs, strap a palm around his massive nine inches, and begin to pleasure him with a few north and south strokes.

He lets out a roar of gratification, turning a rose red hue in his cheeks and forehead. Effectively, the actor lifts his hips once, obviously ready to burst his pent freight. Following this single hip-thrust, another roar of satisfaction exits his mouth. In a matter of seconds, gooey-white streams of seed shoot out of his nail and splatter against his torso. The shit clings to his tight and hairy stomach, and his pecs are ornamented with his own cream.

Although he becomes spent, I'm selfish and continue my task. Bolt after bolt continues to mar his bottom. My constant plunging builds a delightful rhythm. Sweat flings off of my shoulders and nipples, searing my keeper's skin. The heat between us is still volcanic and inexorable.

To my surprise, the actor chants up to me, "Shoot it all over me, Daddy ... Do it."

On cue, feeling a pivotal tremor sweep throughout my nucleus, knowing that I am about to expend my load, I swiftly pull out of his rump, lose the plastic protection, and begin to man-handle myself with exuberant skill.

Handy gratification changes to desirable chaos. Seven fist-humps turn into a dozen. Two longing moans are now heard within the bedroom. I arch my back, aim my dog at his splay of sticky and sweaty chest and … sap fires out of my shooter in elongated cords. The ooze mixes with the actor's juice, combining in pools on his steamy flesh.

Following my blow, Daddy pulls me down to his skin and says he's going to keep me around just so I can fuck him whenever he wants me to. He kisses my nose, a cheek, and my lips. He ruffles my hair, and adds, "You make a good Daddy, Bobby."

I know he's playing, toying with me, and I enjoy it. "Glad you liked it. Role-reversal is kind of fun."

He pushes onxy-colored hair out of my eyes and smiles up at me. The Hollywood heartthrob whispers, "You're special … Someone I could fall for."

"Don't get all crazy-involved with me. I'm just a fling for you. Other guys my age are dying to get your cock inside them."

"I'm too old for flings. You're the only one I want."

He makes me melt. Something happens between us that I don't fully understand because maybe I'm too young and won't comprehend what he's saying for years to come. Daddy calls me his pet, his livewire of fun, his soul mate and …

I cling to his skin, breathing heavily. Our lips combine, and he keeps my sweaty torso against his own. The hug is intimate and real, and I can barely move under his strength. Truth is I don't want to go anywhere.

DAMIANI CUFF-LINKS TO A PO'BOY
By Derrick Della Giorgia

I will confess it took me a good thick thirty seconds to get it. My English, after ten years in New York was much better than any other Italian's I knew – so my American friends said anyway – but the rest of my life spent in the heel of the boot still interfered when things got too local. "N'Awlins. N'Aaaawliins." I kept repeating to myself, making sure nobody from the tables around me could hear my phonetics exercise. N'Awlins stood for New Orleans. Of course! A huge smile of satisfaction formed on my face now that I could finally go through the menu and decide what I wanted to eat and drink. It was my first time in the jazz city, and I owed it all to my hard work. When it was announced that the Neuroscience conference was going to be held in New Orleans, I couldn't believe it. It was usually the boring San Diego or the lifeless Washington to host the greatest minds from all over the world during this annual event, when every research scientist showed his results and commented on them with the colleagues that studied similar things. I was very proud of my project on the involvement of a serotonin receptor subtype in the pathogenesis of anxiety and could not wait to present my results at the conference in Louisiana. At age fifty-five, I had finally accomplished what I'd been dreaming of my whole life: move to the States, direct my own laboratory and produce data of extreme relevance to the neuroscience community. I was eager to celebrate all that in the most beautiful city of the United States. N'Awlins.

The weather was perfect. A little paradise. Every noise in the French Quarter melted perfectly with the narrow streets, the balconies submersed by the plants and kept alive by the big wooden fans, the occasional piano notes evaporating out of the windows, the sweet slowness of the people walking. If I loved New York for crumbling and dispersing me at the feet of its skyscrapers, I adored New Orleans for concentrating all my emotions with its rich net of sidewalks, corners and allies. I could write a book about it already, and my plane had only landed two hours before.

"Po'boys …" I knew that one! It sounded so sexy to me, too. I wanted to eat a po'boy … bite the po'boy … taste the southern flavor. I had picked the most famous gay bar – as it was advertised in a local magazine – a couple of blocks from Bourbon street and its early morning smell of puke and piss before the bleach canceled the signs of the night feast. I wondered if the fact that one could drink in the street was really the only reason why young Americans loved old New Orleans. That was what I heard! Perhaps, they didn't realize that it was the only American city where French was still spoken? The only city that named its streets also in Spanish and French, besides English? Where superstition and religion were so mixed you couldn't separate one from the other? Those were my thoughts as I kept absorbing more and more of the jazz city. I could be a boring nerd; I was aware of that, but I was also capable of switching to a kinky and domineering master as long as I had a nice young smooth body under my hands. I loved exactly the opposite of what I saw in the mirror. Fifty-five, six-three, sexy 100 percent Italian, big hands, great brain, hairy on my chest and my legs – I had learned to shrink my stats to a single line, fruit of my sleepless weekends spent in the chat-rooms in the attempt of finding company after twelve hours of neurons and pipettes. I loved unexpected sex, unthinkable places, unimaginable boys, being begged and faked innocence and inexperience. I loved boys that wanted to be taught something, minds that could recognize my savoir-faire, my knowledge and my hunger for young ass.

"Are you ready to order?" The waiter I had already noticed surprised me as I was concentrated on the fried oyster po'boy, but there were at least ten more po'boys to evaluate. My table was in the north corner of the garden and slightly protected by a huge green plant I'd never seen before. That was why I hadn't seen the twink coming.

"Actually, not yet. But, I'll have a Mint Julep in the meantime. Please." The sun of 11:00 am was piercing the garden, and the warmth had made me thirsty. Plus, I had all day to have fun and get drunk; the conference started the day after in the afternoon. I put my coat in the suitcase – to hide the winter I came from – and undid my tie, showing off my custom made light blue shirt and my Damiani cuff-links. Then, I took a long hard look at the petite body in front of me. I didn't have time for regrettable misunderstandings. I wanted some, and that waiter was the closest available merchandise. I didn't let him turn his back on me before he noticed my gelid stare – as my young assistants usually referred to my penetrating blue eyes – was about to invade his most intimate privacy.

"Here is your Mint Julep, Sir." His voice returned with an insecure tone. He looked as if he wasn't sure what to make of me yet; he was noticeably intrigued by my manners and figure, but he was caught unprepared by my age. The kid must have been twenty something, totally unaware of anything happening outside his bar or his pants.

"Thank you. Aaaand …"

"Are you ready to order your food or do you need some more time?" He interrupted me without being able to avoid staring at my hands and my upper arms. Especially my deltoids and biceps when they were activated to grab the drink. He was willing to serve me; the idea was still forming in his head, but his body had already spoken.

"I think I'll have the fried oyster po'boy. It sounds very interesting." I folded the menu and gave it back to him, exclusively for the pleasure of seeing his eyes freeze on me again when my arms moved closer to him. He was definitely an easy prey. Youngish clean boy, green eyes, brown mid-length hair, well kept body, perfectly fitting the sunny easy afternoon ahead of me.

"It is very good, indeed. Anything else, Sir?" He moved his head backwards a bit, and the sun hit his eyes, reviving their green and revealing some light freckles on the sides of his delicate nose. He squinted and pursed his uncertain lips.

"That's all for now. Thank you."

"My name is Sean, if you need me. I'll be right back with your po'boy." He turned and walked back inside, across the almost empty garden. His skinny legs moved elegantly in a very masculine way, and his little ass followed them like a green fruit.

After exterminating the po'boy – which was a very satisfying experience – and halfway into my third Mint Julep, my only thought was trying to get Sean's ass. Or a blow job, a hand job, something! I was drunk. With my bare feet on the chair in front of me, I let my left hand go up and down the bulge that my grey suit didn't seem capable of hiding anymore. I picked the drinks menu from under the glass of water I hadn't touched and positioned it on my thighs, to protect my genital privacy. Safer as I felt in that little corner of paradise I had provided myself, I shut my eyes and tuned my ears to the chirping birds all around me. My left hand pressing harder and harder on the flesh pushing in the opposite direction. For a second, I thought about getting my cock out and jerking off right there, as if I'd been invested with some sort of special power. What was life good for, if one couldn't satisfy his most basic needs in the most inappropriate situations? It made me happy to think I'd reached happiness. My foreskin was slightly pushed back in the movements of that hidden erection, and my trimmed pubes got trapped in between the expanding parts. I opened my eyes and fixed the problem with my left thumb, as I held the menu with my right. I wanted someone to bite. I searched for Sean with my head, and from far away, he noticed me. He trotted toward me and pressed play on his recorded restaurant-101 speech.

"How was it? Would you like to order anything else?"

"I would like another drink, but I can't make my mind up." I made it clear I was tortured by the problem and never moved the menu or my left hand from the overheated area of my body. When my erection had reached an extension that was easily noticeable, I indicated a drink with my right index and asked, "Is this one as sweet as Mint Julep?"

"Hmm …. which one is it? ... let me see …" And since I didn't move an inch from my obscene position, he sat on the chair next to me and bent over me to read about the drink I was asking about. He felt uncomfortable enough to make my mind blow up. His hair smelled like herbal shampoo, and on his arms, my favorite vein showed up, unexpectedly. They were not muscular at all, just fit, and I wouldn't have imagined in a million years that he could display such a brachial vein, spontaneously.

"I would say it is sweet, Sir." He nodded and stared at me waiting for a decision. His whole slender body unstable for the excitement.

"I'll get that one then, please. And another thing. Do you know where can I find cigarettes around here?" I lifted my hand, exposing my real problem.

"Next block. There's a store that sells them. I can offer you one now if you don't mind smoking menthol." He put down on the table his worn out order book and reached in his pocket, igniting my desire even more with that wormlike movement of his torso and legs.

"That's so nice of you. Thank you. I'll have a menthol." I grabbed it and put it in my mouth. The only other guy in the garden had left, and I pretended undivided attention now.

"Where are you from, Sir?" He surrendered to my arrogance, complacent.

"Italy."

"Nice. I figured you weren't from here." He looked at my face, but also quickly checked below my waist.

"Do you like to suck Italian cock?" I shot out without hesitation, responding to my bodily need of sex. "You must like to suck Italian cock, 'cuz I would love for you to suck mine right now."

"Wow … that was direct!" He kept holding his left hand with his right, in a very submissive and respectful position.

"Do you? … You look like you could do a very good job, kid!"

"All right … let's say I wouldn't mind sucking yours." He had finally overcome his common sense and given up to my persistence.

"You are more than welcome." I pointed to my painful swelling with both my hands.

"HERE?" he whispered, loudly.

"I dare you."

"I can't. See me when I get out."

"See this, better." My cock bounced like a flag in no time after I undid my fly, landing on the side dishes part of the menu. Uncontrollable. Swinging with every throb from French fries to the price of coleslaw.

"Do you wanna get me fired?"

"I wanna get you on my cock:" I pulled his hand and ordered him to work. He was short of words and received my stick in his palm, cradling it with his long slender fingers, anxiously looking around not to get caught. "That's nice, light my cigarette now." And as in cheap porn, he obeyed my order.

"I love it."

"Suck on it then."

"I really can't do that here." He shook his head repeatedly.

"Shut up and suck!" I grabbed his hair, and I pulled him down. His mouth was already open half way the trip to my cock and took it in as if willing to swallow it. His humid hole on me felt like a cigarette after a thirteen-hour flight – much more intense than the one I was smoking; his head rested in my hands as I held him in a way that I could stare at his green eyes as he worked my shaft and licked my sperm nest. I directed him as I wanted, making sure he passed his lips from my foreskin to my head very slowly, so I could feel the tension generated by the circle of tight flesh formed by his mouth. I kept pushing him down and lifting him up, accordingly to my respiration and taking advantage of his light body. My puppy was a good one and quickly learned to use his hands to cling on to my belt and my knees in a desperate attempt at not drowning. "Meet me in the toilet." I extracted my dick from his warm saliva bag and fixed my pants as I walked away from him cleaning his mouth.

In the little hot room, I took his shirt off and dropped his pants to his ankles. Then, I told him to stand against the white tiles of the old bathroom. He innocently and passively – as I'd instructed him to act – waited for approval. His chest was flat but ripped, and his nipples were of the smallest kind, the way I liked them. Little buttons on his perfect skin. I squeezed them between my thumb and index finger before my hands slid down on his stomach and on the silk light blue shorts he was wearing. His body was completely smooth; no trace of hair anywhere. So smooth you almost wanted to look for hair in the hidden places. He arched his back and got on his foot tips, flexing his calves that from the side looked like little hard balls below his skinny thighs. I caressed his key bones and gave him my first kiss, biting his lower lip as he opened his mouth.

"Fuck me, Sir, please." He finally requested, begging me as if it was his last desire. His cock was hard and pushing against his left leg, so with my hand, I teased his head. On my chest, his white hands searched for the strength and power he'd seen in me.

"I think I have to, kid." I hugged him tight, licked his neck and lifted him in one piece. As our mouths tried to devour each other, I tore his shorts off and helped his knees get on the sink, his face resting on the mirror he found himself smashed against. With the calmness that always accompanied me, I used my Italian shirt to dry up the sweat that the temperature of the N'Awlins toilet had trapped in my chest hair and on my abs.

"I love your hairy chest." He moaned from under the mirror, in which he inspected my naked torso.

"Let me taste this fruit …" His butt cheeks were so small and tight that looked like a hard white peach hiding inside the mighty pit. I put my tongue to work on that fruit and dug inside to get all the juice as he desperately tried to touch himself in that position.

"Put it in. Put it in, now, please."

In no time, the lube he had provided me was smeared all around the edge of his hole, and I was latched on to his bony hips. I dove into his pool. It slid right in without any friction and we automatically adjusted to the new rhythm.

When I foresaw his imminent explosion, I controlled the oscillation of his body with my arms and possessed him even harder.

"Are you still in there, Sean?" A man assaulted us from behind the locked bathroom door.

"YEAAH!" My pupil said, recognizing his boss's voice.

"The fried oyster po'boy for table number seven is waiting for you. Hurry up!"

"YEAAH! Be out in a minute!" He moaned again and sprayed his milk on the mirror.

"Here we go, kid." I announced and sat his ass in the sink to make him receive my cum. He closed his eyes and religiously waited for the hot shower to cover him. Nor I disappointed him, pouring my flow on his chin, his chest, inside his shallow belly button and finishing up rubbing my cock on his thighs.

UNCLE BEN'S WILD RIDE
By Rob Rosen

Uncle Ben drove a truck. That, in a nutshell, was about all I knew of him, besides the fact that he wasn't, in fact, my real uncle. He was my mother's sister's ex-husband. I hadn't seen him in years, not since I was a little kid. Still, I had vivid memories of him. After all, he wasn't like the rest of my family. Not by a fucking long shot. He was, I suppose you'd say, larger than life. Like a lumberjack. A real man's man.

But, he'd dropped out of our world years ago. I assumed, as a trucker, he wasn't well suited for married life. Too much time away from home, away from my aunt, away from us.

So it was with some joy, and a bit of trepidation, that I received a postcard announcing his arrival at my house the following Saturday. He was driving through on his way to points unknown, wanted to stop by to see his favorite nephew. No forwarding address or phone number, so I had little choice in the matter.

Still, I was glad for the opportunity to see him again. And curious. Not to mention nervous as all hell. Why now, after all this time? A lot had changed since our last encounter – most notably, I wasn't a little boy anymore, and I was a man who liked men. What would a trucker have to say about such a thing?

I figured I'd find out soon enough.

He pulled up, as planned, in a gigantic silver truck, blaring the baritone horn to announce his arrival. I opened my front door and waited, my heart beating hummingbird-fast in my chest. He emerged from the cab seconds later, looking much as I'd remembered him, though older, naturally. He, like the truck he road in on, was huge, standing about six-three or so; all of it, from what I could tell, rock solid muscle. His plaid shirt and blue jeans strained at his bulk. His face was still handsome, perhaps a bit wrinkled, but that only added to his presence. As did the salt and pepper beard on his chiseled face and the graying head of hair that poked out from under his baseball cap. But, it was his eyes, those big blue eyes, which I so clearly remembered from my childhood. They crinkled, like Santa Claus's, when he smiled. And boy was he smiling now – from ear to friggin' ear.

"Kenneth!" he shouted, with a wave, as he bounded up the path to my front door.

I waved back and smiled at the behemoth that was barreling down on me. He reached me seconds later with a vice-like bear hug that knocked me breathless. His immense arms easily encircled my significantly slighter body as he lifted me a good foot off the ground. I felt five years old all over again. It was, surprisingly, an enjoyable feeling.

"Uncle Ben," I said, when I'd managed to catch my breath and he'd at last set me down. "It's great seeing you again."

He looked at me from head to toe and smiled. "You, too, Kenneth. But look at you. You've grown some."

I laughed. "Yeah, well, twenty years will do that to a person. Oh, and I go by Ken now. It's not so, um, geeky sounding."

"Geeky? No way. Just look at how handsome you turned out."

I blushed and invited him in. He had to duck and squeeze his arms to his chest to fit through the door. It was like having a Sasquatch over. Suddenly, everything in my house seemed small and insignificant, especially yours truly.

I gave him a quick tour of the place. "You done good, boy," he said, when we'd arrived back in the kitchen, a cup of joe offered and eagerly accepted.

"Can't complain," I said, and then delved right into what I'd been thinking since his arrival. "So, Uncle Ben, what brings you here? It's been a long time."

He didn't answer, at first, choosing instead to sip his brew and stare over at me. At last, he replied, "Yeah, I guess it has been. Sorry for that. I thought it best, you know, so as not to upset your aunt anymore than I already had."

I looked at him, quizzically. "Aunt Phyllis? She's never mentioned you, remarried a few years after you guys got divorced and happy as a clam, as far as I can tell. What did you do that could upset her?" Ah ha, I thought, a family secret. Things seemed to be getting interesting.

Uncle Ben, unfortunately, shifted the subject as if it were a gear in his truck. "You know, I would've dropped by sooner, but this is my first time through these parts. My route just recently got shifted. Your mom told me where you lived, and here I am. Guess it's kind of a surprise, huh? Again, sorry."

"No, it's no problem. Really. I'm glad to see you," I told him, truthfully. Still, he was hiding something. I could see it in his face. "So, you spoke to my mom? She never mentioned it. Strange."

He coughed and wiped his face on his sleeve. "Yeah, well, strange seems to run in the family." It wasn't an insult. We were an oddball collection. I was no exception. Still, he hadn't answered my question, just redirected it. So, for the time being, I gave up asking and simply enjoyed his company.

Uncle Ben had barely changed one iota. He was still the same happy go lucky, big hunk of a man that I'd so fondly remembered. If anything, he was even more endearing. Like a fine wine, he'd improved with age. But, there was some connection between us now that was different. I couldn't quite put my finger on it, but I felt we were more alike, despite our outward appearances.

Hours into our chat, I thought to ask him, "How long will you be in town for? Do you need a place to stay?"

"I have a pick-up tomorrow about an hour from here, and then I'll be on my way. So, I'll only be around tonight. If you're free, we could do dinner, maybe drinks."

"Of course, that would be great," I said. "And I hope you're planning to stay here in my home."

"Well, I usually sleep in my truck, but if it's no inconvenience …"

"None at all. You're always welcome here." He smiled that great, big smile of his, smacking me on the back for good measure.

After dinner, however, I was in for something of a surprise.

"How about a drink, my boy?" he asked, jovially.

I looked around. I knew the neighborhood intimately. Still, I steered him to a bar down the street, rather than to one of my regular haunts.

"Flander's Pub?" he asked, with an evident frown. "What kind of place is this?"

"Um, it's an Irish pub. Are you up for a stout ale?" I gulped at the thought of stepping foot in the place.

"Ale, yes. Here no. Take me to someplace you'd normally go."

"I, um, normally go here."

He looked at me with a grin that said that he clearly didn't believe me. He grabbed my hand in his giant paw and said, "Son, I know. I've always known. Since you were a boy."

My stomach flipped. Since I was a boy? Was I that obvious, even back then? Is that possible? In any case, there was no point denying it. "I suppose those dresses gave me away, huh?"

"And the dolls. But other things, as well," he said, with his heavy arm around my shoulder, leading me away from Flander's Pub.

We walked two more blocks before I said, "Okay, but you asked for it." I led him into The Bear. No, it wasn't necessarily one of the regular places I visited, but I had been there on several occasions before. And, as the name implied, it was a bar for big men. Big men like my uncle. I thought, at least, he'd feel at home.

I wasn't mistaken. No sir, no how.

Uncle Ben, as was to be expected, was an instant hit, with little, old me quickly fading into the background. Oh sure, he tried to keep me in the conversations, but I felt like a kid at Thanksgiving dinner, relegated to the children's table and promptly ignored. It was, however, enjoyable to watch him interact. My uncle was a born schmoozer. He could just as easily have been at a football game or a board meeting.

But, he wasn't; he was at a gay bar.

My mind reeled. Was this the connection I was feeling? Was this some family secret I was left out of? To tell the truth, I hadn't a clue.

"Um, Uncle Ben, it's getting late," I eventually said, after what seemed like hours of drinking and conviviality. "Mind if we head on home? I'm beat."

The other bears fairly growled at my request. Papa bear was holding center stage, and that's where they wanted him to stay. And, from the looks of it, that was fine with Uncle Ben.

"Oh," he said, the smile briefly fading. "Maybe just one more drink, huh, Ken? Why don't you head on out; I'll see you in the morning."

My heart sank, but I smiled just the same, telling him I'd leave the door unlocked. He hugged me and kissed me on the cheek. Seconds later, I was on my way home, full of questions and short on answers.

I was asleep as soon as my head hit the pillow, I didn't, however, stay that way for long. I was awakened by a strange noise. A moaning, it sounded like. I got up to investigate. It was emanating from my guest room. Uncle Ben had returned, and it appeared that he had company, male company at that if I was hearing correctly.

I returned to my room. My head was spinning. Uncle Ben was gay? Or maybe it was a trucker thing. I'd always heard that they got lonely on the road – and any port in the storm, right?

Despite my better judgment, I decided to do a little spying. The guest room was my computer room, but I also had a laptop in my bedroom. My PC had a webcam hooked up to it, and it was always on. Meaning, I could see what it was viewing at all times through my laptop. In other words, I could watch my Uncle Ben. "Bad Ken," I chuckled to myself. "Bad, bad, Ken."

I sat in bed and logged on to my laptop. With a few presses on my keyboard, I was hooked in to my webcam. Uncle Ben left the lights on. The webcam was focused straight ahead, namely at the bed. And there, in crystal clear color, was my uncle going at it with someone I'd seen him talking to at the bar. Both men wore nothing more than their jockstraps and were lying prone on the bed, their mouths meshed together, hands roaming. The other guy was about my uncle's age, maybe a bit younger, it was hard to tell at that angle. He was nice looking, in decent shape, but he was no Uncle Ben – not by a long shot.

Naturally, I found myself staring at my uncle. It was hard to look away, not unlike a train wreck. Only this time, instead of twisted metal, it was twisted muscle; and it was writhing all over my guest bed. Both men were way hairy, both with massive bodies, both hotter than hell, even if one of them was my uncle, albeit through marriage.

I felt a twinge of guilt at what I was doing. Then again, I felt a twinge someplace else, too, and it was overpowering my conscience. I set my laptop to the side, peeled off my underwear, placed the laptop on my knees and grabbed a hold of my swelling cock, my plumb-sized head already leaking salty jizz.

I stared intently at the screen as the men removed each other's jocks. And there, before my very eyes, was my uncle's enormous prick. Like him, it was gigantic and thick. His balls were enormous, too, hanging down until they touched the sheets. Even his companion was in awe, I could see. And let me say, the stranger had nothing to be ashamed of himself, sporting a good seven, thick inches of veined meat. His balls, however, were the type that held close to the body, the kind that were hard to pull on but easy to spank. Luckily, my webcam had a zoom feature. Each cock filled my screen as I scanned back and forth. My own six and a half inches were being furiously pumped as I watched – a flash of tingles riding shotgun up my back.

My uncle went from mouth to neck to tender nipple. He pulled and sucked on them, causing the stranger to arch his back, to moan and gasp. He slapped the guy's chest and made his way down the hairy body to the sweet spot in the middle. On all fours, he took the guys thick prick in his mouth. That, however, was not what I was staring at. I zoomed the webcam to my uncle's wide, hairy ass. His legs were spread, his hair-rimmed asshole and monstrously large, hanging balls swaying while he stroked his rod. My own cock was getting a working as well, my fist pumping the cum up from my balls, sweat now trickling down my face.

Uncle Ben, when he'd had his full of the guy's dick, pounced on my bed and straddled the other guy's face. I couldn't see how much of that huge cock was being sucked in and down, but the guy's cock stayed straight up and hard. Meaning, he was enjoying the offering. Lucky fucker.

And though it seemed clear that Uncle Ben was in control, it was the other guy who was smacking my uncle's hard, hairy ass, repeatedly, as he sucked his cock. And it was the other guy who spit into his hand and worked several fingers up and into my uncle's asshole, pumping it while Ben worked the guy's nipples, torturing them between his thick fingers.

Then, the biggest surprise. Uncle Ben hopped off the bed and out of sight of the webcam. He returned with a condom and a small bottle of lube. It was quickly rolled onto the stranger's dick. My uncle was a bottom, at least for the night. It was a surprise for me, not expected at all; then again, none of this was. Not by a mile.

My uncle squeezed the lube into his upturned palm, then greased his ass up, squatting over the other guy's waiting prick, facing the cam as he did so. Uncle Ben had obviously bottomed before. He placed the guy's rigid cock against his hole and then slowly sat down on it, until the entire dick was fully entrenched up his ass. A look of pure joy spread across my uncle's handsome face, his gray mane shaking from side to side, his broad chest quivering, belly tight as a drum. I groaned and pulled on my balls as I watched him get fucked, hard and fast.

Uncle Ben rode that cock for all it was worth, pumping his ass up and down and up and down as he played with a nipple in one hand and his enormous prick in the other. The smile never left his face. I watched as his huge balls bounced and then progressively grew tighter. He was close, as was I.

When he was ready to come, he ground his cheeks into the guy's crotch, bucking and rolling his ass around as he stroked his thick hunk of meat, growling all the while, eyelids fluttering. And then, as the first stream of white spunk erupted from his dick, he threw his head back and moaned, rattling the very walls, the sound rocketing through my speakers and then my head.

And then, I watched as his cock bounced and shook and convulsed. He spurted over and over again, thick cream spewing from that gigantic cock of his. Within seconds, I forcefully came as well. I moaned one last time, sending a gush of warm cum up and over my furry stomach and chest. He collapsed on the stranger, I on my bed. Newly exhausted, I shut my laptop off and placed it back on my nightstand. Once again, I fell fast asleep.

When I awoke the next morning, my house was silent. I scraped the dried cum off my stomach, feeling just a stab of guilt. Then I beat off thinking about what I'd witnessed the night before. It was a strange dichotomy of shame and pleasure. Mostly the latter.

I took a quick shower and stumbled into the kitchen. Uncle Ben was up, alone, fixing us both some much-needed coffee.

"Did you have a good time last night, Uncle Ben?" I asked, not facing him.

"Yep, sure did," he said. "Those were some mighty nice guys. By the way ..." he paused as he poured the java.

"Yes?" I said, expectantly, taking my cup from him.

"I wish you'd stop calling me Uncle Ben. It sounds so ... so ..."

"Geeky?"

He smiled that joyous smile of his and let loose with a rattling belly laugh. His stunning blue eyes did that Santa crinkle I so adored, and then he said, "Yeah, geeky."

"Okay then, Ben," I said, echoing the laugh. "Mind if I ask you a question?" I finally looked up and stared him in the face, eyes locked at last.

"Sure, Ken. Shoot."

"How did you know that I was gay when I was only a kid? I didn't even know it then."

He sipped his coffee and nodded his head. Then he set his cup down and answered my question. "Because, Ken, it takes one to know one." He smiled and reached out to grab my hand for a big, manly shake. "It takes one to know one."

BOUNTY HUNT
Diesel King

Victor Emmanuel sat outside of the dilapidated white house on top of the steep hill for almost three days. In that time, he had seen some of everybody going in and out of that house. From the most respected of businessmen in the city to some of the shadiest motherfuckers in the world. On a couple of occasions, he almost blew his cover because of some of the scum coming out of the house had a high bounty on their heads. But it was the one that stayed inside of the house that Emmanuel wanted to get to first.

"Philip Carteret," Emmanuel groaned, stretching his long legs in his old oversized Cadillac.

He was the one with the highest bounty on his head. He was also the most accessible. That was until Emmanuel got his hands on the big boy of the West Coast:

Marcantonio Martino.

Philip Carteret wasn't a bad start. He had a bounty on his head worth $50,000. Carteret had made a ten-year career out of eluding the police. He started out as a small town drug dealer in suburban Sacramento before raising the stakes with his four-man cartel in Oakland. Oakland was in the middle of a turf war, and Carteret lost three of his men there. With his tail between his legs, Carteret relocated to San Diego where he built another empire from scratch. And when Five-O got a whiff of his funky scent, Carteret ran to Mexico where he quickly learned that he couldn't cut the mustard. He chose to lay low back here in the States, on the East Coast trying to go straight. That was short lived. He made a triumphant return in the last several months, running a house of ill-repute in the crime-infested neighborhood near Elysian Park in Los Angeles.

Victor Emmanuel emerged from his classic Cadillac looking like an old-school player shortly after midnight, scratching idly at his lean belly and took one last puff on a cigarette. Before taking the assignment, the skinny forty-seven-year-old black man could proudly boast that he hadn't touched a death stick in three years, but it was the only thing around he could do to take the edge off without whacking off right there in the middle of the street.

"I guess this motherfucker is going to make me come in and get him," Emmanuel groaned in his rich deep native Creole accent, looking up at the exceeding long case of stairs it took to get to the house.

He had meticulously gauged the flow of traffic over the last three days around the white house, learning that around midnight was the slowest. Yet, everything else around the neighborhood seemed mildly busy with drug dealers and other kinds of street vendors roaming about.

Before Emmanuel could put his fist to the door, one of the pallid boys working at the house answered the door. He looked legal, Emmanuel gauged. He was a little on the scrawny side as if sexing for pay wasn't his only pastime. He stuck his tongue in his rosy cheeks and said, "Dicks gets discounts," referring dicks as cops.

"I'm not a dick." Emmanuel clarified, playing with his soft dick in his pockets.

"Suit yourself." The young man said, walking off as he wanted Emmanuel to pursue him.

Emmanuel said nothing as he followed the young rose-cheeked boy through the house and into a bedroom where Philip Carteret, a young thickset sepia-colored man, was in a pair of red and black heart-shaped boxers sitting up in his bed surrounded by piles of money.

Going by the file Emmanuel had on him, Carteret was about twenty-nine years old and stood five-foot-nine. And as he could see, he had reddish-brown hair.

"Hey, Philip, I brought my customer back."

"I'm not your customer, kid," Emmanuel said.

Philip fanned the rosy-cheeked boy away.

"I have more of a stable downstairs if you don't want that nancy. Pick one out and bring him back up here to pay on your way out." Philip said nonchalantly.

"I'm not here to take a swim in your supply."

"How can I help you then?"

"I hear that you're doing some good business, and I want in."

Carteret looked back at Emmanuel, knowing exactly what was running through his mind. He thought that Emmanuel was either a cop or some crazy motherfucker that kept his ear to the street.

"Sorry old man, I don't divvy up my profits." Philip smirked.

Emmanuel reached for his back waist and pulled out his handcuffs. "Well, I guess I have to go back to my old job of bounty hunting then."

Carteret glanced over at the burglar bars on the window while reaching behind him hoping that there was a gun behind the pillow.

"You moved it, remember?" Emmanuel noted.

Emmanuel walked backwards to the dresser and pulled out a revolver from one of the drawers. Though, the house sat atop a hill, the window had no curtains, and Emmanuel had sharp eyes, so he could see everything that was going on.

Carteret slowly got up from the bed, putting his hands in the air as if he was surrendering before he dashed for the door. Carteret, in his haste to get to the door, slipped face first onto the hardwood floor. Emmanuel got on top of him and cuffed him. While Carteret was down on the floor, Emmanuel whipped out the warrant for his arrest and threw it on the floor next to him, so Carteret could see it for himself.

"I'm sure that we can work something out."

"Too late," Emmanuel growled, picking the man up with one hand, tossing him on the pile of money. "I don't divvy up my profits either."

Emmanuel glanced over at the bed where Carteret was laid out. He could clearly see that his dick was trying to break through the slit in his boxers.

"Well, there is a way we can work things out." Emmanuel said, walking over to Carteret.

"What are you doing, man?" Carteret asked, trying to get upright before falling back into the bed.

Emmanuel answered by reaching into the slit of his boxers and grabbing a hold of his hardening dick.

"This big dick is good for poking, man." Carteret defended, "sweet mouth and sweet ass. I bet back in your heyday you had a good bit of both."

Carteret laughed. Emmanuel stroked the piece of manhood in his hand, grinning back.

"Great minds think alike. I was thinking the same thing. I was thinking that you had some sexy-ass lips and a phat juicy booty. I was thinking to myself when was the last time you had some of that on the receiving in of that stick?"

"Hey, man, what do you mean by that?" Carteret got nervous.

"You're a smart man, Philip, figure it out." Emmanuel said unzipping and unbuckling his pants with one hand, letting them drop to his ankles to reveal his magnum-sized dick commando style. "Better yet, ask which one of us isn't in handcuffs?"

With the revolver still in his hand, Emmanuel removed his pants from his ankles and his shirt and jacket from his body.

"Hey, man," Carteret grinned. "I can take care of that personally, no problem. But only if you let me go after the fact."

"And what's in it for me?" Emmanuel inquired.

"Eight K, which is everything on the bed," Carteret pointed out.

Emmanuel nodded, placing the revolver on the windowsill and tossing Carteret on the bed. "Don't try anything stupid because I will fuck you up."

Emmanuel, completely nude, the way nature intended, turned Carteret around and climbed on top of Carteret and fed him his dick. His mouth felt wonderful, Emmanuel thought, positioning himself to hump his face.

The way Carteret was able to take his big dick down to the hilt like that fully convinced Emmanuel that Carteret was no mere amateur size queen. He probably built his empire sucking on many dicks rather than slinging drugs or pimping, which he boasted his reputation on.

"Damn! Your mouth feels like some new cunt." Emmanuel barked to Carteret's disgust, just like Emmanuel suspected as he started to fuck his mouth.

After a decent ten minutes, Emmanuel pulled out and willed himself to spray his massive load across his handsome face.

"Four thousand," Carteret sounded off angrily, trying to spit out some of the cum that landed on his lips.

"Here comes the full eight then." Emmanuel said, getting off of Carteret and flipping him on his stomach.

Emmanuel pulled Carteret's boxers off his ass. He then began to gently rub his calloused hands across the smooth white mounds before trying to stuff his meaty fingers in his mouth.

"Don't warm me up. There are some condoms and lube in the top dresser drawers."

Emmanuel didn't say anything. He just walked over to the dresser, put on a lubed condom and slathered on some more lube. He slowly walked over to Carteret and the bed, and climbed on top of him, rubbing his purple tip against his puckered hole.

"Shit!" Carteret cried on his stomach as Emmanuel prodded him with half his inches.

"Take it, man," Emmanuel growled, digging deeper and deeper into Carteret until his balls and bush were crushed against his butt hole.

His hole was tight, but Emmanuel soon worked it into a welcoming gap with no walls stopping him from drilling Carteret the way he wanted to. That didn't stop Carteret from fighting back, lifting his ass and pushing it back against him cussing up a storm against the squeaking bed.

Young stuff, Emmanuel thought, can take dick for days!

He fucked him long and strong, listening to Carteret's groans and his thighs slapping against his bubbly ass. He didn't care whether Carteret came or not as he shot his load and filled the tip of the condom. He then collapsed on top of him, slowly pulling out as his dick softening in his ass.

When he was finished, Emmanuel politely covered Carteret's ass with his boxers as he got dressed. Afterwards, Emmanuel counted all the money that was on the bed and found out that it was a little more than Carteret led on.

"You lied." Emmanuel said, standing Carteret up, tossing the money in a nearby pillowcase and taking him out of the room.

"What I lie about?"

"You were two K short of a pipedream."

Carteret pleaded with Emmanuel all the way out the house, telling the world that Victor Emmanuel took advantage of him.

When Emmanuel got Carteret in the back of his Cadillac and got in the driver's seat, Emmanuel reached back, squeezed the hardened nub between Carteret's legs, and said, "Get comfortable; we got a long ride ahead of us."

FATHER FIGURE
Diesel King

Benito felt like such a little ho carrying the chilled pie down the street. He could see if he was still eleven years old and was doing it as a helpful favor to his single mom, walking beside him carrying an armful of groceries. Oh sure, Benito might be joned by his little running buddies for being so poor that his family had to catch the bus to get the groceries or that he was such a "little big man" for carrying the dessert like some little fag instead of flexing his muscles by carrying all the foodstuff. But, at least he could walk down the street gaining the respect of most of the older folks that lived around the way. Folks that was certain to spot him a quarter or two for doing them such a "huge" favor later on.

But, at twenty-two, though, Benito knew that it was just sad, carrying a homemade Banana Cream Pie wrapped in a plastic grocery bag like some low-rent baker making a fucking delivery. He wouldn't have even been on foot if his mom wasn't so stingy with her car keys. If she hadn't, he probably could've held onto what was left of his dwindling manhood around his old running buddies turned gang bangers who littered the streets with their tricked-out low riders, making catcalls at him like he was some kind of good pussy.

"One little favor," the tall lanky Chicano boy cussed under his breath, repeating his mom's famous plea as the gang bangers joned him about packing some long and thick cream-filled éclairs for his sweet pie hole.

It was all her fault, Benito thought, scratching his wiry moustache, one little fucking favor.

Benito's mom was always yapping about doing this one little favor for her. But yet, like clockwork, that one little favor always seemed to come around every hour on the hour.

Benito sweep the floor. Benito wash the dishes. Benito put the clean clothes up.

Benito couldn't say to the contrary because her ace in the hole was her legendary guilt trips, complaining that she was the only one bringing in any money into the house. She needed all the help she could get. He was grown. He could move out, but if he chose to plunk down on her couch, the least he could do was help out. She was right, of course, considering that Benito sucked at being a curbside drug dealer and at selling himself to rich broads hungry for a dick, leaving his mom not only to support him, but also Benito's girlfriend and newborn son.

So Benito had no problem thumbing through his *abuela's* old cookbooks to find a pie recipe. He didn't mind hopping the bus to get all the ingredients. Nor, after he saw how tired his mom was from working all day, did he put up much of a fuss about going ahead and making it for her. This was even after he discovered that the pie wasn't even intended for them but instead for the single man that just bought the house down the street. He was cool with it just the same. He didn't even mind her sashaying her way down there to make a play for him. He figured the more she was out of the house the more time he could get with his girl. But, when his mom thought it would look more authentic to send him down there to deliver it, appearing as if she was too busy with house chores to deliver it herself, Benito was on the verge of cocking an attitude with her before she asked him to do this "one little favor."

Benito had just made it behind the fence to ring the generic doorbell when he saw the man come up behind the screened iron door. Even though his mom and every other woman around the rough neighborhood had been drooling over the man since he moved in, Benito, seeing him for the first time, was shocked to see how short he was.

"Yeah," the light-skinned black man barked gruffly, looking and sounding like an old bulldog. "What the fuck you want?"

Benito, who towered over the man, shrunk down to the size of an ant stammering to get his words out.

"My-my-my mom wanted me to-to bring y-you this." Benito said presenting the plastic bag covered pie with both hands as if he was a child.

"What the fuck is it?" The man said cracking open the door and poking his portly hand to seize the pie.

He wasn't a huge man. He just had incredibly rounded shoulders and a diesel-cut chest with distinct prison muscles that still bulged out of his tight shirt and well-fitted jeans.

"A banana cr-cream pie ... t-that she made ... sh-she wanted to be n-neighborly."

"You got some kind of stuttering problem, son?"

The man said his words so harshly, Benito was afraid that he was about to crap in his pants.

"No, sir," Benito said barely stumbling that time to get words out as his hands trembled violently with the pie still in his hands.

"Then, stop acting like you're scared, then. Damn. I ain't going to bite, partna." He said aggravated, forcing Benito to hold the pie with him.

"I'm not." Benito said, trying his best to sound like the man he was used to being, but then his dick got stiff in his sagging pants smelling the man's fragrant cologne.

"Who's your mom?" The man asked, not ready to take the pie away from him.

That knocked his boner cold, and he was able to talk more steadily. "She's the one that lives about six houses up the hill in the green and yellow house."

"The green and yellow house, huh?" He said, sticking his head out the door and looking up in the direction Benito was pointing.

"Yeah," Benito said, with the beautifully-scented cologne whiffing up his long nose.

43

"The long-haired Latina with the huge tatas," the man said with a devilish grin branded across his wide face, showing off his shiny bald head the two gold hoops pierced in each ear. He had a smoky-colored goatee (black, white, and gray) and part of a tattoo that started around his neck and disappeared underneath his shirt.

Benito nodded, with the guy stepping back in his house, using his foot to keep the door open as he took the pie inside with him.

"No disrespect, man." The man apologized seriously, and then smiled again. "But she not only got the looks, but she can cook, too?"

"Yeah," Benito lied, knowing that his mother couldn't boil a pot of water to save her life.

"Is it any good?"

"Shit, yeah," Benito told him. "She got the recipe from my *abuela*."

The man smiled looking at the pie in hand. It wasn't until he looked at Benito still standing there that he thought to invite him in to join him for a slice as a thank you for delivering it, not knowing what to make of the stuttering from earlier.

Benito was reluctant, but agreed, wanting to taste his creation.

"What's your name, boy?" The man asked, moving the pie through the living room and setting it down on the dining room table.

"Benito."

"Benito," the man said with a Spanish inflection that could be heard on his way to the kitchen. "*Boricua*?"

"*Chicano*? What's your name?"

"Mr. Melvin Collard, like in Collard greens," Mr. Collard said, moving back into the dining area with a couple of saucers and a butter knife.

He cut the pie, doling out small slices to each plate.

44

"What do you think?" Benito asked, after taking a couple of bites of his delicious creation.

"Yeah," Mr. Collard salivated. "Your mom can throw it down. Let me ask you, kid – how old are you?"

"Twenty-two," Benito answered.

"So be straight with me. Is your mom doing this just to be neighborly or is she doing this," he pointed to the pie on his plate, "to get my attention?"

Benito could have ratted out his mom, but he knew that Mr. Collard knew what was up by brandishing a stupid grin. So instead, Benito announced, "Let me just say this. There aren't a lot of men over the age of thirty living in this neighborhood, so when one moves into the neighborhood, everyone within a ten block radius definitely takes notice."

Mr. Collard laughed. "I bet they do. Too bad there all young enough to be my daughter."

"How old are you?" Benito asked abruptly, he couldn't see the man being older than forty-five and even that was excessive given the small amount of gray and white strains sprinkled about his face.

"Aren't you forgetting something?"

"Sir," Benito guessed, not accustomed to using the word that often.

"Good, you got some manners. To answer your question, I'm sixty-one."

Benito was short of letting out a cuss word looking at the handsome man when his ears were flooded out by the rattling of barrage of bullets a couple of houses over.

Benito stayed low to the ground, making his way over to the burglar-barred window as his elder, Mr. Collard, walked over to it unfazed by the gunfire glory. It wasn't hard for either of them to see that it was a rival gang doing a drive-by shooting at the parked cars as some of the local street gang members attempted to fire back at the speeding vehicles.

Mr. Collard laughed, looking down at Benito.

"What so fucking funny, *hommes*?" Benito said, letting his Mexican accent override his typical American dialect. "They're shooting to kill."

"Nothing, man," Mr. Collard said, as one of the cars in the middle of the street stopped to have an in-depth shootout with one of the parked cars. "When you showed up on my doorstep, I sort of pegged you for one of those boys that got around on his knees."

Benito wanted to get up and cuss the shit out of the old man. Instead, as Benito tried to get up, he lost his balance and accidentally grabbed a chunk of Mr. Collard's sturdy thighs, which he quickly let go of.

"Needy, too," Mr. Collard laughed some more.

"That shit ain't funny." Benito said defenseless.

"Yeah, it is," Mr. Collard looked down at him.

"Benito was tempted to get up and go at him again but promptly decided better against that. Benito saw there had to be something hugely off with this man as he stood unmoved in the curtain-less window watching the shooting action in the street move to the house right next door.

"Yo, what're you doing?" Benito asked fearfully, looking up to find Mr. Collard undoing his jeans like he was getting ready to come out of them.

"I figured that while you're down there you could put this in your mouth and shut your sweet-ass up for awhile." Mr. Collard said with his jeans opening down to mid-thigh, letting his soft musty dick flop out.

It wasn't the longest ruler in the kit, but Mr. Collard definitely had a nice admirable bulk, with its width of that of can of shaving cream at the bottom along with these gigantic lime-size nuts.

"I don't swing that way, man." Benito said like he was scared that the dick eying his face was ready to attack.

"Tough shit," Mr. Collard said, stroking his meat. "Either you get down with the program, or you get your ass shot up in the streets."

Benito would have easily chosen to get out of the house if the action wasn't just one house over. Because even if Benito could make it out the door, he had to fumble with the gate to get out, and if he got past the gate, he would have to sprint down the street in another direction. Even if he jumped those hurdles, he risked being shot in the back for being suspected as a possible snitch.

"C'mon, man, please," Benito pleaded.

"I told you how it goes down in my cage, man." Mr. Collard said against the rapid succession of bullets flying about next door. His reference to his house being a cage only confirmed to Benito that he had been to prison. "If you don't like the rules, you're more than welcome to leave."

Before Benito could say anything to the contrary, Mr. Collard was peeling off his shirt exposing a handsome torso envious of men half his age. The only distinction was that his chest and rounded hard belly were thickly covered in these wild strains that were the same smoky-colored as his goatee obviously more pronounced.

"Please," Benito said with tears swelling in his eyes.

"Please, can I have some more porridge, sir?" Mr. Collard mocked in an Old English accent, laughing.

Benito thought this was crazy. He had never seen another piece outside of his limited porn collection, and he was being asked to suck dick as if he was one of those hos in the videos.

"What? You think your crying is going to change my mind or something? I spent forty-four freaking years in the slammer, and I didn't blink twice about running trains on sissy punks like you."

"P-p-please, don't do this!" Benito folded at the serious terror in his voice.

"There's that sexy stuttering again." Mr. Collard noted, as he unexpectedly seized a chunk of Benito's hair. "Do it again."

Benito shuddered at the sudden jolt to the back of his head, causing his swelling tears to automatically pour down his face with more to follow because of the excruciating pain. Mr. Collard beamed at the masochistic beauty behind this, leaned over and darted his tongue between Benito's trembling lips as the gunfire rattled on.

With his strong painful grip still present at the back of the boy's head, Mr. Collard finished his thought with, "You know why I don't mind running freight trains on punks like you? Well, after sweet boys like you get turned out by your first stroke of pipe, it's nothing more profitable than pimping out a fiendish dick-whore!"

Benito wanted to speak but couldn't find the voice to do it. He was deathly afraid of what was to become of him on one front and on the other absorbing the shock that this most masculine man kissed him.

"I ain't gay, man." Benito finally found the courage to speak.

"They weren't either," Mr. Collard said, rubbing his hand-held crotch against the pair of lips beneath him.

"No," Benito called out, struggling to get away from Mr. Collard as the gunshot seemed to be quieting down from their high.

"You might as well make it easy on yourself and open up." Mr. Collard let it be known, fighting back. "Or I might decide that I just want to plug some butthole with no lube."

Benito stopped fighting. He thought about his outs and understood that there weren't any, especially since he wasn't sure if

Mr. Collard locked his front door after he let him in, as most of the doors in the neighborhood were locked inside and out with a key.

"That's better," Mr. Collard grinned, guiding his thick jock through the warm trembling lips of his unwilling submissive. "Don't you dare fucking bite me either, you here!"

Benito begrudgingly let the hard salted flesh enter his mouth. As the fat piece of man-meat made its way through, Benito instantly wanted to throw up around it. This was all new to him. He didn't know that the thin strip of foreskin covering the back of his dickhead was going to taste like molded cheese and potent nose spray. He didn't know that the sheer width of Mr. Collard's dick would make his jaws sore from the stretching alone. And just when he thought he was making some leeway, trying to breathe around the awkwardly big thing, Mr. Collard grabbed the side of his face and started raping his throat like it was whore pussy.

"There you go. That's that good boy pussy. Watch those fucking teeth and shit." Mr. Collard barked, not knowing that Benito was slipping in and out of consciousness with a hard-on in his jeans.

Benito was spilling spit and snot out of his nose and mouth with Mr. Collard going in for the kill, slamming his powerful hips into his mouth, heaving his heavy balls onto his pointed chin. Benito didn't know if he was going to live or die from this ordeal, but he was certain that something had to give the way Mr. Collard was grumbling incoherently through his clenched teeth.

"Open up, bitch." Mr. Collard reported after a deep, laboring exhale. He was breathing hard and fucking throat like he was a rabid jackrabbit desperately needing to get off, holding steady the head beneath him with his sweaty hands. "Oh, that's it! Aw, that's the shit!"

Benito came back into full consciousness as he began to struggle harder against Mr. Collard who began to slow down, swell in his mouth, and start up again with the violent plunges.

"Drink my fucking babies, punk!"

A second later, Mr. Collard blasted off, shooting an explosively hot and thick load the throat of the newly broken-in twenty-two-year-old.

"Oh, damn," Mr. Collard breathed. "And don't spill a fucking drop."

Even as Mr. Collard came, Benito couldn't help but to feel the powerful dick spurt off more throbbing shot down his throat as he worked his mouth overtime to take in the unique fluid.

"There you go. I knew you were a punk in training. You just needed that father figure to teach you how to appreciate dick." Mr. Collard said coming down from his high point.

As Benito was trying his best to pinpoint his feelings of what to make of his first time giving head, he heard Mr. Collard let out a great sigh and then felt his hand push him back off of him and onto the floor.

"Get on you back, pie boy." Mr. Collard commanded.

Benito was reluctant to oblige because he didn't know why he was ordered onto his back. As much as he could come up with, Benito thought that the shooter were moving over to where they were and under the window was probably the safest place.

"What's going on?" Benito asked, trying to clear his throat of the flood of cum, noting that it had been awhile since he heard any gunshots.

"Don't worry about it." Mr. Collard said straddling Benito's chest and putting his softening dick back to his lips. "I need you to do your job of cleaning up this mess you made and take off your pants."

The last thing on Benito's mind was that a blowjob wasn't enough, figuring that Mr. Collard's dick was still soft in his mouth, and that as old as he was he needed one of those blue pills to get going again.

Benito reached around over Mr. Collard and undid his jeans the best he could. He got them midway down his thighs to his knees. He tried kicking off his boots, but both managed to get tangled up on his heels.

It wasn't hard for Benito to put the pieces to the puzzle about what was to come next. Yet, he seemed surprised when Mr. Collard's dick sprung back to life like a comatose patient back at warp-speed recovery. Mr. Collard then preceded slid back down Benito's legs, bringing his pants down to his ankle along the way before knocking off his boots and headed off into the kitchen.

Benito could have made a break for it, or at least tried, but he was still more in a state of shock than anything else. He had never thought of dudes that way, and he sucked and swallowed another man whole like he was some kind of ho. He couldn't see how refusing Mr. Collard again was going to make him any less gay, especially if he was right in suspecting that the door was locked from the inside.

"This shit is as good as gold." Mr. Collard announced seconds later with a nice two-finger scoop of lard, smearing the stuff on Benito's naked pink bootyhole.

Benito didn't know what to make of the weird feeling back there. It was going from a creamy stiff solid to a melting liquid as Mr. Collard roughly fingered him. Benito couldn't believe how much Mr. Collard's fingers hurt digging up in him. Benito tried playing it cool, keep it in, but the pain got to him a bit, and he let out a yelp.

"What you crying about over there, huh?" Mr. Collard asked sexily. His fingers were still invasive yet a lot gentler. "Are you thinking about this dick inside of you?"

Benito hadn't a chance to respond to the contrary before he let out a sensational roar that caused him to arch his back and his virgin hole to open up. Mr. Collard had found that spot inside him that would turn a he-man into a sissified bitch.

"Stop," Benito cried. "I feel like I'm about to pee."

"Go ahead." Mr. Collard dared him.

Benito thought he would several times but was never able to. He just brought his ass up to those fingers invading him. He was feeling good that they were touching this thing inside of him that he never knew existed, and yet there was something about the pain that made him hot, made him moan.

"Sounds like it's time to pork the pig."

Like a pro that had done this about a thousand times, Mr. Collard raised Benito's legs and got right between them, placing his chunky dick at the top of his crack. Mr. Collard smooth slid down to the slick-wet deep valley to where his thick dickhead kissed the furrowed opening. He wasn't even ready to push in when the hole just flared open and let him slip the head in. The boy was just that slippery.

"Relax," Mr. Collard coached.

The virgin was easy to slide into because of the lard, but he was beyond snug against the hefty invader.

"Ohhhhh," Benito bemoaned softly.

Mr. Collard smacked him on the ass. And against his conscious will, Benito opened up and let the dick dive deeper into him, cutting him like a special ops knife, screaming and hollering against every painful inch. But once Mr. Collard felt he was secure inside Benito, smothering his balls into his crack, Mr. Collard reached behind Benito's back, scooped him up by his shoulders and hoisted him up on the table.

"There you go." Mr. Collard said, reaching around cuffing the front of Benito's thighs.

Mr. Collard pulled back and sank into his suffocating hole again and again, pounding out his sweet spot with every stroke as he tried not to work himself into such fantastic frenzy so soon.

Benito was up there feeling light-headed, trying his best to make sense of what he was feeling. It was obvious he was on the other side of getting fucked. Benito just wasn't sure if he wanted to pull away from the ravenous monster or wrap his legs tighter around the waist that was digging him out.

"C'mon, bitch, throw it back at me." Mr. Collard growled as sweat sparkling off of his thick mat of smoky hair. "You know you enjoy riding this dick."

Benito hated to admit it against the rising tide of pleasure, but Mr. Collard was absolutely right. Benito knew slinging pipe felt good, but he had no idea that he could feel right at home on some dick. Even going so far as to think that maybe he might give some of those cream-filled éclairs outside a chance to shove it in his pie hole.

Before long, Benito let loose, really getting into it, throwing his ass back on Mr. Collard after the sound of his strong thighs slamming against his ass got the best of him. Mr. Collard rewarded him by reaching around his lifted legs and pinching his nipples, giving him another powerful sensation that sent his head spinning around the room.

"What are you doing to me, pa?" Benito asked, sound like some hot foreign bitch.

"You like your ass getting dug out by a real man?" Mr. Collard asked.

Benito had no words, just incredible moans and groans as Mr. Collard found new places inside of him to touch for the longest time. Mr. Collard went from this sort of smooth and rough fuck to just hammering out his hole in these balls-deep thrusts.

"Ah, shit," Mr. Collard grunted hard. "I'm about to come up your butthole."

Benito felt Mr. Collard pile-drive him hard before he came to a screeching stopped, holding his hard steadily dick in place. Even though Mr. Collard came to a stop, Benito was surprised that there was still movement down there, as he soon realized that his asshole was quivering uncontrollably over the dick that had been assaulted it most of the afternoon.

"Take my babies, punk. Ahhhhhhhh!" Mr. Collard screamed holding Benito down, shooting a nice powerful nutt deep into the asshole he was fucking when the automatic trembling of ass muscles proved too much.

Benito just lay there sweating, letting his body just drink up this insane amount of white hot seed that painted his inner walls.

Benito was pants heavily trying to catch his breath when he looked over at the pie lying beside him, reminding him of the reason he was down here in the first place.

"Oh, damn. I got to go," Benito said nervously, getting his clothes together.

Eventually, Mr. Collard unlocked the door and let him free.

"Hey, son," Mr. Collard called out as Benito was halfway down the walkway. Benito turned to look back. "If you're mom's pie is as good as that in there, tell her I wouldn't mind being that father figure to her either!"

WHITEOUT
IN MOONLIGHT
By Mark James

Frank used to tell me, what we need most, we can't tell nobody.

I was nervous about being home for the holidays, wasn't just a small town boy anymore. I was in college now. And, Frank's on parole now, a part of me whispered.

Yeah, I argued with myself, but he didn't do it. He wouldn't do anything like that. But, I couldn't help thinking – nine hitchhikers in nine months. And, where they found those boys, running around naked in the cold, crying, it was like every spot was a spoke in a wheel, and Frank's cabin – that was the hub.

A hard wind rocked my car. Snowflakes slid over the glass between me and Frank's front door. For a second, it looked like a log cabin in those globes you shake, where everything stays still, except the snow falls nice and slow. I felt as if somebody was shaking me like that, except nothing inside me was staying still. My heart sure God wasn't going nice and slow; and if I waited ten more seconds, I'd lose my nerve.

I leapt from my car so quickly I nearly slipped on wet gravel. Tramping through the falling snow, I rehearsed what I'd say as soon as he opened the door: "Hi, school's great. I'm not leaving till I suck your dick."

Before I could knock, before my cold fist hit hard wood, the door slid open.

"Thought you'd catch your death sitting out there, boy." Frank eased out of the shadows, filled his wide doorway.

Now that I was face to face with him, all the words I'd rehearsed flew out of my head. "Hey, Frank."

"First night home. And I get to see a young old face." He tilted his head, gave me the sideways look I remembered. "A real pretty one."

I plunged my cold hands deeper into my pockets. "Thought you'd been home a while."

"That right, boy? You been keeping tabs on old Franklin?"

If anyone could get away with keeping tabs on a man like Frank, it was I. I'd heard about his rough side, but I'd never seen it. "No." I squinted up at him through the snow. "Just heard stuff around town. Look, if you got company or I'm bothering you, I can …"

"You can what? Look at the sky. About to piss down snow like a baby what's been holding it all day. You ain't going no place."

I knew he was right; the sky was the color my dad called hard, mean, get your ass inside grey.

"You busy, Frank?"

He crossed his arms over his wide chest, leaned comfortably in his doorway, his body thick and bulky under a blue flannel shirt. "Nope."

Just like that I was rock hard.

He did that to me. It could be how he was standing, how he talked; it came at me, out of no place, drove me crazy.

"So what'd I do to get a hot shit college boy to drive way up here?"

"You ain't gotta do nothing, Frank." I knew I'd fallen back on how I used to sound before I was a college boy, before I knew it made me sound like a hick. "Just wanting to see you is all. Okay if I come in?"

He faded back into the dark; his deep voice came from the shadows. "Been waiting for you to ask."

# # # # #

The inside of Frank's cabin had always been forbidden territory, kind of like that one tree in Eden they weren't supposed to touch.

I'd walked up to his cabin I don't know how many times. He always met me outside, took me fishing, showed me secret places in the woods, talked to me about anything. But as soon as the sun got low, he'd send me on my way.

Before I left for school, he'd joke that the day I saw the inside of his cabin was the day I'd stop being a virgin.

"What they been showing you up at that fancy college?" He held his hand out for my jacket. "Didn't I teach you no better than to be out in city boy clothes when a storm's blowing in?"

I stripped out of my thin leather jacket and gave it to him. "Drove all the way." Of course I did. What else? Walk a hundred and fifty miles?

"And if that nice car your daddy got you broke down, guess you'd just zip up in this fancy candy wrapper and freeze your balls off." He shook his head. "I worry about you, boy."

The half confused, half irritated note in his voice made it okay somehow. "I know. You always did."

"Go on and sit by the fire." He turned his back on me, opened the small closet. "Get your boots off. Thaw out some."

The solid mahogany floor was smooth under my feet. The fireplace was so big, it looked as if I could step through and come out the other side.

Logs, dark brown with age, stacked on top of each other, rose up into sturdy walls. A black leather couch roosted low in front of the fire, like a prehistoric beast warming its rough hide.

Next to the fire, a chair leapt in and out of shadow, looking big enough to fit a giant and his two closest friends. A bear skin rug sprawled before the blazing maw of the fireplace.

Sinking down onto the couch, I wondered how it would feel to lie on the rug naked, Frank on top of me and …

"You heard me, boy?"

Oh shit. He'd said something and I'd missed it. At least he didn't catch me staring at his crotch. Again. "What?"

"How's your daddy?"

I shrugged. "People still need sewing up, so he's got work."

He slid into the chair by the fire, seeming to fill every inch of it. The flames lit only half his face, the other half hid deep in shadow.

I'd asked him maybe a dozen times, but he'd never told me where he got the scar under his right eye. In the fire's soft light, the white zig-zag scar seemed to work back and forth, like he was a thunder God and lightening lived under his skin.

"School all right?"

School's great, and I'm not leaving 'til I suck your dick. My feelings twisted like ribbons in a high wind. "It's nice there. Everyone's nice. My roommate's nice."

He looked into the fire, gave me that sidewise look I'd seen a thousand times. It meant either he was thinking hard, or he was about to say who you think you foolin' with, boy?

"Sounds real nice." His hard face creased into a grin. "It's me, boy. Franklin. You been telling me your secrets since grass been green." He leaned his big body over the arm of his chair, reached out and pushed damp hair from my eyes. "Talk to me."

For the first time since I'd driven into town, I felt as if I was home. I thought I might even have the guts to tell him what I'd thought about for a hundred and fifty miles.

# # # # #

"School's a whole bunch of city folks." I slid down, stretched my legs, reaching for the glossy black fur at my feet. "Get their panties all in a bunch if they can't take a cab two blocks." I shrugged. "Weird. Act like they never seen outside before."

"You meet any nice college boys?"

"Kind of."

"Christ. You even talk like a city boy, now." He waved a big hand at me. "That like being sort of drunk? Did you or didn't you?"

"I met this one guy. We went out a couple times."

"And?"

"We had drinks, dinner, saw a movie."

"Then what?"

I slid my eyes away from him, to the fire. "Nothing. We went home."

Frank leaned back; the scar under his eye slipped in and out of shadow, like a phantom storm was brewing inside him. "You ever me tell a lie and get away with it, boy?"

I thought about it, sank lower on the couch. "No. Not with you."

"Go on and tell me the rest of it. Who sucked whose dick first?"

Heat rose to my face. "He did."

"You like it?"

I saw he was listening hard, almost holding his breath, like a hunter sighting his target. "I liked it, but I didn't. I mean, it felt good but ..."

"You come in his mouth?"

"Yeah. Then I did the same for him." I stopped because I didn't know how to say the rest. Frustrated, I threw my head back against the couch. "I don't know. It wasn't like how I thought, is all I mean."

I looked over at the small window. Grey light crept in. Snow swirled against the glass; fragile sounds, like kittens lost in the storm, scratching the glass.

"You mean it wasn't hot like when you jacked off thinking about it back before you did anything, right?"

I got that rush of excitement you get when someone says what you're feeling, and they get it exactly right. "Yeah." I lunged forward, threw up my hands. Words tumbled out. "It was just me coming in his mouth, then he came in my mouth, then I went home."

"And jacked off and thought about something that made you come real hard."

It wasn't a question, so I didn't answer. I didn't tell him I'd gone home and thought about him. I didn't have to. The truth hung in the air between us.

"Don't look so long faced, boy. It'll happen. And even better than your one hand daydreams."

He reached over and pushed my hair back again, let his hand linger a little, then he drew back into firelight and shadows.

It was quiet for a while, just the crackling fire, restless wind outside, like a small army of ghosts. I watched him pace over to the window, his broad back to me. In the dancing shadows, he was the stillest thing in the room.

I wanted to ask him if prison had been real bad, if he'd done okay in there, if he was glad to be back in Birchon. I didn't know how, so I settled for vague and meaningless. "Been all right, Frank?"

"You think I done anything to those boys?"

Him asking about the hitchhikers like that from out of nowhere caught me off guard. "Why would a man like you have to force a boy to be with him? I always thought that was dumb."

He turned to me, rubbed his crotch mildly, as if he had a deep itch he couldn't get at, so he was just rubbing to get what relief he could. "Is that right?"

I smoothed out the wrinkles in my jeans, pressing hard so he wouldn't see my hands shaking. "Yeah. Just what I think is all."

"What about you, boy?"

I looked up at him sharply. "Me?"

"I'd have to force you to be with me?"

I shook my head, and as it always does when we least expect it, the truth slipped out.

"I always thought you were real ..." I stopped talking so fast, I nearly bit my tongue.

"Thought I was what, boy?"

Oh God. Guess if I was going to say it, now was the time. "Real hot."

He squinted at me through the shadows. "You ain't no kid no more, and you sure grew up to be one fine looking boy."

Before I could say anything, he filled the chair by the fireplace again, like a stealthy shadow coming out of hiding, getting more real with every passing second.

"There's things you don't know about me, Billie."

My heart pounded. "What kinds of things?"

Like it was something he'd thought about for a long time, he said, "I'm different than any man you ever knew."

I gathered all the runaway words in my head and blurted out what I'd been thinking all the way home from school. "I know, I came up here to ..."

"I know why you're here." He pressed a big finger to his lips. "Shut up and listen, why don't you?"

Oh God, I thought. Don't let it be the hitchhikers.

"I'm not like your friend up to the college," he said. "If I let you suck my dick, I'm never gonna suck yours."

I got so hard so fast I had to shift a little.

"And if I fuck your ass, you're never gonna fuck mine."

His legs were spread wide. I glanced at his crotch and saw he was rock hard, and not trying to hide it. "How come?"

He smiled when he saw my eyes on his package. "Cause that's how I am. You suck my dick, I fuck your ass, and I take care of you. You're my boy. I'm your man."

I'd heard about this, but I'd never expected to find a man in real life like that. Not in a place like Birchon. "Is this that thing where I call you Sir?"

He gave me his sidewise look, and this time I knew for sure it was who you think you foolin' with, boy? "I don't care what you call me. But if you're with me, and I tell you to suck my dick, you get on your knees and do it. I want your ass, you bend over and give it to me."

Hearing him say that made my cock so hard, it hurt. I wanted my jeans off, not so I could jack off, just so I could give my cock and balls room to breathe.

"I been waiting on you a long time, Billie. If you heard anything you like, crawl over here and kiss my boots."

How many times had I thought about this? Dreamed about it? Come hard thinking about writhing under his hard body? But none of it had been like this. "What if I don't want it like that?"

"Then you spend the night in my bedroom, and I sleep on that couch." He looked into the fire. "But if you crawl over here boy, come sunrise tomorrow, you ain't gonna be no virgin."

Frank was right. I'd never seen this side of him before. It was hot and scary and made my cock throb, and – oh my God – his cock looked so big and thick under his jeans. What was I doing?

I was already on my hands and knees, crawling across the soft rug. I'd never kissed a man's boots in my life, but there, in front of the roaring fire, I pressed my lips to his boots. My cock got impossibly harder; for the first time in my life, my ass throbbed, clenched, felt empty.

His fingers were in my hair, a soft caressing touch, and his breathing was harder, faster. "That was good, Billie. Real good. Been waiting a long time to see you do that."

He curled his fingers into my hair and pulled me up till I was on my knees. His dark eyes told me he'd waited even longer to see me on my knees between his spread legs. "You wanna suck my dick, boy?"

"You know I do, Frank. I wanted to for a long time."

Digging his fingers deeper, he pulled my face into his crotch.

I inhaled his scent, my unsteady fingers on his hard legs, my lips rubbing the outline of his cock. "You going to let me?"

"Depends on how good you ask," he said, holding my face down, lifting up so his cock was hard and warm against my lips. "Let me hear you ask for what you need, boy."

I pressed closer to his jeans. "Can I suck your dick, Frank? Please?"

He pushed me back. "No."

My whole body was caught up in a storm of aching need; I couldn't understand that simple word. "What?"

"Who you think you foolin' with, boy?" He jumped at me so fast, I nearly fell back before he grabbed my sweater and dragged me close. "All you want is to suck me off? I can get that any day of the week down to the Miner's Pit. Thought you crawled and kissed my boots because you wanted more."

Confusion whirled my thoughts, tossed every fantasy about Frank through my mind. "I do." As soon as I said it, I knew it was true. "I want more."

"Then ask for what you need." He loomed over me, his dark eyes heavy on me, demanding, uncompromising.

I thought about the fantasies and how they were all the same, how they were never about me, always about Frank, what he wanted, what he did to me, what I would have begged him to do to me. "I want to kiss your feet, lick your balls." Words gushed out of me. "Suck your cock, bend over and beg you to fuck me." I looked up at him, scared I'd gotten it wrong somehow, that I'd blown my chance.

He kissed me. "That's my good boy. Franklin's gonna give you everything you need tonight."

He unzipped his jeans, pushed down his drawers, spread his legs.

I took his thick cock head between my lips, heard him moan softly, felt him lift his hips to me; it felt so good, so right to be on my knees, making him feel good.

He slid his cock in and out of my mouth, his hand in my hair, pulling my head down on him, making me taking him deep down my throat.

It was hotter than any jack-off fantasy I'd ever had because I'd never thought of Frank just taking me. It didn't feel like he was fucking my mouth; he was using me, satisfying himself, and knowing that made my cock swell and press against my jeans. I moaned.

Frank grabbed the back of my neck. His hand was big, like a giant clamp pushing me down on his cock.

He moaned, spread his thick legs and shoved his cock down my throat so far I choked. I tried to pull back, but his big hand kept me clamped firmly in place.

My universe narrowed to three things: Frank's cock in my aching throat, his panting and moaning, and the deep throbbing ache in my swollen balls.

He pulled back, pressed his slick cock head to my lips. I licked, even though I was still gulping for air.

"Good boy." He pushed my hair back. "You'll get used to it."

When he sat back, I chased after his cock.

He slapped my face lightly, pushed me away. "No. I'm not wasting a load down your throat when that virgin ass is waiting on me."

I heard him, but I couldn't help licking and sucking his heavy balls, pulling them into my mouth before I said, "I don't want this to stop. Please."

He pulled me up hard; I saw the cords bunch in his forearm. "I'm gonna give you what you need tonight, boy. What you want, that's not gonna matter a whole lot."

"But I ..."

"Fuck, boy." He ran his hand down between my legs, fondled my cock through my jeans. "You always did talk too much. Shut up and get naked for me."

It was like I'd been speeding along and a giant speed bump had sent me sailing into space. I looked up at him. "Just like that?"

His eyes turned hard; not mean, just hard, like maybe I was about to see the rough side of him. "You don't wanna start the night pissing me off, Billie. You want my cock up your ass before you feel my strap on your ass, don't you?"

His soft voice, the hard shine in his eyes, the way his big hands were hanging down between his legs, looking relaxed, but probably ready to whip across my face or grab my balls like a vice – all of it added up to two words in my mind. "Your strap?"

He leaned closer. "Yeah. I got a real thick leather strap upstairs. Mark you up real good. I don't mind fucking a welted up ass, but I don't think that's how you want it the first time." He studied me a second. "Or do you?"

I looked into the fire and did what my math Professor called a 'quick sum.' I was in an isolated cabin with a man whose boots I'd kissed, a man who'd choked me on his cock, a man who'd gone to prison for raping nine boys hitchhiking on the wrong back roads. Was I seriously considering saying no, I wasn't going to take off my clothes? Bad equation.

"I don't want it like it that," I said slowly, shifting my eyes to his face. "Unless you think that's how it should be for a boy who wants to be with you."

He grabbed my sweater again, both hands this time, and kissed my mouth rough, mashing my lips against my teeth. I saw his cock twitch. "I'm gonna enjoy the hell out of that virgin ass. Get naked."

# # # # #

It made me unbelievably hot, standing there nude, looking at Frank sitting there, his muscled legs spread, his thick cock sticking up out of his jeans.

He patted his legs. "Come here, Billie."

I eased down; he helped me straddle him, so he was between my ass cheeks, and my cock was between our bellies.

"You ever sit on a man like this before?"

"No."

"You like it?"

I rubbed my hands over his soft flannel shirt, felt his warm, somehow unyielding muscle underneath. Leaning close, I kissed him and said against his lips, "Yeah. I like it a lot."

I writhed on him, rubbing on his cock pressed up against my ass. It felt so good. I couldn't remember wanting anything more than I wanted him inside me.

My hands on his broad shoulders, I lifted up, and tried to sit on his thick cock. I writhed until his cock was pressed up against my hole and pushed.

"Don't," he said.

When nothing happened I pushed harder.

And screamed.

"Christ." Frank wrapped his thick arms around me and pulled so hard I fell against him, made the heavy chair rock back and hit the wall.

I felt like I'd got on a rollercoaster blasting downhill, a train of cars on the edge, about to fall off the track. "Oh my God." I heaved in a deep breath. "I can't. I'm sorry. Jesus."

"Easy." He rubbed my trembling arms, kissed the side of my neck, trailed his big hands down my back. "Can't do it like that, boy. I'll rip your virgin ass in two."

He kissed me, unbuttoned his shirt, and put my hands on his skin. I was quiet for a while, ran my trembling hands over Frank's chest, followed the dips and hollows of his sculpted muscle, trailed my fingers over his hard belly. "You're so big and hard everywhere." In all the years I'd known Frank, I'd never touched him. Not like this. "Like there's rock under your skin."

He laughed, ran his calloused hands over my ass, kissed my neck. "And you're nice and soft all over, like you got velvet for skin."

Considering I'd just sucked his dick, after I'd begged him to fuck me, it was stupid, but I blushed anyway. "I used to live for you to say nice things to me."

"I know."

Wiggling gently against his hard cock, I leaned into him, whispered, "I want you so bad."

He ran a finger between my ass cheeks so lightly I barely felt it, like a soft breath. "My new boy needs to let his man open this virgin ass."

He took my face in both his strong hands and kissed me, sliding his tongue into my mouth, his fingers caressing my cheeks.

"Up," he said. "Lie down. Spread your legs for me."

# # # # #

Was I scared? Yeah. But not as scared as I would have been if it wasn't Frank.

I got up off him, and lay down. The bear skin rug was soft and warm under me, a light caress all along my naked body.

He stood between my legs, used one booted foot to spread my legs wider.

Looking down at me, he unbuttoned the rest of his shirt and slipped it off. I'd seen him shirtless lots of times, but not like he looked tonight. Every muscle in his chest and arms was tense, like he was a hunter, about to bring down his prey.

When he was naked, he slipped into the darkness without a word. I lay there in the heat of the fire, legs spread, waiting for Frank to come back and slide his thick cock into my virgin ass.

Was this really happening?

Outside the wind whipped snow against the cabin. Yeah. It was real. If this was my dream, the sun would be shining outside; there wouldn't be shadows and grey light, and I'd be sure I was doing exactly the right thing.

He came back, a bottle of lube in one hand. His cock was thick and shining, and I was suddenly sure of one thing. I wanted him.

"Ready to give me what I waited for all this time, boy?"

He was between my legs again. I looked up at him, spread my legs even wider. "I don't want to be a virgin anymore." I licked my lips. I'd told Frank a lot of things, but nothing like this. "And, I want it to be you."

He tossed the lube on the couch and knelt between my legs.

I looked up at his hard body. It seemed like there wasn't an inch of Frank that wasn't hard muscled. I wanted all that pressing up against me, grinding me into the rug.

"I'm gonna open you up, boy." He pressed a slick finger to my hole, rubbed in slow little circles that made my cock throb. "Before I'm done with you, this little virgin hole's gonna be stretched wide."

I pressed down on his finger, wanted to feel him inside me. "Make me your boy."

"Give it to me." He pressed hard, slid his finger all the way in me.

I stifled a groan of pain.

"Relax." He slid his finger out real slow. "Tell me what you thought about all the way home from that fancy school." His finger went in and out, slowly. "Tell me what you were thinking about sitting in my driveway for ten minutes, boy."

I opened my mouth to tell him, but nothing came out. Even now, with my legs spread wide and his finger deep in my virgin hole, I couldn't bring myself to tell him. "I don't know, Frank. I was all mixed up."

"How come?"

His finger inside me was driving me crazy. I squirmed, my hips going up and down. "I wanted you so bad, but I couldn't tell you."

He slid his finger out and lay on top of me, his cock nestled between my legs, his face inches from mine. "And, you think I didn't know?"

He kissed me, long and deep. I slid my arms around him, down his hard back, aching to touch every part of his sculpted body.

After forever, he pulled away, and looked down at me, watched me writhing against him. I felt him reach down between us and guide his thick cock to my ass.

When I felt his fat cock head pressing into me, I panicked. "I can't, Frank." I hissed in breath, planted my palms on his muscled chest and pushed as hard as I could. "Please. I'm sorry. I was wrong. It's going to hurt too bad."

Frank froze above me like a sculpture caught in mid-motion. My breath caught in my throat. The man I knew was gone; a dark-eyed stranger was on top of me, a man who'd take what he wanted, then abandon me naked and crying to the howling night. "How come you're acting like you got a choice, boy?" the stranger said.

I trembled all over. "What?" Air sobbed in and out of my lungs. "I don't want to."

He looked at me as if I'd said something funny, but he was being nice and not laughing in my face. "You don't get it, do you?" He leaned over me, his hard body pinning me to the rug, whispered in my ear. "You stopped being a virgin the second you asked to walk in my door. Ain't I told you what would happen if you ever came in here?"

I pushed harder against him; it was like pushing a brick wall with a feather. "But Frank ..."

"Don't tense up, boy." He pressed himself into my virgin tightness. "Just gonna make it hard on yourself."

His cock head slipped into me, stretching me wide. "Oh my God."

"Nice and slow." He kissed my trembling lips, and the stranger was gone; it was Frank's low calm voice saying, "Not gonna give you nothing you can't handle."

He inched into me. I looked down and saw his cock half inside me, his hard body resting on his thick arms, like he was doing a push up, and I was under him.

"Look at me, Billie."

I met his eyes.

"Don't that rug feel good under you?"

"Yeah." I was still breathing hard. His cock pressed into me relentlessly.

He pushed in another inch – God – maybe two. I gasped.

"Don't fight me, boy."

"I'm scared."

"You got nothing to be scared of. I ever hurt you?"

Then his lips were covering mine, and he was sliding into me. The pain was turning into a tingling that started at the base of my spine, moved out through my body.

He kissed the side of my neck and slipped all the way into me. I could feel his balls touching my ass. "Good boy."

I reached up, touched his face, my fingers light on his rough skin. "I didn't know it would feel like this."

He let out a low groan of pleasure, slid out of me, then buried himself deep again in a smooth, long thrust. "Like what, boy?"

I wrapped my legs around him, rested my hands on his shoulders, looked into his eyes. "I feel like ..." I bit my lips when he slid out of me, then thrust into my ass again, every inch of his cock making a hot friction that made me lift my hips.

He looked down at me. "Like what?" His cock was deep in me, and he was grinding his heavy, swollen balls into my ass.

I ached for him to fill my ass with hot cum, to feel it leak out of me. "It feels like you took me, and like that's how it's supposed to be between me and you."

He pulled all the way out of me, and pressed his cock head to my hole, holding me down. "You liking how it feels? Me taking your hot little virgin ass?"

I lifted myself to him, writhed against his slick cock head. "Better than anything I ever thought."

He laughed and sank deep into me. Then he did it again and again, and I moaned and writhed under him.

"That hole good and stretched now, boy?"

I was throbbing and aching. I grabbed my hard cock and started jacking off. "Yeah. I need to come so bad."

He slapped my ass hard enough to sting. My muscles clenched around his cock. "I tell you to do that?" He pushed my hand away.

"But I wanna come."

He slid all the way into me and eased down 'til his hard body was pressing me into the rug, his lips bare inches from mine. "I told you, Billie, what you want isn't gonna matter a whole lot tonight."

Then he kissed me and fucked me, slid his cock and in and out. I felt him swell inside me, felt how thick and hard he was and heard his ragged breathing in my ear, hot on my neck.

"Gonna open that ass right up, boy."

He fucked harder and faster into me, each stroke shaking my whole body.

Hot spikes of pleasure and pain rocketed through me, making me want his hard body pressing me down.

I felt a shudder run through him, heard a strangled moan, then he was panting and grunting.

He rammed into me so hard, I screamed, thought I'd split down the middle, then his hot cum was jetting into me.

While his cock twitched and spurted hot load after hot load into my tight ass, he grabbed my face and kissed me hard.

He stroked into my ass a few times, before he got up and fell into the chair beside the fire, his head thrown back, breathing hard. "Fuck, boy."

I don't know why I did it, but feeling his warm cum leaking out my ass, thinking of how he'd taken my virgin hole, made it impossible not to. I rolled over, belly crawled the two inches separating us, and kissed his feet.

He laughed deep and slow before he reached down and pulled me up onto him. He let me straddle him, pulled me against him, pressed my head down to his shoulder. I wrapped my arms around him.

My cock was still hard, but I was satisfied in a way I'd never felt in my life.

His big hand caressed my back. "I hurt you. I didn't mean to. You're a hot fuck."

Outside, the storm raged on, threw snow against the solid little cabin.

"You're awful quiet, boy. You all right?"

"Frank, if you could force a boy, would you?"

"You mean like a hitchhiker, some kid caught between hoot and holler, and don't nobody know his name, and ain't no one gonna care if something bad happens to him?"

I swallowed. "Yeah. Like that."

He held me tight in his strong arms. "Nope."

Did I believe him?

I thought about 'quick sums' and how in geometry, the shortest distance between two points is always a straight line. But, what if those two points were truth and love?

I looked past Frank to the window, thought about the dark-eyed stranger who'd been in his body for a few seconds.

The moon sent silvery beams through the storm. Bare limbs on trees lost their harsh angles; sharp edges faded off into grey. I thought maybe that's all the truth we could stand to know in life – whiteout in moonlight.

ACQUISITIONS
By Kale Naylor

"This is your last chance."

Brown's words echoed in my head as I gazed at myself in the bathroom mirror of Marino's, Chicago's most exclusive five-star restaurant. This wasn't supposed to happen. I was to land a killer job with a premiere ad agency. I'd work hard, pay my dues, prove my mettle as a fresh-out-of-college phenom, and I'd be one of the city's top ad execs before I was twenty-five. My buddy Keisha has an old saying, "If you ever wanna make God laugh, tell him your plans."

In actual fact, I was living from paycheck to paycheck in a shoebox apartment, earning my modest wages as the whipping boy for a sadist. How I became the sad desperate visage in the mirror, I was still trying to figure out. What I did know was that if I didn't land the Sharpe account, I was out of a job. The problem? No one lands the Sharpe account. Brown has been trying to court Sharpe for years. Sharpe has a rep for being one of the toughest businessmen in town. I got myself to blame for this one. But, you'll promise to do the impossible when you're desperate and threatened with being fired. Brown's smirk still haunted me. We both knew I wasn't going to land this account with his campaign ideas.

I splashed some water on my face and released a deep breath. Couldn't think about any of that now. I had miracles to perform. Clenching my briefcase handle, I slowly meandered back into the dining area, scanning the vicinity for my target. Though his rep preceded him, I had no idea what he looked like. Seeing as he was essentially the death of my career, I kept an eye for anyone sporting a cloak and scythe. Of course, I should've kept an eye out for the waiter I nearly plowed into.

"Sorry," I gasped.

I made it back to my table and hid my beet red face behind the menu from the nonplussed customers. My respite would be short-lived, for minutes later, he made his entrance. Even in this establishment full of Chicago's wealthiest patrons, he stood apart. His aura of power and confidence identified him better than a name tag could. With a square jaw and gelled sandy blond hair, his Brooks Brother's suit did little to hide his powerful wrestler's frame. Initially wearing a scowl, his baby blues suddenly gleamed, and his right eyebrow arched when we made eye contact. His thin lips curving to a slight smirk, I suddenly felt like a mouse who had just been cornered by a ravenous feline.

"Mr. Sharpe," I greeted. "I'm Colin Trent. It's a pleasure to meet you."

We shook hands. His stone vice grip was cool and refreshing against my warm sweaty palms.

"I apologize for my tardiness," Sharpe said. "I fired my assistant last week, and I've been left to tend to my own schedule."

"I appreciate you meeting with me."

"My pleasure. I've rather come to enjoy shooting down Brown's top guns." He scanned me and shook his head. "So Brown sent a benchwarmer this time. He must be in worse shape than I heard."

Disarm the opposition and keep them off balance, smart tactic.

"Well actually, sir, I have some great concepts, which I think will interest you," I replied, promptly removing the mockups from my briefcase and placing them on the table. "We know that Sharpe Athletics values its legacy as being a family company and one of tradition, ever since your great-grandfather founded it. So we went with a familial theme. As you can see, we have a good looking All-American family at the park engaged in various sports activities with your gear being prominently showcased."

He shook his head and snickered, "Oh Brown, still unable to figure out what the client wants. Look, you seem like a nice enough kid. Let me give you some free advice, start job hunting, you're going nowhere fast working under Brown. Have a good evening."

"WAIT!" I cried. "I can understand why this wouldn't appeal to you. You don't strike me as the kind of guy who wants to rest on your laurels or live on your family's reputation. You want to blaze your own trail, establish your own identity."

I removed the second set of mock-ups from my briefcase. Sharpe carefully studied the sleek redesigned logo and pics of the scantily clad collegiate models who were engaged in a sexually charged game of tag football. Perhaps it was wishful thinking on my part, but I thought I saw a smirk on his face.

"Brown didn't sign off on this did he?" Sharpe said.

"What makes you say that?"

"Because he only signs off on ideas he personally would've thought up. The young and sexy approach. Not exactly original, but it's well executed here."

"If you wanna look like the beautiful people and attract the beautiful people, you'll have to get in shape. You wanna get in shape, buy Sharpe's. Buy Sharpe, look sharp."

Sharpe scratched his chin as he studied the two most risqué pics in the set. In one portrait, two of the female models were embraced in a sensual hug. The other featured two buff shirtless hunks locked in a sexually charged tackle.

"Interesting how you went for the homoerotic slant with these pics."

"I hadn't noticed."

He grinned, "Sure you hadn't. Okay, I need a drink. What's your poison?"

"No thanks sir. I don't drink when I work."

"You will if you want to land this account."

Truth was that I hadn't had a drink in months. I had come to learn (the hard way) that I can't hold my liquor and what little I can hold makes me very stupid and very horny very quickly. Case in point: Keisha's party where I threw myself at her brother – her very heterosexual brother – before passing out in the driveway. This meeting just got more problematic.

Miraculously, I kept a steady head while I pitched the campaign. More miraculous than that was that I continued to pique Sharpe's interest. His tie loosened after the third glass of wine, a faint smile remained fixed on his face.

"It's too bad Brown didn't send you sooner," he said. "It would've saved everyone a whole lot of time."

"Does that mean …"

He nodded. "Only on one condition. You help me celebrate by helping me crack open a twenty-five-year-old bottle of scotch I've been saving for a proper excuse."

"Wow, that bottle is older than me. I don't know. I'm feeling kinda sloshed. I'm a lightweight, Mr. Sharpe."

"It's Aidan. Come on, Colin. You can't keep me hanging."

Tell him no, I said to myself. Don't push your luck.

"You only live once," I said.

It was official; I was a moron.

I lost count after my fourth glass, but at that point, I didn't care. Hours after returning to his loft, we remained draped over his leather sofa, cackling like hyenas while trading college prank stories.

# # # # #

"And, that my friend is why you never leave crazy glue in a frat house," Sharpe, I mean Aidan, said.

"That's too funny," I snickered. "Okay, either I'm really wasted or my watch says it's after one. I need to go."

With a strong hand planted on my slender chest, Sharpe shoved me back on the couch. "You're not going anywhere."

My head spun. I was virtually powerless when my client straddled my legs and removed my tie.

"What are you doing?" I moaned.

"Isn't it obvious?" he replied while unbuttoning my shirt. "Now that I've lured you back to my place and have gotten you considerably inebriated, I'm going to undress you, carry you to my bed where I'm going to fuck you mercilessly."

"I don't think we should."

"Don't think. Besides, you want this account don't you? This bulge down here tells me you want it, period."

He wasn't wrong, which is why I didn't put up a fight when he tossed me over his shoulder and carried me into his bedroom like a bagged prize. The pungent mix of scotch, cologne and musk made him intoxicating. I lay helpless as his esurient eyes absorbed my slim nude form, like a wolf eyeing a lamb before devouring it. Expecting his touch to be rough and cold, I was thrown off guard how soft and sensual his caress was. My body shivered, his grin indicating I was experiencing the desired effect. His tongue alternated between lapping at my neck and my nipples. Both being erogenous zones, I was being driven into a frenzy. However, I was powerless and forced to endure the pleasurable torture.

It didn't take me long to realize his goal. This wasn't just about getting his rocks off. He wanted to conquer and dominate me. He meticulously and mercilessly licked away at each weak spot he discovered. My begs and moans only encouraged him. He was a man who took pride in his work. He unceremoniously parted my legs and plunged his tongue into my biggest weak spot.

"FUCK!" I yelled.

"I knew it," he chuckled. "The way you were squirming, I figured you had a sensitive hole."

My fingers ran through his dark sandy hair as he expertly worked my ass over with my tongue.

"Fuck me!" I moaned.

"What was that?"

"Fuck me! Fuck me hard."

"I don't know," he teased. "I don't know if you've earned this cock. I don't think you've worked for it yet."

I clenched his massive rod with both hands and devoured it. It was his turn to gasp and moan.

"That's it," he groaned, "suck that cock." He massaged the back of my neck while I slurped away at his massive pole. "That's a good boy."

Without warning, Aidan clenched a handful of my hair and yanked me off his cock.

"Oh, I could get used to you," he said.

"Right now I just wanna get used to that cock."

"Eager. I really like that."

He hooked his massive arms underneath my legs and hoisted me onto his dick. He slammed me against the wall. Our tongues intertwined as I bounded up and down off his meat. I was in heaven. His hot rod slid in and out of me effortlessly. I clenched down on his dick, which elicited a grin from Aidan. In response, he tossed me onto the bed and mounted me. His hips pumped like a piston, slamming mercilessly into my prostate. I dug my fingers into his chiseled ass and met each thrust. This is what real fucking was. The previous hookups didn't even rate. This was primal, spiritual, unyielding, it was an act of God.

I glanced to the right and spotted a mirror hanging over the armoire. We were a sight. Our sweating bodies were intertwined like the two Greco-Roman wrestlers in the picture hanging on the opposing wall. Aidan glanced at the two of us in the mirror and chuckled. Deciding to take charge, I rolled on top and straddled his waist. My clenched ass bounced up and down off of his rod like a paddle ball. The larger man groaned, but I pressed against his chest to keep him pinned.

"I'm getting close," he moaned.

"Go for it!"

Moments later I felt him unleash torrents upon torrents of his hot cream inside me. That was all it took to send me over the edge. My cock spewed a steady stream all over my client's torso. I slid off of his rod and collapsed on top of him. Drunk, exhausted and spent, I was only conscious for a few more seconds before passing out.

# # # # #

My fluttering eyes were greeted by the harsh sunlight from the bedroom window. The fugue slowly dissipated, and the memory of last night's activities returned with a vivid vengeance.

"Fuck me."

"Aren't we insatiable."

Sharpe emerged from the adjoining bathroom wearing nothing more than a thin red robe and a Cheshire grin. He slapped my ass, "Lighten up kid. You got nothing to be embarrassed about. Trust me. However, after last night, I decided not to go with Brown."

"WHAT? Why?"

"You."

"Ah hell!"

Sharpe snickered, "You misunderstand. You were impressive, in and out of the sack. You're smart, eager, and you think on your feet. And if Brown is too feeble to see the talent, he has working for him, then I don't want him handling my business."

"You don't understand. If I don't bring in this account, Brown's going to fire me."

"That brings me to my next point. As I mentioned at dinner, I've been searching for a new personal assistant. I think you might take. I'll pay you twice what you're making at Brown's, which I'm betting isn't much. Among the many perks and benefits is that you get to work directly under me, in more ways than one." He pushed my tousled hair from my eyes. "What do you say?"

"So when do I start?"

My new boss grinned and opened his robe, "No time like the present."

FIELDER'S CHOICE
By HL Champa

There was nothing like the first few days of spring to put a smile on my face. The campus that had spent the winter slumbering in a blanket of grey skies and mushy snow was now alive again. But, there was only one way to know that spring had well and truly arrived. The first sighting of the college baseball team was always the biggest and best clue that the season had changed. They arrived en masse, taking the field to begin preparing for their season. The rowdy voices echoed off the brick wall of the building, their laughter and jokes filling the silence of the staid admissions office. At first, I balked at having my window so close to the playing fields. But, now I saw it as one of the few perks of my new job. I hated having to wear suits and ties, and I hated the mountains of busy work and the never-ending meetings. On top of that, the college had seen fit to shove me into a crappy makeshift office with mismatched furniture and a fake wall. My only solace was the window. It let in a lot of sun and gave me an increasingly great view.

Despite the growing stack of papers and backlog of work on my desk, I found myself distracted by the noise and movement going on outside. Although the day started off dank and cloudy, the sun had finally broken through the clouds, causing the temperature to spike. That week, the team started their routine of grooming the infield dirt and preparing the chalk lines for practice. For the last few days, I'd spent countless valuable minutes with my face near the window, watching boys half my age exercise and do manual labor. I should have been ashamed of myself, but I didn't feel bad at all. My divorce had been final for nearly five years. I had barely dated, spending way too much time avoiding who I really was. I deserved a distraction. Hell, I deserved a lot more than that. But, the fantasy would have to do for now.

I sat up higher in my chair, trying to catch a glimpse of my favorite first baseman. Finally, he came into view, striding out of the dugout with the casual confidence only a twenty-year-old could possess. He stood a few inches taller than the rest. His lanky frame was just a bit thin but still revealed bunches of tight muscles. I watched intently as he stooped over his rake, pulling and pushing the red dirt back and forth to smooth out the divots the cleats left behind. His shirtsleeves had been cut off, showing off his perfectly sculpted arms. His laughter rang out through the air, the deep rumble making my ears perk up. I rolled closer to the window, getting a better angle on the situation.

He really was a gorgeous kid. His dark brown hair was short but messy; his hands seemed so big even at a distance. I swallowed hard at his legs flexing back and forth, his tight pants clinging to each amazing curve while he chatted away to his teammates scattered near him. It was suddenly hot in my office. The ventilation was anemic at best, but I knew most of the heat was coming from inside my pants. A slight sheen of sweat was forming on my back, my cheap dress shirt stuck between my shoulder blades. I shrugged off my jacket and loosened my tie. My eyes went back out the window. I was shocked to find my first baseman staring straight back at me. He had stopped working, his large frame leaning lazily on his rake, his eyes registering my presence. I watched, breathless, as his full lips curled into a smile. His attention was soon stolen, his eyes gone as quickly as they had come. A knock at the door startled me fully back into my day.

"Hey, Alex, are you ready to go to lunch?"

It was Debra, my co-worker, salad in hand. I sighed, throwing one last glance out the window before I opened my drawer and pulled out a crumpled paper bag. Thinking about another ham sandwich in the break room, I sighed again. It wasn't the tasty treat I was looking for, but it would have to do.

The next day, I woke to rain and wind pounding on my windows. My mood immediately dampened. The baseball team retreated to the gym during bad weather. Rolling over in bed, I resigned myself to spending my day without my favorite escape. Maybe I could finally get some work done. Lord knows I had fallen hopelessly behind.

Instead of buckling down and working hard, I was caught up trying to find out more about my ballplayer. It was difficult, since I knew nothing about him; not even his name. I had to search out old baseball programs and once I found his picture, I finally learned who he was. Travis Miller. The name felt too plain, too ordinary for him. I stared at his picture for longer than I should have, before I got itchy fingers. My need for information grew every day the rain fell and the view out my window stayed bleak. I learned his major, class schedule and home address. But, it wasn't enough. I found out where he lived on campus, what his grades were and how many times he'd taken a class pass/fail.

The week stayed rainy, and it wasn't until Friday that the baseball team reemerged from their exile. The ground was muddy and soaked with water, but that didn't stop them from standing far apart from each other and throwing baseballs back and forth. I looked out the window, watching the fluid, easy motion of his arm. He barely looked at the ball when he caught it. It was as if he were on autopilot; until the ball thrown by his partner sailed past him and went careening off the wall of the building where I was sitting. My heart skipped a beat as I watched him running straight towards my window, his legs pumping hard. The ball skipped up against the base of the building. Before I knew it, Travis was standing right in front of my window. He bent down to pick up the ball and stood up, his eyes staring right through the glass at me.

I froze, unable to move an inch in my chair. I expected him to just run off, but he didn't. He just kept staring, his eyes fixed on mine. A deep flush rose up in my face. His smile surprised me, as did his apprising gaze. His hand reached out and touched the window, just for a second. His hand truly was large, his fingertips leaving smudges on the thick glass. It felt as if he was touching me, a jolt of electricity shot through me. He turned and ran away, returning to his buddies and their game of catch. Nothing had happened, but it felt as real as anything ever did. Turning away from the window, I tried to calm down. But, my breath was ragged and quick. I could feel my cock stirring in my pants. It had grown painfully hard. My reaction felt out of proportion; my response to something so simple felt excessively profound.

The rest of the week went by without incident, Travis too distracted by playing to give me another glance. It didn't stop me from peeking, spending time watching the athletic display of my cute young man. I secretly wished for another glance, another flash of a smile through my portal to brighten my day. However, it was all business on the other side of the glass.

I worked late the next week, to try and catch up on all the work I'd been shirking. By Friday, I was almost completely caught up, but it was after five when I finally finished the last stack of forms for the next semester. My file cabinet drawer slammed shut, when I heard the glass shatter. The shards were all over the floor, a dirty baseball coming to rest in the corner. Voices and footsteps were in panic outside, but when I went to the window, I didn't see anyone. There was a dustpan in the break room, but I just stood stunned, looking around the damage in my office. I'd have to call the maintenance department to board up my window. So much for my decent view.

I tiptoed over the glass. As soon as I put my hand on the doorknob, there was a knock on the other side. I pulled the door open tentatively and saw him standing there. Travis, my dream boy was standing outside my office, his baseball glove still in his hand. My mouth was open, and my heart was in a skipping panic.

"Hi. I'm sorry about the window. It was totally my fault. The ball just got away from me."

I stood helpless as he stepped past me into my office. Surveying the damage, he stooped to pick up the ball that was in the corner. He tossed it repeatedly into his glove, looking down at me from across the room.

"We were just goofing around. Dave told me not to throw it so hard."

He kept talking, but I was barely listening. It didn't seem real, to have him right in front of me. We had been close that day at the window, but the glass stood between us. I knew I should say something, but words failed me.

"Here, let me help you clean this up."

He set his baseball glove on my desk and stooped down to pick up glass.

"You don't have to do that."

My voice sounded weird, like it belonged to someone else. He looked up at me, his hand full of sharp pieces of my beloved window. He stood up, pausing to deposit the trash into the metal can next to my desk.

"It's the least I can do after being so clumsy."

He kept scooping up the glass as he spoke, putting the shards into the nearby trashcan. But, what he'd said didn't make any sense, so I decided to call him on it.

"That's funny. You don't strike me as the clumsy type."

My boldness had returned, my heart finally getting itself under control. I stared into his eyes, which were the palest blue I had ever seen. His smile returned, a sly look in his eyes told me I was on to something.

"Okay. I admit it. It wasn't so much of an accident."

"Then, why did you break my window?"

I knew what I wanted him to say, but I was nervous about his response.

"I've seen you staring at me, at us, for the last few weeks. After I got a closer look, I knew I needed to meet you, Alex."

He surprised me when he said my name out loud. He took two steps closer to me, his large hands wringing together in apparent nervousness.

"There are easier ways to meet me. All you had to do was make an appointment."

"It's not an appointment I want from you, Alex."

"Then, what do you want, Travis?"

"I'm pretty sure I want the same thing you do. You've been paying pretty close attention to me out that window. And, you already know my name. Unless you are just a really big baseball fan."

His hand touched my shoulder, the heat of the contact making my mouth fall open. My brain was screaming for me to be reasonable, but my body was ignoring the protest.

"I love baseball."

It was a lie, but he didn't need to know that.

"Sure you do."

Before I could say another word, his lips fell to mine. His arm curled around my back, pulling me into a deep embrace. His mouth was softer than I ever imagined. The eagerness of his youth was evident, a refreshing change from the last indifferent mouth I had kissed. I was more surprised by the hand on my ass, squeezing gently as he pulled me closer still. I could barely breathe when he let go of my mouth.

"I have to admit when I first saw you watching me I was a little freaked out."

"So, what changed?" I was truly curious, as the whole situation seemed surreal.

"When I looked in your window that day, I thought you were one of the cutest guys I'd ever seen."

"Come on, Travis. Does that line ever work?"

"No, because it's not a line. It's true. Don't tell me you've never heard that before?"

His mouth on my neck distracted me from answering. I had to admit he was persistent. And, I liked it. I also liked his teeth scraping against my skin, the sucking pull of his mouth no doubt leaving a mark. He pushed me to sit on the edge of my desk, his legs pushing my thighs apart.

"No. I've never heard that before."

"Well, now you have, Alex."

Despite my better judgment and my cynicism, I swooned a little at his earnest appreciation. He really was charming.

"Travis, you are too cute."

"I'm more than just a cute kid, you know."

His hands yanked my hips forward on the desk, his hands moving to my belt. For a moment, I panicked, suddenly unsure of what I was doing. His fingered fumbled slightly on the button of my pants, the zipper easing down slowly as he assaulted my mouth with another deep kiss. His long fingers slid into my boxers, a moan escaping my lips when I felt him touch my hardening cock. He wrapped his fist around me as his tongue moved deeper into my mouth. I gripped his shoulders for dear life, my hips moving off my desk without thought. I whimpered when his hands left me, leaning forward to nibble his lips as he dropped to his knees in front of me. He pulled my pants down my legs, while I practically tore off my shirt, tossing it aside without thought. For a moment, I was scared; worried what this perfect guy would think of my less than perfect body. But, I looked down and saw him staring at my cock with worshipful eyes. I couldn't help but moan at the sight.

"Fuck, Alex. What a cock."

I propped myself on my elbows to watch his face, to read his expressions as he moved. His hand gripped me tight, his thumb passing gently over my weeping slit. I watched in awe as his delicious lips wrapped around the head of my cock, his tongue meeting my sensitive flesh for the first time.

I expected him to be timid or clumsy, but he was neither. His tongue moved over me slowly, but he was confident in all his movements. My eyes shut tight when I felt his lips move lower and lower, the head of my cock bumping against the back of his throat. I couldn't keep my hands out of his rumpled hair, gently guiding his bobbing head as he sucked me hard. It was beyond me to be quiet, my moans filling the small room. Again, his enthusiasm overwhelmed me, his hand gripping my thigh as he moaned with every sweep of his hot tongue. I felt the familiar tremble run through me, as I got closer and closer to coming.

He pulled his mouth back, standing up to shuck his shorts and shirt off. I stared up at him, his well-muscled chest and stomach giving me more of a show than I had ever gotten out the window. The muscles that were hidden from the sun were paler, but no less impressive and taut. I got off the desk, and stood in front of him. My tongue itched to taste his sweaty skin, so I let my mouth pass over each perfectly formed muscle. As I moved lower, I stopped to lave over each bump of his abs. My hands explored what my mouth couldn't, feeling his muscles strain and relax as I touched him.

It was my turn to drop to my knees, my face right in front of his young, hard cock. I marveled at it, admiring its every detail. The thick drop of liquid at the tip begged to be licked away, and I obliged. His ragged breathing gave away his nerves, despite his calm façade. I let my tongue swirl over the head of his cock. It felt thick and silky soft, his salty sweet taste filling my mouth. I sucked him gently into my throat, easing down slowly. His hands fisted my hair, his hips pushing forward, trying to urge me on. Trying to keep us both on the edge, I teased him, not giving him too much too soon. His strong ass tensed under my hands, his powerful body a mass of tension and effort. His voice wobbled, but it still sounded so good.

"Oh God, oh fuck."

I just smiled before devouring him fully, my nose touching his flat belly. But, his reprieve didn't last long. I pulled back, rubbing my lips against his weeping head, avoiding his advances.

"Please, Alex, I can't take much more."

I went back to what I was doing, but my own desperation was outweighing my need to exact my revenge. After a few more deep thrusts of his cock in my throat, I stood up. His mouth was immediate on mine, kissing me frantically. I fumbled through my drawers, reaching for the condoms and lube Debra had stashed there as a joke for my birthday. Travis gave me a long, deep kiss before I turned him roughly, causing a yelp to escape his lips. I wasn't usually forceful, but something about Travis made it easy for me.

"Bend over that desk, Travis."

He leaned forward; my sweaty hands trembled slightly as I fumbled with the bottle top. He gasped when he felt my cool, lubed fingers pressing against his asshole. One of my fingers slipped inside, just a bit. But, it was enough to make him cry out and make my hand drop to my needy cock. Travis leaned further over my desk, his ass moving higher, my finger easing deeper. My voice sounded rusty, deeper than usual.

"Do you want more?"

"Yes. Yes, Alex. I want more."

I pulled my finger nearly all the way out of his ass, and when I pushed back inside him, I replaced one finger with two. He looked back at me, the sting of pain written all over his pretty face, but as he relaxed, he started pushing back against my probing fingers, his body adjusting to my thrusts. His head fell forward, his hands gripping the edge of the desk as his hips moved back towards me in a steady rhythm. He whimpered his disappointment when I removed my fingers from his ass, but the latex-covered head of my cock soon placated him. I teased him a bit, until I felt him press back into me, his eyes back on mine.

"Oh, God, please fuck me, Alex."

His words pierced right through me, splitting open my desire that had been dormant for too long. I inched inside of him, my thick length stretching him open little by little. I couldn't do anything but sigh and moan and watch him take me. After a few moments of resistance, my hips hit his ass, my cock inside him as deep as it would go. I held still, letting Travis get used to the feeling. His moaning and the throbbing tightness of his ass were overwhelming me, so I moved back slowly, feeling the intense pull of his snug ass. My need for him took control after that, and I grabbed his hips in my hands and started thrusting into him. My thrusts were erratic, my timing interrupted by his ass pushing back hard against me. I didn't care; I knew neither of us would last long. My fingers wrapped around his cock, jerking an unsteady beat while I drove into him. Travis stopped rutting back against me, and I felt his cock start to twitch. Hollering out, his whole body stiffened, his dick spurting into my hand as I continued to pound him. My own climax soon followed, my hips slamming hard into Travis as I stuttered out unintelligible words of pleasure.

My body lay heavy on top of him, our sweat mixing as we panted in silence. I withdrew from his body, the condom tossed into the trash. I slumped back into my chair, hardly able to move. Travis stood up, gathering his clothes while I waited for my heart to stop trying to escape my chest. I watched his shorts slide up his narrow hips; his chest flushed and wet from our exertion. I couldn't resist staring at his hot body. I stood and pulled him close, our lips meeting gently, before my tongue plunged into his mouth. He pulled back and looked at me, his sweet smile kicking me in the gut.

"That was amazing, Alex."

"You're not so bad yourself, Travis."

"So, am I off the hook with the window?"

"I don't know. I might need more time to think about it."

"I'm sure if you let me, Alex, I can make it up to you."

He nuzzled my neck as I pulled up my pants, my thighs still trembling slightly from my orgasm. Travis really was a good kid, too good to only have once.

"I have no doubt, Travis."

After we dressed, he helped me clean up the rest of the glass. He picked up his baseball glove but hesitated before he walked out. His face was serious as his grabbed me, kissing me hard.

"What was that for, Travis?"

"I don't know. Just because."

God, he was so damn cute. He took the baseball that had cracked my window and handed it to me. I rolled it between my hands, looking up into his sparkling blue eyes.

"Thanks, Travis. For everything."

"No problem, Alex. I guess I'll be seeing you."

"Yeah, you know where to find me."

He walked out, his cleats echoing off the linoleum floor. I picked up the phone and called the maintenance department. I needed my window, after all.

CLASSIC
By Landon Dixon

The guy was a classic, like that black '66 Lincoln Continental he kept all for himself in one corner of the sprawling used car lot. He was around fifty, with dark hair streaked white at the temples, clear grey eyes, a lush, red mouth, and a tall, lean body tanned a deep-brown. I was half his age, but I was hot for car-daddy.

He was one of the reasons I'd taken the job hustling autos around, washing them, cleaning up around the place. Him, and the fact that I was still tuition and textbook-shy of getting into my second year of college. My real father had decided I was old enough to support myself.

From the first day I set foot on the lot, I tried to be the best employee a used car dealership had ever seen. That might not be saying much, given the rep of the joints, but I stepped it up a notch, putting a shine so fine on the cars you could comb your nose hair in the mirror finish. I made sure there wasn't so much as a pink slip blowing around the big lot, no garbage on display other than the 'vintage' K-cars. And, I was the fastest guy from garage to lot behind the wheel, 0-100 yards in less than ten seconds, depending on the job the mechanics had done in temporarily patching up the engines for resale.

And, I got noticed by Mr. Wallace Stern, and rewarded – a pat on my blond head and a pay boost from minimum wage to ten cents above minimum wage. That was after one month on the job. After two months of killing myself, me and my bank account were really still in no better shape; I was no closer to closing the deal with Wallace as I'd been when I started work.

I knew the guy was as queer as the warranties he offered on some of his wrecks, but I just couldn't get him to take a look under my hood, get his motor racing. Despite the fact I was parading around in form-fitting tanks and shorts, letting the hot summer sun soak into my tight, toned chassis, sheen my lithe limbs with a glistening coat of sweat. I've got a cute little bubble-butt and a freckle-sprinkled face to match. But Wallace's hands were too full running the car lot, apparently, to get them dirty on little young me.

So, at the start of month three on the job, with summer closing fast, along with my chances of a second-year of college, I opted out of the good kid program. If auto-man didn't want to give me a ride, I was going to take him for one.

I started moving around with all the pep of an early-model Firefly, leaving streaks behind on the paint jobs after washing, letting garbage fly around the lot like the banners and bunting, grinding gears and trailing rubber whenever I jockeyed cars into sales position. I was already looking for a more permanent job, anyway, one that would take me through the fall, winter, and spring and, hopefully, into summer school the following year.

To give myself a bigger boost in that respect, I boosted some cash out of the showroom till on a couple of occasions. Nothing too much, just enough to allow me to get along with some kids my own age on the weekends. But the third time I tried it, Wallace put the hammer down.

"What do you think you're doing, Troy!?" he demanded, suddenly appearing from around the corner of his office.

I'd thought everyone had gone home; I'd seen Wallace drive off in his Lincoln. But, I guessed he stopped and came back for something, and caught me green-handed.

"I-I was just, uh, replacing some money I'd taken out for lunch. I know I shouldn't have, but ..."

"Like hell you were! You were stealing, like you have on two previous occasions. Don't think we haven't noticed the shortages in the till."

He glared at me, his hands on his hips. He was wearing a blue, pinstriped suit, a plum-colored silk tie, black shoes as glossy as his Lincoln. I was sure I could outrun the older guy. So I took off like a VW Rabbit, accelerating past him and out the side door and along the building, headed for the fence and freedom in the field beyond at the rear of the lot.

But as soon as I hit asphalt, I spotted Wallace's Continental idling by the garage, and I got a better, more vengeful idea. I skidded to a stop, yanked the front door open, jumped in.

Unfortunately, and surprisingly, Wallace had wheels of his own, besides his sweet ride. He caught up with me and grabbed me by the arm and yanked me back out of the car, suddenly all over me like he'd never been before. "I'll teach you to steal!" he rasped, swatting my ass with the flat of his hand.

I was jolted up straight by the blow. I'd never expected anything like that ... never expected it to thrill me like it did. I was wearing a thin pair of jean shorts, and the man's blade of a hand impacted my ass hard and heavy and heated. I surged with sudden warmth, from my tingling cheeks on up and around, my cock leaping in my shorts.

"You need to be taught some discipline, college boy!" Wallace hissed in my ear. "And, here's your second lesson." He smacked my bum again, even harder this time.

I jumped up onto my toes, stung, stunned. My whole body flushed with shimmering heat, my cock swelling right along with the rounded flesh of my swatted bottom. I'd never been spanked before in my life, never before realized it could feel so excitingly erotic. Wallace gripped my left shoulder with his warm left hand, his right hand fanning pure exhilaration into my butt cheeks.

He smacked my ass again and again. Then he loosened his grip, thinking maybe I'd learned my lesson. But, I was just getting educated; I was a bad boy, desperately needing the strong, guiding hand of a Stern daddy in the worst way. "Fuck you, old man!" I sneered, making like I was trying to wriggle out of the guy's grip.

His grip tightened, his straight, white teeth gritting together. He pulled me back, pulled the rear suicide door of the Lincoln open and flung me inside, jumping in after me.

We had a little more privacy inside the running luxury car, and Wallace used it to really lay down the law. He perched on the leather bench seat and dragged me over his knees, whacked my upturned bottom like I was a little kid. I gulped, jerked, the wicked blow feeling so sensational on my rump, shivering me with pain and pleasure. I draped over his legs and soaked up the flaming heat of his hand and body.

He gripped me by the back of the neck with one hand, raised the other right to the roof and whistled it down on my derriere. The cracking sound blasted the interior of the vehicle, easily drowning out the purr of the powerful engine beneath the hood. I shuddered with every strike, my cock pressing hard and throbbing into the man's legs.

I'd discovered the wanton appeal of spanking quite by accident, and now I deliberately sought more sexual punishment. I twisted my head around and shouted, "Fuck you and the car you drove in on, asshole!"

Wallace's face was already pink with exertion, and now it flared red with anger. He tore my shorts down, popping my trembling butt cheeks out into the open – just like I'd hoped he would. His bare hand smashed my bare ass, shooting me full of raw bliss.

He struck again and again, whaling my rippling mounds, battering them red as his face, hot as his temper. He only stopped when he finally noticed me undulating against his legs, pumping my pumped-up dick against his thighs.

That's when his head cooled down enough to figure out that maybe I wasn't quite getting the message he was trying to dish out. But he got my message, loud and clear. While he held his burning hand up in the air, I kept on pumping his legs, my butt and cock burning.

He lowered his hand, dropped it softly down on my bum, gently rubbed my battered cheeks.

"No!" I hissed at him. "Spank me! Teach me!"

He lifted his hand, smacked it down on my rump. He rained blow after blow onto my ass, shattering my buttocks, my conception of traditional sexuality. The car shook with his savage blows, like me. I was a length of molten steel over his knees, my ass the superheated core, Wallace the unrelenting blacksmith, hammering me into and out of shape.

I bounced on his knees, my cheeks jumping numb. My cock spasmed. I was ready to erupt, which is exactly when wise Wallace ceased his beating, and got all touchy-feely with my glowing cheeks again. The guy knew when to hard-sell, when to soft.

He caressed my buttocks with his swirling fingertips. I could hardly feel it, yet felt it enormously, the tenderness amplified a hundred-fold after the beautiful brutality. He traced tantalizing joy all over my throbbing ass then dipped his fingers into my cleavage, spreading my buttocks.

He blew cool air onto my blazing seat cushions, breathed warm air onto my exposed asshole. I shuddered across his legs, my head and body swimming with delight.

A finger slid against my pucker, and I moaned. His finger wiggled into my manhole, and I whimpered. He plunged deeper inside me, gripping my cheeks with his other fingers.

"Fuck me! Please, fuck me!" I gasped, unable to control myself. I wanted that mature man's hard cock punishing my butthole, like his hand had punished my buttocks.

He pulled his digit out of my ass and then helped me get into position – knees on the backseat of the car, hands on the backrest. He crouched in behind me, and I arched my young bum at him, as he unfastened his suit pants and pushed them and his silk shorts down, drew out his stiff prick.

I stared back at his cock. It was as long and lean as the man himself, as smooth. "Spank my ass with your cock," I said.

He whacked my left cheek with his dick, my right. It was nowhere near as hard as his hitting hand, yet it was so much more intimate, his hood and shaft smacking the bare skin of my butt.

I dug my nails into the leather seat, biting my lip. He struck me with his cock again and again, shooting sparks through my ass wherever he impacted, making my own prick quiver with delight. My buttocks trembled uncontrollably, spanked in the most erotic manner possible.

Wallace at last stopped the wicked onslaught, drew some non-engine lubricant out of a pocket and greased his cock, my crack. His slender, slippery fingers glided in between my cheeks and rubbed, making me tingle from head to toe. Then tense, as he pulled out his fingers and pushed in his cap.

I reached back and gripped my cheeks, spread them. They were burning in my sweating hands, and I fully realized just how hard I'd been impacted by the man's strong hand. I bit into the backrest, digging my fingernails into my blistered butt flesh and tearing myself open, begging Wallace to stick and stroke me.

His hood squished against my starfish, shot through, bursting into my anus. Followed smoothly and oh-so-sensuously by his long, hard shaft. He filled my ass to the max, cock stretching my chute, surging me with a wonderful warmth. Then he started fucking my bum, thrusting his prick back and forth in my anus.

"Hit me! Spank me! Fuck me!" I yelped.

He whacked my rippling cheeks with his free hand, other hand holding tight to my waist, cock pounding into my hole. I was rocked to and fro by the frantic rhythm of his banging, my body ablaze like my bum, brain melted down to a puddled mess of pure pleasure. I grabbed onto my cock and jacked, the spanking and spearing driving me wild.

Wallace hit harder, fucked faster. The crack of his hand on my ass, his thighs against my cheeks, became one, filling the sweating, rocking car and our ears. He rammed me in a frenzy, flailing my butt.

"Jesus, yes, Troy!" he cried, jerking in back of me.

I felt his cock spasm, shoot in my anus. Just as my own cock exploded in my fist. Hot sperm flooded my chute, hot sperm flying out of the tip of my prick. I danced around on my knees like I'd been hooked up to the battery of the car, volts of pure ecstasy shocking me over and over.

I collapsed down into his lap afterwards, and he held me tight, whispering soothing words of sweet love in my ear.

"You're going to be a good boy from now on, aren't you?"

I kissed him full on his plush, red lips. I'd be going to college in the fall for sure now, I knew, and would work hard to get good grades. But I'd still need a good spanking every chance I could get.

So, I grinned evilly at Wallace, asked, "What's the fun in that – Daddy?"

DADDY DETECTIVES
By Landon Dixon

I was sitting in my office, twiddling my thumbs and thinking of diddling, when the kid sashayed inside.

He was nineteen, maybe twenty, with sandy-blond hair and bright blue eyes and a full, red mouth, a smattering of freckles splashed on his adorable, innocent-looking face. He was small for his age, built willow-thin, dressed in a blue jean jacket, white T-shirt, and blue jean pants. He looked like he'd just stepped off the bus from Hayseed, Kansas.

I wasn't far off.

"My name is Jimmy Orton," he said, his voice little more than a lilting whisper. "I'm from Rochelle, Kansas."

I raised a hand out of my lap, waved him closer, watched him perch up on one of the wooden chairs that fronted my desk. "And my name's Hart Murdoch, from right here in the City of Angels. What can I do for you, Jimmy?"

He looked as if he didn't have enough dough to stuff in a men's room pay toilet, but I liked his look, nonetheless.

He clutched his little hands in his lap and writhed his fingers around, glancing up at me from behind long, curling lashes. "I'm looking for my daddy," he finally mustered the courage to state.

I arched a quizzical eyebrow, creaked forward in my chair, picking up a pencil. "What's the guy look like?"

Jimmy batted his eyelashes some more, licked those rose petal lips of his. "Well … he's about fifty, with curly, salt and pepper-colored hair. He's got grey eyes and a long, straight nose and a rather wide mouth."

"Uh-huh, go on," I grunted, making with the lead etchings.

"Well, he's well-built, fairly tall, likes to wear blue, double-breasted suits and red ties."

"Uuh-huuh," I said, looking across the desk at the kid.

He gulped nervously, grinned. Then he popped off the chair and walked around my desk, stood right next to me. "Does that description ring a bell, Mr. Murdoch?"

I snorted and leaned back in my chair again, folded my hands back together. "Yeah, it rings a few bells – alarm bells. You just described me. But, I don't do handouts, kid, so take your sob story down the street to someone who's buying."

He slid into my lap, bolting me upright in the chair.

It all happened so fast it made my head whirl. One minute: dull, dusty day with nothing to do but watch the flies tap dance on the windowpanes; the next: a young, pretty boy dropped into my lap, on top of my now swelling interest in his particular case.

Jimmy flung an arm around my neck, snuggled his tight, little buns in firmer and warmer over top of my hard-coming-on. "Have I been bad, Daddy?" he asked, voice soft and caressing as a velvet kid's glove. He slid his left thumb in between his petulant lips and sucked on it. Then pulled it out all wet and shiny and offered it up to me.

It was the best offer I'd had in a long time, and I almost jumped at it. But then my training caught me up short. "Just how old are you, Jimmy?"

He smiled. "Nineteen. Twenty in August. How old are you, Mr. Murdoch?"

I smiled back, reaching up a hand and gripping his, drawing that shapely, succulent thumb down closer to my hungry mouth. "Old enough to be your … daddy," I said, then sealed my lips around his glistening digit, and sucked on it.

He beamed, feeling my tug all through his trembling body. His other hand tightened around my neck. And when I popped his thumb out of my mouth, he lowered his head, and we both sucked on it, licked at it, swirled our tongues together.

I gripped the kid in my arms and mashed my mouth against his, thumb forgotten, wanting to swallow the yummy little teen whole. My cock throbbed under his squirming bum, as he wrapped his other arm around my neck and kissed me back. His lips were soft and warm and eager, moving against mine.

I pulled back, breaking the breathless seal, allowing one or both of us to come to our senses. This was a place of business, after all; we'd only just met; we were generations apart.

But, none of that stuff made a lick of difference, the mood we were both in. In fact, it only aroused us even further. Jimmy stuck out his kitten-pink tongue, and I batted my tongue against it. He moaned, breathing hot and bubblegum fresh into my face. I caught his luscious tongue between my lips and briefly sucked on it, before crowding my urgent sticker into his wet, red mouth, thrashing it around.

I filled his kisser to bulging, his cheeks flowering outward with my searching tongue. He took it all with delight, my hands on his slender, tender neck, then my tongue. He tilted his head back, and I licked his hot, young flesh, lapping at his gaily bobbing Adam's apple, stroking up to his chin and surging back into his mouth.

"Oh, please, fuck me, Mr. Murdoch!" he gasped. "I want your big, hard cock in my ass, Daddy!"

These teens and their impetuosity.

Jimmy arched up in my lap, and I helped him skin his jeans and white Jockeys down off his legs and sneakers. His cock sprung up hard and long from its nest of fuzzy blond pubes, as smooth and clean-cut as the rest of the guy. I gripped it, stroked it, feeling the pulsing excitement of the young man all through my body and soul.

He moaned, his bare legs trembling across my legs, his cock jumping up even harder and longer in my pumping hand. "Please, Mr.

Murdoch!" he bleated, pretty face twisted in sexual anguish. "I'm so close to squirting already!"

These kids and their hair-trigger dicks.

I pushed him up, and he arched his bum off me, allowing me to unbuckle and unzip and push my own pants and shorts down. He licked his lips when my hard-on flopped out, a wicked grin on his face.

Then he plopped back down in my lap, legs on either side of me, the two of us face-to-face, cock-to-cock. He grabbed both our erections in his darting hand and squeezed them together. We groaned as one, our cocks burning together.

I reached past him and fumbled a desk drawer open, pulled a tube of lube out. The cleaning lady could at last stop wondering why I kept that there. I squirted some gun oil onto my prick, let Jimmy rub it into the veiny, pulsing appendage. Then I raised his bare bottom and scrubbed his smooth, happy crack with a pair of slippery digits. He groaned, dick jumping up appetizingly close to my mouth.

But, there was dirty business to get to, and I'm not one for putting things off. So I grasped my cock in the upright and locked position and let Jimmy spread his fuzz-dusted cheeks and sit his pucker down on my arrowhead.

"Yeah!" I growled, feeling his starfish squirm, loosen, burst open to receive my bloated cap. Then the rest of my shaft, as the kid dropped down in my lap with an oomph, burying my bone full-bore in his butt.

He flung his arms around my neck and kissed me all over the face, a blissful expression on his beautiful pan. I grasped his buttocks and bobbed him up and down on my pole, his anus hot as a coke oven, tight as a vise. I thrust my hips up to meet his bouncing bottom, driving my cock back and forth in his chute.

He rimmed my lips, licked the sweat off my upper lip, joyfully getting impaled on my stake. My face and body burned fire-red, thighs thumping downy cheeks, cock reaming gripping anus.

I tore a hand off a mound and grabbed onto his cock, started pumping in rhythm to my pumping. His prick was iron-hard, ready to go off.

"Oooohh ... Daddy!" he wailed, shuddering on the end of my spearing cock, spurting hot sperm out of the end of his.

I stroked him, fucked him, joined him ecstasy, his clenching butt cheeks and sucking chute pulling me past the point of no return. I cried out, exploding inside him, blasting his bowels with my burning seed.

We were drenched in sweat and cum.

He kissed me goodbye and popped off my cock and pulled up his pants and exited my office just as unexpectedly as he'd arrived.

And I'd thought he was looking for a daddy for the long haul?

# # # # #

I went looking for him.

And for a hungry dick that knows his way around town, it didn't take me long to sniff out the kid. He was up on the desk of one of my colleagues in the snooper business, Barnes Ketchum, sucking Barnes' cock as if he expected to pull a rainbow out of the guy's turgid schlong.

Barnes is a slim, silver-haired fox with pale blue eyes and an all-over tan. Just the kind of daddy in the kind of profession Jimmy apparently preferred. I slapped the kid's bare ass, and he almost choked on Barnes' cock.

"Aw, and he was giving such a good interview," Barnes sighed, looking at me and winking.

Jimmy twisted his head around and stared at me, his youthful face flushed red from exertion and embarrassment. "Oh, hello, Mr. Murdoch," he gulped. "I, uh, just thought that, you know, two daddies might be better than one. I'm all alone in the big city, you know."

"Smart thinking, kid," I congratulated him, running my hands over his cheeky impudence with fond remembrance. "Looks to me like you'll have all the daddies you can handle in no time at all."

I unbelted and unzipped, dropped my trousers along with the foreplay. My cock poled out straight and true and throbbing. Jimmy wheeled around from Barnes' shining prick and gripped my dong at the base, his hot little fingers and warm palm making me shiver. Then I shuddered as if I'd been groin-shot, when the kid slipped his moist, red lips over my mushroomed knob and mouthed me almost all the way down.

"Pretty talented for a youngster, a hick from the sticks, huh?" Barnes commented to me, greasing his already dripping gun, his gleaming eyes fixed on Jimmy's fine, upraised rump.

"Yeah," I grunted, sifting my fingers into Jimmy's soft, blond hair and riding his bobbing head with my hands. "He's got everything this town is looking for. I think he's going to do just swell."

Barnes poked the hood of his pecker into Jimmy's pucker. The teenager jumped on my cock, teeth biting into my shaft. I got him sucking again, pulling his head back and forth, his mouth wet-vaccing my pole. As Barnes sunk slow and sure and steady into his ass, right tight up to the balls.

Jimmy's moan of pleasure reverberated up and down the length of mouth-sealed prick and all through my body. Barnes started fucking the kid's ass, undulating his hips, gliding his cock in and out of the sweet, pink chute I'd savaged not so long ago.

Jimmy kept right on sucking my cock, though, tugging, scraping, wagging his tongue across the underside of my pulsating dong. I pumped my hips in rhythm to my colleague's, fucking Jimmy's mouth as he sucked. The kid rocked back and forth atop the desk, me at one end, Barnes at the other.

If he'd never been in a threesome before, been plugged in both manholes at once, he showed no signs of squeamishness or sheepishness. Rather, he was downright enthusiastic, taking it at both ends and reveling, wallowing in it. He grinned up at me, mouth full of my cock, Barnes plunging his butt full-length.

The phone rang. Nobody answered it. Business could wait, this couldn't. A kid like this comes around only two or three times in a dick's life, so he's got to take full advantage. And, Barnes and I were taking full advantage, taking it up another notch.

The silver fox dug his manicured fingernails into Jimmy's waist and pumped his lean hips faster, harder, ramming Jimmy's bum, churning the teen's chute. I reciprocated, pumping my hips more feverishly, driving my dick deep into Jimmy's velvety mouth, right down his throat.

He gagged only a little, spit spluttering out of the corners of his overstuffed mouth, his flared nostrils gasping for air, watery eyes looking up at me, down at my shifting, glistening shaft between his lips. Barnes rammed, and I rammed back, Jimmy getting banged at both openings and taking it like a man.

The temperature soared in the stuffy office. Even Barnes' normally laconically composed face registered heat and sweat and feeling, as he drove Jimmy like a madman, pistoning the kid's anus. It was all I could do to keep up. But, I did, almost tearing out chunks of Kansas sun-ripened hair from Jimmy's scalp, slamming my cock back and forth in his lovely kisser, bouncing my balls off his drooling chin.

The kid's face cheeks billowed with the force of my cock splitting his mouth, his ass cheeks rippling with the force of Barnes axing his chute. It was quite a sight, distant second only to the wicked feeling of fucking the kid's crimson, creamy mouth and throat. It was far too good to last for too long. We dicks aren't the patient type.

Barnes hammered asshole a couple more times. Then he tilted his head back and howled, jolted by orgasm, jerking on the end of Jimmy's bum. I could just imagine the blissful blasts drenching Jimmy's tunnel, having just been there myself.

I flung my hips into Jimmy's face, cock flying in his mouth. And then it was my turn, again, to cry out and come. I shuddered, jumped, ball-batter busting loose and blowing taps on Jimmy's tonsils.

I danced around like the jitterbug was back in fashion, coating Jimmy's throat, filling Jimmy's mouth, with burst after burst of hot, salty man-juice.

The kid frantically gulped, his Adam's apple actually doing the jitterbug, taking just about all I had to give him. While getting filled to overflowing at the other end, Barnes dousing his bowels over and over and over.

Jimmy stays with me sometimes, sometimes with Barnes. And sometimes with some other seasoned, sexy men he's found on his travels around the city. He's made intimate friends all over the place, no shortage of daddies to love him.

ACCOUNTING ON TROUBLE
By Landon Dixon

They call me a one-man audit wrecking crew, always looking for trouble on the balance sheet or income statement, whenever I strap on the green visor and start counting the beans.

Except for these two guys out in the darkened parking lot of Brandon Petroleum way, way after closing time. They were calling me names like 'asswipe' and 'pansy' and threatening me with great personal bodily harm unless I laid off the tests and procedures, gave the company my unqualified audit opinion on the P&L statement.

It was to laugh. And, I did. Right in their cruddy faces.

Here's how it all began.

I was handed the income statement section on the year-end BP audit. And, a bunch of guff from the partner-in-charge about how I shouldn't go looking for trouble because there was none to be found. BP was a big client for the firm, after all, fees gushing up in the hundreds of thousands.

The guy might just as well have waved a red flag at a bull in Merrill Lynch's china shop. My integrity comes without a price tag, my dedication to ferreting out the truth in the numbers, unstoppable and inexhaustible. Sure, it was 'busy season,' and the audits were backed up like the old man's bowels, but that wasn't my concern, nor were the firm's client relations efforts. I swear allegiance to a higher god – the capital markets.

So, I started to dig into the books. And, it didn't take me long to hit oily accounting practices. Their revenue recognition procedures were right out of the Gordon Gecko School of Greed, the Minister of

Finance Department of rosy optimism. Everything was being booked as revenue to shore up the earnings numbers, from handshake deals at strip bars to phone-in pledges from prison cells to geological reports that didn't hold water much less oil.

And on the flip side, expenses seemed to be an endangered species at BP, to be quarantined off the income statement and capitalized on the balance sheet. Every outlay was an 'asset,' every pay-off a profit-earning center to be amortized over more years than it took apes to evolve into CEOs.

The net effect was an income statement as bubbly and exuberant as a tar sands tailings pond. And it stunk just as bad.

I had a meeting scheduled with the CFO the following morning to see how he could throat-dance his way out of the mess I'd uncovered. And it was the night before, when I was leaving the company offices after logging another eighteen-hour shift that the boys from the 'service department' showed up.

They accosted me in the parking lot, shoved me up against the late-model Trabant that a first-year articling accountant's salary allowed.

"We don't like the way you're doin' the audit," the goon on my right rasped, jabbing a squat digit into my chest.

"Then take it up with the professional standards board," I replied politely. "That's what they're there for. Do you need their fax …"

"We're takin' it up with you, bright boy," the goon on my left gritted, gripping my Giant Tiger suit in a death-grip, tearing the cheesecloth. "We want you to lay off the questions. We want a clean report on your P&L section. *Capishe*?"

Capishe must've been the brand of garlic he'd just eaten. I shook my gourd, my arm free. "Threats don't count," I intoned. "I do."

A shot to the gut was their response to that shocking reality. I doubled over like yesterday's stock report. Then I came up swinging, audit bag and all.

I'd been gripping the heavy tan leather satchel all along (it was packed with paperwork for the car ride home), and now I brought it up in an arc, catching the one goon under his jutting blue chin and sending him airborne. He took it hard – cracking his conk on the asphalt when he back-splashed down.

The other goon bounced a right off my jaw, making my teeth and synapses chatter. But he'd forgotten I had my hand in my pocket – an auditor never travels without his calculator. This one dated back to the Ka-Ching Dynasty, a five-row abacus time-worn by the sweat of a hundred truth-swearing accountants before me.

I brought it out of my pocket, rammed it into the pig eyes of the goon. Wood shattered and beads blasted and retinas detached on brutal impact. The goon staggered backwards, clawing at his blinded orbs, and I delivered a stunning final judgment on the pair's haphazard efforts – a size-twelve Florsheim between his legs, into his tiny beads. He went down like the Titanic, minus the four-hour running time.

But, that wasn't the end of it. They'd played the hammer, now they brought on the honey.

I unlocked my cell in the flophouse I call home and flicked on the lights. The Murphy bed was down, a silky blonde stretched out on its mice-chewn sheets. She was as naked as the facts they were trying to cover up at BP, built soft and sensual with more hills and dales than the Pembina Valley.

"Hello," she purred, warm syrup on an unyielding stack of pancakes. "Won't you join me – for a meeting?"

"I'm booked solid to the end of the month. Try me again in the spring."

She wasn't taking no for an answer. She spread her legs, showing me there was no question.

I dropped my audit bag on the plank floor and walked over to the hot plate, set a can of Chunky soup down to boil. I looked back around. She was still there, stretched out on my bed, doing a pretty good job of feeling herself up. I don't know what she needed me for.

"Okay, sweetheart," I growled, striding over and jiggling her upright. "I've got two hours of shut-eye to get done. And, I can't do that with a blonde stain on my sheets."

She slapped me, kissed me. Her tongue slithered into my mouth like a sewer snake down a drain. I was having none of it.

I spun her around and heaved her out the door, sent her clothes sailing out the window after her.

Then I slapped my hands together and grinned. That can of Chunky was going to hit the spot, all right.

# # # # #

Calvin C. Castor was a good-looking gent. About six-foot-two, slender, with silver hair, a Grand Beach tan, deep brown eyes, and a smooth, charming manner.

He gave me a chair, some platitudes about how much he valued the relationship between our firm and his, and a glass of mineral water. I took the chair and the water, shrugged off the platitudes.

"I've got 652 variance analysis questions to go through with you, Castor," I grunted. "So save your breath for the answers. If you can make them up fast enough." I grinned savagely, and the man's hair turned a whiter shade of pale.

He put up a good front, but so did the Germans at Stalingrad – at first. By question 234, he was breaking down like a Tiger tank on the winter outskirts of Kursk. My barrage of audit evidence had punched a gaping hole in his flimsy defense of rationalizations and half-baked justifications.

I'd broken men before under the glaring heat of my one-man inquisition, and Castor was about to join the heap of charred and twisted psyches I'd left rotting in prison cells and corporate boardrooms clear across the province.

"Lunch at the Wellington Club followed by golf at St. Chester's – January 16," I recited off my pad of green seven-column. "You amassed a combined bill of $926.85. And instead of expensing the amount to 'Bogus and Miscellaneous,' you capitalized it as part of the 'Jericho Project,' thus turning a hit to your income statement into a miss on your balance sheet." I looked up, the diamond-piercing glare of audit indignation in my righteous orbs. "I won't even comment on your handicap for proving you played golf on January 16."

"Please! No more!" Castor wailed, crumbling like the walls his phony project was named after. "I can't take anymore!"

He piled out of his calfskin executive chair and staggered around his teakwood desk and collapsed on his silkworm knees in between my legs. "What do you want!? I'll give you anything! Just, please, stop the questions! You're boring the life out of me!"

I looked down at the desperate man clutching my thighs. His pampered face shone with perspiration, his manicured mitts shaking. Someone with a soul instead of a ledger might've taken pity on him. "I'll put that down as 'NE' – no explanation. Moving on …"

His hands slid up my legs, brushing my groin. His fingers lingered, feeling the sudden jump he'd elicited. He looked up at me, down at the swelling bulge in my pinstripes. He grinned.

"You want oral answers, I'll give you oral answers – just the kind you want." He unzipped my pants and pulled out my semi-erection, palmed it.

I inadvertently jerked, spilling my pad, as his warm, smooth hands topped my lap. I had to give the man credit; he possessed the necessary skills his blonde bimbo assistant from the night before had been so painfully lacking. He'd stumbled onto the one tool in my arsenal I couldn't always control – in the right hands.

Even auditors get aroused. And sometimes, the long, grinding hours of the busy season limit a man's self-pleasuring social life. I hadn't jerked off since October.

Castor tugged my entire pent-up manhood out into the open, oohing and ahhing as appropriate. I measure up, skill-wise and skin-wise. He cupped and gently squeezed my balls, his other polished hand gliding up and down the ever-expanding length of my cock. Until I'd poled out to my full 210.5 millimeter potential, the man working me like an annual convention.

"God, you're built!" he breathed all over my cock, stroking with just the right twist of his wrist. The Jeremy jerk, I think that particular technique was called.

I gripped the arms of the chair, watching the man finally put his thieving hands to good use. There was no way to stop it, so I let it ride along with his mitt. We men of numbers have to take our pleasure where we can get it, and this guy was adding up just right on my dick.

He bent his silver head down and kissed the bloated purple tip of my club. I jerked. He teased the tip of his bleached pink tongue up and down my slit, and I bit my lip.

"Pre-cum tastes good," he murmured, stringing a sticky length out from my cockhead then sucking it into his mouth like a strand of salty spaghetti.

I braced myself, knowing what was coming next.

I still almost tore the limbs off the chair, nonetheless, when Castor blossomed his full, red lips over my shiny helmet and took me into his mouth. His kisser was hot and wet as any subordinates' and I shuddered, the man sucking on my knob.

He twisted my nut sack, making my balls bubble, his pulling lips doing wonders on the end of my cock. And then he got greedy, like the corporate cocksucker he was, lowering his head over my groin and merging more and more of me into his mouth. He didn't stop his hellaciously heated descent until his pretty lips met up with his pretty hand.

"Audit satisfaction!" I barked, taking one for the team.

Castor might've bitten off more than he could chew, but you'd never know it. His watery eyes stared up at me, his cheeks bulging with dong. He bobbed his head in answer to my unspoken request, sucking on my prick, deep-throat style.

A lesser man would've broken under the CFO's awesome rebuttal to all of my questions. But I held firm, in my resolve and in his mouth. He sucked hard and quick and tight, slow and loose and sensual, a talented snake-charmer of the highest order.

He gulped the cum I was leaking, milking my balls with his plying fingers. His mouth plummeted down, pulled up, lips tugging and tongue dragging. Until he showed me what I'd never shown him – mercy.

He yanked my tool out of his maw with a wet, slobbery pop and mouthed, "Fuck me up the ass! Give it to me in the ass like all the shareholders want to do to me!"

He had a point there. And I had a point – eight glistening inches out from my groin. He rose to his feet and unbuckled his kangaroo skin belt, pushed down his pants and satin shorts. His own cock was a frozen staff. He liked meeting man-meat as much as I did. He swirled his hand up and down his impressive length, then pirouetted and gripped the edge of his desk, presenting his ass to me.

It was a nice, neat package – tight and taut and twin-mounded. He plucked a tube of lube out of his breast pocket and tossed it back to me. "Oil up," he quipped, the CFO of Brandon Petroleum. "And get some retribution. Stick it to me hard!"

There was more than one way to skin a con-man, all right. I used the lube, greasing my gun. Then I slipped a pair of slickened digits in between Castor's padded cheeks, scrubbed. He groaned, pressing back against me.

I kissed his pucker with my cockhead. He reached back and spread his ass-ets, and I plowed through his starfish and plunged deep into his honey hole.

We both groaned, me giving it to him full-length, he taking it full-length. There was snow on his roof, but there was still fire in his bowels. I grasped his hips and pumped mine, fucking the man.

He arched his back, sucking on my plundering dick with his gripping ass walls. My knuckles went white on his hips, my glaring orbs watching my prick slide back and forth in his chute, the sexual pressure building in my balls.

I pumped faster, harder, really ramming the rat. The desk shook, his cheeks shimmied. He bleated for more. My thighs cracked off his ass, giving him the spanking the Board of Directors and Mama Castor should've years before.

"God, yes! Fuck me! Fuck my ass!"

My actions spoke a thousand times louder than his twisted words. I hammered into his bung, pistoning his rump, rocking like that water-dipping bird except with a dick where his beak was.

Castor didn't pull on his own prong, excited enough to let me do all the dirty work. I grunted and growled, semen bursting out of my balls and steaming up my pipe. I jerked, jolted by the rawest and most honest of auditor emotions, jizzing Castor's anus over and over, overflowing his cheek banks.

I blew off months of accumulated ball batter, jumping around on the end of the man's ass with a joy I seldom experienced and never admitted to. Until at last I was empty, drained like after the Uniform Final Examination, my performance straight A's across the board here, as well.

Castor delicately bent down and pulled up his pants, tucked in his dick. "I ass-ume we have an agreement?" he arrogantly assumed.

"Your plea bargain is with the Securities Commission," I countered, shaking off my rod and reholstering. "I'm taking my audit findings all the way to the top, you to the bottom – for a second time."

I didn't get the tears and dicksucking I'd gotten earlier, to my surprise and considerable consternation. Instead, Castor just grinned, showing off those pearly whites that had felt so good tucked in behind his lips when he'd played on my skin flute.

"Hate to tell you, but I flipped on the intercom when I went into my 'act.' My secretaries have heard every grunt and groan of your cornholing." The grin widened to shit-eating proportions. "Having sex with a client is behavior unbecoming an independent auditor, isn't it? Could get you expelled from the Institute of CAs before you even get in?"

So, I didn't blow the whistle. I swallowed it. Along with one solid pound of pride and liter of bile.

Castor's company was kaput by the second quarter, the man himself fled to some remote, sunny beach part of the world where extradition treaties were as rare as snowflakes.

Shareholders and employees got reamed. But at least, I'd done some reaming of my own. Unbeknownst to them, they could take some small measure of satisfaction in that. I know I did.

NIGHT OF THE TWO MOONS
By Jay Starre

Kikuru knelt just outside the bathing chamber and waited. The young samurai captain had been rigorously trained and was quite capable of enduring Prince Namari's obvious stalling tactic, or at least he believed himself so.

His superiors, the ruling Shogunate in the capital at Kyoto, believed Kikuru capable, or they wouldn't have dispatched him on this crucial mission.

He'd been required to relinquish most of his elaborate ceremonial wardrobe, along with his precious sword, at the entrance to the prince's chambers. He was dressed now in only his cotton under-garment and his warrior's kilt. Bare-chested, bare-headed, and barefoot, he knelt with knees under him and palms face-down on his muscular thighs.

His men, a full two hundred armed to the teeth, waited just outside the entrance to the Summer Palace. The Prince's own guard numbered a mere two score, although his attendants were more numerous but, of course, unarmed. It seemed as if Kikuru held all the essential pieces in this game of power. So far, Prince Namari's only strategy had been to fall back on tedious Court etiquette and the vain hope the young captain would merely tire of waiting and leave him in peace.

Four times previously with other captains this strategy had actually succeeded.

Kikuru believed himself different. Young and full of purposeful energy, he'd proved himself on the battlefield against the

Shogunate's enemies and even succeeded in withstanding the cut-throat politics of the military elite that surrounded him.

He managed a small smile of complacent self-confidence as he looked around him. He had never been to the Imperial Summer Palace. High in the mountains, surrounded by woods and enclosed within a spectacular garden, the palace itself was surprisingly simple.

A series of low buildings constructed of bamboo and wood and roofed with cedar shingles, there was no ostentatious decoration to be found, nor even much in the way of elegant furnishings. He faced a paper wall that served as partition and doorway into the Prince's bathing chamber while around him in the open room just outside, there were no furnishings at all. He knelt on a simple woven carpet that covered the bamboo floor.

On closer inspection that very simplicity revealed a carefully fashioned and breathtaking beauty. The door frame was the smoothest rosewood, dark against the beige paper. The roof beams above were cedar logs chosen for the series of swirling knots that flowed naturally from end to end. Even the handles that served to slide open the door were inlaid with mother-of-pearl that glimmered emerald and aquamarine against the brown and beige of the rest of the room.

Even the paper of the doors was more than it seemed. Embossed on the off-white background, a delicate pattern of pond lilies sprayed across each segment from top to bottom, right to left.

Kneeling now for an hour at least and perhaps closer to two, he had noted how the slanting rays of the afternoon sun coming in from the open paper windows on his left had picked out that pattern and transformed it into a flowing stream of light and shadow. And now, the rays of the setting sun had grown slightly red, flushing those lilies into subtle shades of pink.

Movement beyond the doorway caught his attention. Three figures created shadow behind the flushed lilies. Two approached, then the doors were slid open to reveal the prince's bathing chamber. And the Prince, himself.

Kikuru bit back a gasp. A quaver in his bowed lip and a slight rising of his dark brows betrayed him, but only for a moment. His physical self-control was impressive, but it was his mental acuity that saved him from a pitiable display of shocked emotion.

Prince Namari was entirely naked.

"Welcome Captain Kikuru. Please excuse us as my attendants bathe me. The day has been long, and I would prefer to be fresh and clean for our discussion regarding your need to arrive at the Summer Palace with a cohort of armed samurai."

The young captain bowed in place, his forehead touching his knees as he sought to calm his racing heart. Naked! It was unheard of for a member of the royal family to so blatantly parade himself before an inferior in this manner.

Kikuru had immediately understood the ploy for what it was. Not mere arrogance, although this came naturally to a royal family that had ruled Japan for centuries, but rather a canny move to discomfit the young captain.

The Prince's second move in their game. Kikuru could only wonder what the Prince next planned. He steeled himself as his head came up and he dared a direct gaze at the naked aristocrat.

"Your Highness, I appreciate your consideration, and I beg your forgiveness for our intrusion on your privacy." It was on the tip of his tongue to ask if the Prince would rather he retire to another room while he bathed, but believed this would signal weakness.

The Prince smiled. Kikuru's heart tripped. In a broad, flat face, the mouth was a splash of round pink, the lips curling as they spread apart to reveal even white teeth. It was a melancholy smile, gentle and yet just a touch condescending. It was beautiful.

He dared a glance at the Prince's nude body. Squat power. Broad shoulders and large hips, thick muscle along the limbs, feet planted with firm confidence. Lengthy prick dangling between the big thighs like a somnolent snake.

At the thought of actually viewing the royal manhood, Kikuru flushed and felt his own prick stir and swell under his clothing. He took slow, deep breaths and succeeded in cooling the heat that rose up from his crotch and into his face. He steeled himself for whatever came next, certain if he could maintain his composure thus far, nothing else would vanquish his determination.

Little did he know.

The two attendants were already busy dipping large copper pots into a steaming cauldron of water resting on a stone fire pit in the far corner of the chamber. They wore simple undergarments of wrapped cotton but were otherwise naked. Both were slender young men close to Kikuru's age. Neither offered him even a glance as they went about their business.

The Prince stood in the center of the room facing the kneeling captain. His gentle smile remained in place as he quietly gazed at him, large almond eyes unabashed and unashamed. His stance was solid, similar to that of a warrior at rest but prepared for action.

Warm water cascaded over his nude body. The dying rays of the sun slanted in from open paper windows to paint him in glistening shades of liquid amber. Kikuru observed with quiet composure, although the hefty power of the naked aristocrat was so beautiful it dazzled him. The bare chest was smooth and full and without blemish. The shoulders bulged with supple muscle.

The attendants discarded their copper pots as one took up a bar of soap and a small scrub brush and the other lit a half dozen paper lanterns. Kikuru realized all at once it was dusk. How long had he been kneeling there?

His thoughts were brought back to the moment as the pair of attendants began to soap up and scrub Namari. The Prince's hair was released from its knot and fell to his shoulders in wet tendrils. Raven-black for the most part, the odd strand of grey stood out, as did the few wrinkles around the corners of his expressive eyes on the smooth roundness of his face.

Perhaps the Prince was reading his mind. His next words seemed to indicate the possibility. "I am now in my fortieth year. I judge you to be perhaps half that. You are very young, Captain Kikuru."

The kneeling warrior thought carefully before he replied. Certainly the Prince was pointing out their age difference as a way of indicating his own superiority in the arena of wisdom and experience, while hinting at the captain's lack of both due to his youth.

"Yes, Your Highness, I am indeed young, although my superiors have judged me capable." He didn't want to appear to be defending himself, or boasting. It was a delicate game they played.

The Prince beamed. Kikuru's heart beat a little faster as he deemed that a compliment on his own measured response. Increasing his pulse, too, was the sensual display being played out before him. The two attendants raised the Prince's muscular arm and soaped it, revealing the smooth pit beneath, which for some reason seemed inordinately exciting.

More exciting yet, were the sudsy rivulets that ran down the Prince's sides over his powerful hips and smooth belly. Those rivulets dipped into and out of his perfect navel, then lower yet into his crotch. Sudsy water slid over the length of his sleeping manhood to drip off the hooded crown. More suds gathered in the place where his hefty thighs met and his full seed-sack nestled.

Once more he marveled at the shocking fact he was allowed to watch as the intimate ritual was performed before him. He endured, prick rising and throbbing under his kilt and thoughts muddied by lurid notions he struggled to hold at bay. Still, his expression remained calm and his body composed.

A low rosewood stool was placed before the Prince, and he turned partially away from Kikuru to face the open windows that overlooked the palace garden and pond. One foot, surprisingly peasant-like in its broad flatness, came up to settle on that gleaming stool.

The captain's eyes followed the rivers of suds as they flowed down the wide back, over powerful lats, down the valley between shoulder blades, and then to pool at the juncture of muscle that inserted into the jutting buttocks before flowing farther downward over those large but graceful mounds.

With one leg up, the deep crevice between those royal cheeks was open. A trail of suds followed the ravine, slowly and with determination as Kikuru watched with absolute fascination.

The puckered hole was conquered by those traveling suds before the flow dripped onward between the hefty thighs and over the low-hanging pair of royal balls.

So fascinated was he by this, he was almost startled by the sudden movement of the bathing attendants. All at once, they were squatting in front and behind Namari as soap and brush moved over his powerful body.

The one behind soaped the lower back, massaged it with his brush, then ran his soapy palm over the jutting mounds of the Prince's ass, following it with the brush. The captain felt his fingers begin to shake slightly as the servant's hands slid between the ass-globes and lathered that deep valley.

He had to admire the two attendants as they performed their duty without the slightest hint of hesitancy or embarrassment. A hand ran over the soapy hole without pause, followed by the massaging brush. Kikuru flushed as the Prince actually arched his back and bent over just enough to open up the royal ass-crevice, obviously enjoying the intimate attention.

In front, the second attendant was hidden for the most part by the Prince's raised thigh. Kikuru could only imagine the care he lavished on the royal prick! Now, his hands were definitely trembling.

"Rinse and leave us. Captain Kikuru and I have business."

The pair scurried to the steaming cauldron and filled their copper pots with more water. Namari did not turn to face the captain, but remained with one foot on the stool and his gaze focused on the view beyond the open windows.

The attendants were quick to perform this last service. Namari stood quietly as the warm water cascaded down his naked body and rinsed away the last of the suds then murmured a polite thanks just before the pair left.

They were alone.

The Prince moved. Several confident strides brought him to the open windows. Once there, he placed both hands on the oak sill and leaned forward to gaze up at the night sky. Planting his bare feet wide apart, his buttocks were parted and once more the royal hole was exposed for Kikuru's viewing.

It was almost as if he was presenting himself! The young captain's prick was at full mast, obscene thoughts crowding out more rational ones.

"Come, Captain. I would have you see something wondrous."

Kikuru rose, the lean muscles of his lower body protesting after prolonged immobility. But he was a warrior and his body a well-trained instrument. He could move at in instant's notice.

The soap's muted scent assailed him as he approached. A delicate hint of lilac beneath a more strident stench of lye. There was also the rich smell of the garden and pond beyond the opening to inhale with quivering nostrils as he finally came to stand beside the Prince himself.

"The night of the two moons. Lovely, yes?"

Leaning out as the Prince had, he could see what Namari meant. Above, in the eastern sky, a full moon hovered just above the canopy of the nearby woods. Below, in the still waters of the pond, its reflection glowed equally bright.

"One is real, the other a reflection. But who is to say which glows brighter, or has more power to stir the soul?"

The Prince was a renowned poet. Kikuru knew this. He was not much for flowery poems, preferring the direct commands of battle. Yet, these words did stir him, most likely due to the fact he was struggling with his emotions and his need to remain in command of them.

"Oil is on the stand. Please, young captain, I would have you apply it as we converse."

Kikuru's heart skipped a beat. Of course the request was a command, and the service any servant would be highly honored to perform. Captain or not, he was a servant of the Shogunate, of the government of Japan. And of course the royal family, even if they no longer wielded true power in the land.

He turned and padded on bare feet over to the stand beside the gently steaming cauldron. A silver flask stood alone. It would undoubtedly contain the massage oil. He took it up and returned to the Prince who had remained feet apart and palms wide on the window sill.

Kikuru hesitated. Should he begin? Where? The thought of actually laying hands on the Prince's sacred body, naked as it was, both dismayed and thrilled him.

"Best if you remove your remaining garments. I would not have you soil them with oil."

The Prince remained focused on the view, no doubt contemplating the esoteric meaning of the moon and its reflection, or thinking other thoughts. Perhaps even considering surrendering to the will of the Shogunate!

Kikuru himself had no choice but to obey the Prince's command. He unfastened his gold and green kilt and stepped out of it. He carefully placed it aside where the bamboo floor was not wet, then before he could give in to his doubts, quickly unwound his cotton undergarment and dropped it.

Betraying him, his prick reared up. A fat pole that slapped against his rippled abdomen, the hood was peeled back and a dribble of pre-cum oozed from the dark piss-slit. Ignoring it, he stepped in behind the Prince and began to apply the oil to his shoulders and neck.

"Thank you, Captain."

His hands no longer trembled now they had work to do. The Prince's shoulders were exceedingly broad and powerfully muscled. The oil fell from the open spout in the flask in a honey-brown rivulet, almost exactly the color of the royal flesh. He kneaded the slick substance into shoulders and neck with adroit fingertips. Somehow, he managed to focus on the task, regardless of the fact his rearing prick took lewd aim at the Prince's parted buttocks and seemed unwilling to retreat.

His hands slid lower, over the broad lats and into the valley of the back. Prince Namari was obviously in supreme physical condition. The royal family had been forbidden to engage in military endeavors or to use a sword or other weapon. Namari had channeled his talents into martial arts of the weaponless sort. Kikuru had been warned he was an adept.

His slick hands moved lower, kneading the packed muscle just above the waist and the jutting buttocks. He took his time there, understanding how this part of the anatomy carried the burden of the body's activity. And truthfully, he was reluctant to move lower.

"So your Masters in Kyoto demand my attendance at Court. I am to be their trained puppet to parade before the eager masses. No doubt some unrest of the peasantry requires this."

Spoken calmly without apparent rancor and directly to the point, the Prince's statement brought Kikuru back to the harsh reality of the situation.

He was there to force Namari, at sword-point if need be, to return with him to the capital. Others had failed in the task, too timid, too awestruck, or too frustrated by the Prince's stalling tactics.

His prick twitched and oozed as he dared to lower his hands, sliding them over the curved mounds of the Prince's buttocks. For some reason, the trembling of his hands, and his body, had entirely ceased. Perhaps it was the supple stillness of the Prince's powerful muscles and skin that calmed him. Perhaps it was the steel determination in his own heart. Perhaps it was the realization that he would do what he must to convince the Prince to obey his Masters.

He was about to discover what was required of him.

The Prince's feet moved wider apart, and he arched his back. The deep ravine between his ass mounds was wide open. Kikuru's hands slid into the smooth valley, oil glistening on the amber flesh, then painting the puckered hole as his fingers trailed over it.

He dropped into a squat and focused on that mighty ass. He poured more oil over the head of the valley where the back and buttocks joined. He stared directly at the hairless hole, noting how it clenched, then pushed outward, oil dribbling over it and from it.

"Pardon my impertinence, Your Highness, but it is your duty to obey the Shogunate. Your duty to calm the populace."

"Duty? We all have our duties, young captain."

With those words, the Prince moved. So quickly it happened even before the trained samurai saw it coming, hands whipped back and found his head. They pulled him forward and drove his face between the Prince's full buttocks.

He snorted in the thick scent of the oil, a sesame seed and rose mixture, before his nostrils were mashed into the smooth flesh of those delectable ass-cheeks. The grip on the back of his neck was firm and powerful, yet he could have broken away if he chose to. He was lean and wiry compared to the stocky prince, but agile and quick, too.

As his lips were pressed directly against the pouting orifice that led to the Prince's inner self, he was forced to make his decision. There was little choice. If he was to succeed in his mission, he could not quail now. He was the type of person who believed life was a battlefield, and in battle one gains nothing through half-measures.

He opened his mouth and stabbed with his tongue. Mewling loudly, he began to fuck the royal hole with the tip of his tongue while pulling the broad cheeks farther apart and exposing more of the deep valley for his roaming hands.

His fingers slid beside his mouth and dug into the Prince's anal lips. He forced them apart as his tongue burrowed within. The hefty ass reared backwards to writhe against his face, while the royal hands continued to clamp the back of his neck and hold him in place.

In a squat, Kikuru's own ass was open. As he ate out the royal hole, his own hole pulsed and gaped open in empathetic response. His prick, already stiff, jerked wildly at his crotch. He flushed all over as he surrendered totally to lust.

"Ahhhh, yes, young captain. You apparently comprehend duty. Come, freely explore what is at your disposal."

He understood the meaning. Encouraged by the heat in the Prince's voice, he dared boldness as his slippery fingers traveled down the smooth valley, between the parted thighs, over the ridged perineum, then cupped the Prince's full seed-sack. He rolled the balls in his oily palm as his tongue darted in and out of the quivering royal hole, then slid his other hand up to the base of the Prince's lengthy stem.

Hard, it reared skyward. Kikuru's oiled fist slowly slid up the prodigious length. He discovered the crown and rubbed oil into the bared slit and head. Tongue delving beyond quivering ass-lips, hand massaging seed-sack, and oiled fingers teasing twitching prick-head, he snorted and mewled in place as his own prick and hole jerked and throbbed in sympathy.

Namari moved ever so quickly again, this time stepping backwards while maintaining his grip on the young captain's neck. Kikuru immediately dropped from a squat to his knees while whipping his hands back to place them on the wet floor and preventing himself from tumbling backwards.

All at once, the Prince straddled him as he leaned backwards on his knees. His lean body arched upward, his stiff prick slapping against his lean abdomen, on display for the Prince for the first time. Royal prick was pushed down and between his gasping lips.

A hand dropped to his muscular chest and fingers found his right nipple. Those fingers tweaked and pinched as prick was fed into his gurgling mouth. He did his best to suck in that fat tool as his nipple burned and his own prick lurched. He was acutely aware of how his own jerking tool betrayed him.

131

It only grew stiffer and lurched more violently as the Prince abandoned his right nipple and attacked his left. The right one still ached and throbbed while the left began to swell and burn.

His bowed lips stretched wide around the invading cock in his mouth. He sucked it in while tonguing the oozing crown and pulsing shaft. The Prince pushed downward, toward his tonsils. Kikuru snorted in a deep breath and opened wide. That slick knob slithered into his gullet.

Fingers attacked one nipple or the other while prick probed his throat. He found himself arching his back and humping the air with his stiff cock, pressing his chest into the painful pleasure of his nipples being ravaged. Cock began to withdraw, and he managed a snort of air.

"Rise, Kikuru. Your Prince requires your humility now, rather than mere duty."

Prick slid from his wet lips. Fingers abandoned his burning nipple. The Prince's hefty thighs came back and away from his lolling head. He understood the command and was up and bounding forward in an instant.

He took the stance Namari had only just vacated. Palms wide on the window ledge, bare feet spread, back arched and compact buttocks presented. In this instance, he fully understood what humility entailed.

The Prince's larger body enfolded his from behind. He moaned loudly as the royal prick slid up between his parted ass-cheeks. One hand cupped his muscled tit while the other dove into his ass-crevice alongside the pulsing prick already there.

The hands were broad and calloused, and similar to the feet, surprisingly peasant-like. They also dripped oil. While one massaged his chest, the other rooted in his ass-crack. Fingers found his snug asshole and rubbed it. He moaned louder and willed his tender sphincter to yield as a pair of those fingers settled on the entrance and drove inward.

It was not gentle. He was gored by those oily digits, both thrusting deep and twisting at the same time. They hooked inside him while moving in circles to stretch and push against the insides of his sphincter.

The rough handling worked. His asshole capitulated, gaping open as those fingers were abruptly removed and the Prince's plump, equally-oiled prick-head thrust immediately into the void. That broad crown burrowed beyond the quivering lips and deep into the steamy gut beyond.

Half the Prince's fat weapon gored him. Kikuru grunted loudly but did not flinch away. Instead, he took a deep breath and thrust backwards. The profound ache of hot prick straining his tender hole only galvanized him. He rammed his lean hips against the Prince's hefty thighs.

Namari chuckled in his ear. His firm hands clasped the young captain at chest and buttock as he began a lusty pump and grind that had his huge prick buried to the balls after only a few violent thrusts.

There was nothing gentle about that anal assault. The Prince fucked him hard, slamming into him from behind, oil squishing as it leaked from his violated hole. It was a little surprising, the near-brute force of it, especially since the Prince had seemed so calm and deliberate in manner thus far. But, the captain did not protest. Rather, he reveled in the savage pounding, giving as good as he got, bucking and writhing against that pummeling pole without the slightest reservation.

If Namari fucked him with brute force, the Prince's hands played a different game. They roamed all over the captain's lean body in a slithering glide. They explored almost tenderly. They traced the emerald and crimson tattoo that splashed across one arm from shoulder to wrist, a writhing dragon with fiery breath and sharp talons. They slid over the rippled belly; they lightly stroked the rearing prick and tickled the oozing knob. They cupped and gently squeezed his dangling balls. They followed the curve of his firm buttocks and slid between his splayed thighs. They came up to his neck and then his face to stroke there.

Kikuru gazed up at the full moon, mouth open and eyes half-closed. Taller than most and packed with lean muscle, he was a fine example of warrior masculinity. His face, though, presented a distinctly different demeanor. Almost pretty, with bowed lips in a small mouth and a delicate nose below expressive almond eyes, that gentle countenance had wrongly emboldened a number of enemies. His nature was closer to the steel of the sword than the pretty bloom of the chrysanthemum.

Namari traced those lovely features with his fingertips as he plowed the young captain's fertile asshole with thrusts that lifted him off his feet. The fingers toyed with his open mouth; they stroked his delicate, flaring nostrils; they followed the line of his pencil-thin brows.

The only remnant of composure remaining to him as he writhed and moaned with the Prince's thick prick deep in his ass was his dark brown hair still pulled back and tied in a knot. Not for long though, as the Prince untied it and ran his oily fingers through the sleek strands.

Then, as Namari fucked him, he whispered in his ear.

"Duty and power, are they not reflections of one another, much as the two moons we gaze at now? Which to chose and at what moment, this is the game we play, all of us from prince in his palace, to warrior on the battlefield, to peasant in his rice paddy."

One hand dropped to seize Kikuru's prick and begin a slow, tantalizing pump. The captain spread his feet farther apart and shuddered from head to toe. The prick up his ass rammed in and out rapidly.

"Are you an assassin, Captain Kikuru?"

"Ohhhhh, no, Your Highness. Uhhhhnnn!"

Kikuru rallied his wits as he took a moment to grunt as prick impaled him fully, princely balls slapping violently against his firm, sweaty ass-globes. He recognized it was time for complete honesty.

"But if I fail in my task, your next visitor from the Shogunate will likely be one."

It was his final move. The threat his masters had promised in the event of his failure was all too real.

He was pushed down and farther out the window, his eyes now focused on the moon's glowing reflection in the pond. Prick ravaged him, in and out and deep up inside him. This fuck was the core of their battle. Even though Kikuru had surrendered to the Prince's, and his own desires, still it was apparent to both the conflict could not be resolved unless the Prince himself capitulated equally.

The hand on his prick pumped faster. The violent ache in his battered ass grew almost too much to bear. His mouth hung open, his tongue out. The exquisite torture was approaching culmination.

"My seed is yours, young captain!"

Prick rammed home and held there. He could feel the pulse of that thick pole as it released a torrent of royal juice up his ass. Victory!

His elation lasted a mere moment before his own surrender followed. The slippery hand pumping his own prick performed its magic. He shot, violently. Cum rocketed upward to splash his heaving belly. His entire body was wracked with such intense pleasure he cried out before fingers stuffed his mouth to silence him.

He sucked on those fingers as the prick up his ass flooded his gut until the copious overflow began to dribble from the battered entrance. He jerked in the Prince's arms as his own spew splattered his body and then dripped to the floor.

He realized the paper lanterns behind them had guttered out. The only light came from those twin moons. Other than their own gasps and moans, all was silent around them.

Namari spoke in his ear.

"The summer is pleasant here in the mountains. It will not wane until the next full moon, and the next night of the two moons. Are you patient enough to last that long?"

The young captain grinned as the fingers in his mouth slid out and he was free to speak. But what could he say? The truth was now his only option. One thing he had certainly learned, naked and without his sword to rely on, was that sometimes power had nothing to do with swords.

"My men will enjoy the cool breezes and the lovely woods outside your gardens. And perhaps, I will enjoy your royal favor now and then. Regardless, my patience is boundless when duty requires."

"Duty, yes. Let us explore the meaning during the next month."

Kikuru understood. Perhaps they both had won on this night of the twin moons.

FINDING SICILY
By Jay Starre

Paul had to admit he was unexpectedly moved when he got off the boat at Marsala. He was setting foot in Sicily for the first time, and no matter how much he'd tried all his life to pretend, he was not just an American. He was also Sicilian.

He breathed in the Mediterranean air, sharp here with the tang of nearby salt flats and hot with a breeze from the island interior. The city itself was fair-sized and boasted an intriguing mixture of sights due to its patchwork past.

First, the Phoenicians occupied the important harbor, followed by the Romans, then the Arabs. The Arabs, especially, had left a lasting mark. In fact, the population of the town included a large percentage of modern Tunisians and its fair share of tall palm trees reminding one of desert oases waving in the breeze.

He didn't linger, though. His destination was farther inland. He'd come to stay with his relatives at their vineyard in the famous Marsala wine district. A rental car provided him transport, and by late that afternoon, he was heading up the gravel drive toward his relatives' rambling ocher-plastered house on a ridge above rolling slopes lined with grape vines.

The countryside had been lovely, with conical cedars lining the road and hay fields, orchards and vineyards crowding in on all sides. It was a richly cultivated province and surprisingly quiet in the lazy summer afternoon. By the time he reached his Uncle Vittorio's vineyard, he'd begun to wonder what he would do for entertainment over the next three weeks.

Little did he know what awaited him.

A trio of cousins all around his own age, in their early twenties, greeted him enthusiastically.

"*Buongiorno,* Paolo," they chorused. Franco, the oldest, took over as he spoke the most English, and they'd been warned Paul was hopeless at Italian.

Franco was tall and lean and cute as hell. Paul felt his dick stirring and quickly reassessed his notion of what entertainment might be available over the next fortnight.

After settling in upstairs in one of the numerous bedrooms, he peered out the open window and took stock of his vacation home. Vineyards stretched as far as the eye could see, with a little pond sparkling in the setting sun on the ridge across from the house and a few stone or plastered outbuildings rearing up here and there. It was all very orderly with the vine trellises marching in lines across the terrain, but at the same time, a bit unruly due to the naturally twisting growth of the vines themselves.

That's when he first saw Vittorio.

A sturdy looking man approached the house, making his way slowly and methodically through the greenery. He halted periodically and reached out to fondle the grape bunches.

In work boots, jeans and a simple grey T-shirt, there was no reason to believe he was other than a farm hand at his chores. But when he faced the house, Paul was struck by the familiarity of his features. He looked almost exactly like Franco. This must be his Uncle Vittorio.

The long nose, full mouth and dimpled chin, the wide-set brown eyes, the broad forehead and full head of rich auburn hair, all mimicked his son's more youthful features.

Grey hair streaked the temples, and lines marched across the forehead, but the vigor of the powerful body belied the marks of maturity. He looked about the same height as his son, but his shoulders were broader and his hips more powerful, while his thighs strained the jeans he wore, intimating that he'd probably been striding through those vineyards since he was a toddler.

He looked up toward the house.

"*Ciao*, Paolo!"

"*Ciao*, Uncle Vittorio."

Straight white teeth gleamed against the olive-brown complexion. The eyes looked directly at him, softly golden. Paul actually flushed. He'd thought Franco was cute, and he was, but his father was downright gorgeous.

"Supper will be soon. Come down, *per favore*."

He nodded, grinning foolishly and oddly tongue-tied. He was slightly confused by his strong emotions. Vittorio had to be in his mid-forties, judging by the ages of his sons, and Paul had never seriously been interested in anyone over thirty. What was he thinking?

It only got more intense. Downstairs, Vittorio embraced him while kissing him on both cheeks. The embrace was not the least bit tentative, lasting longer than Paul expected. It felt surprisingly comforting.

They had dinner around a polished oak table, the three sons and the middle son's visibly pregnant wife, Teresa. They all helped with the setting of the table and the food, although Anna, the plump cook, cheerfully managed them. Surrounded by walls plastered in ochers and umbers, dark oak floors, and whirring fans overhead, it was surprisingly cool, regardless of the lack of air conditioning.

Afterwards, they retired to the patio where an expansive rose arbor curved over them and a soft breeze from the distant ocean cooled them. They talked for a couple of hours, in English with Vittorio and Franco translating for the others amidst good-natured laughter. Even though there was a wide-screen television in the living room, Paul had noticed no one seemed in dire need of turning it on. Vittorio laughed easily. They talked about Chicago where Paul worked as an investment banker, and they talked about their relatives, naturally. It seemed that Vittorio had actually attended college in Chicago, along with his brother who'd married Paul's mother's sister. Paul had assumed Vittorio and his sons were related to him by marriage, but not by blood. Vittorio illuminated him on the truth.

"*Scusi*, Paolo, did you know, my grandfather and your great-grandfather were cousins?" Vittorio said with a broad grin. "And so, we do share blood, good Sicilian blood!"

Later, in his bed, with a large fan whirring overhead, Paul found himself fantasizing as he drifted off to sleep. He was actually the odd man out, with Vittorio and his three sons all tall and tanned and with such rich auburn hair. He was much shorter with jet-black hair he kept trimmed close to his head, light hazel eyes and fairer, freckled skin. Yet Vittorio had claimed him as one of his own, his blood. Romantic but nebulous notions, not of the cute young Franco, but his handsome father, swirled round in his head. All evening he'd drunk in that easy laughter and broad smile like a love-struck teen.

The quiet of the countryside lulled him, and he fell fast asleep, waking much later than he'd planned. Anna was in the kitchen to whip him up a hearty breakfast although the rest of the family were already outdoors.

He stepped out the kitchen door with a steaming cup of thick Sicilian coffee in hand to discover two of the family at work in the large garden just beyond the patio. Vittorio and Teresa. Vittorio worked in khaki shorts and without shirt or shoes. The brilliant Mediterranean sun reflected off bronzed shoulders and a smooth, muscular chest.

"Can I give you a hand?" Paul called out.

"*Buongiorno! Si.* Come."

He discarded his own shirt and shoes and joined Vittorio as he bent to the task of weeding and thinning the lush vegetable patch. They chatted easily as Teresa took her time picking ripe tomatoes, peppers, green onions and other herbs.

The soft, moist dirt in his toes and under his fingers, the smell of the vegetables and herbs and the warm sun all created a sensual excitement he had no idea was possible. Vittorio naturally was a main component of that heated sensuality. Tall and sturdy and much larger than Paul who was not only shorter but had a lean runner's body, he exuded an exuberant but focused strength that was awe-inspiring for the younger American.

Naked except for his shorts, his bare calves and chest were suntanned a dark amber. His big capable hands and feet were work-calloused and adept. The pair worked side-by-side, close enough for Paul to smell the older Sicilian, a mixture of sweat and fine Italian cologne that had him nearly dizzy and springing a boner that just wouldn't go away. It tented the front of his own shorts, and he was sure Vittorio noticed it, but fortunately didn't comment.

Franco arrived after an hour of blissful and sensual grubbing in the dirt to announce he was taking Paul to the nearby coast and a beautiful beach where they could swim. Vittorio smiled and nodded, and off they went.

A half hour drive on Franco's scooter brought them to a quiet stretch of sand and the aquamarine waters of the Mediterranean. Rugged cliffs formed an imposing backdrop under azure skies. Franco wore skimpy European-style trunks, and Paul couldn't help eyeing his smooth body, comparing it to his father's more powerful one.

A large tube bulged the front, which fired up the American's imagination and had him springing wood again as he thought of Vittorio in the garden.

"*Scusi*, but you are gay, no?"

The question came out of a stream of conversation the chatty Franco had kept up since they'd gotten off the scooter and headed down to the water. Paul glanced down at his tented trunks and laughed out loud.

"It's obvious, I guess. Yep I am."

Franco, so much like his father, laughed it off as of no consequence and continued on with his chatter. Paul did notice, or a at least thought he did, a swelling of that tube under Franco's trunks.

That night after another pleasant supper and after-dinner conversation, he went to bed with more than mere romantic notions in his head. The overhead fan and the open window cooled him as he lay back naked on his covers and fantasized about Vittorio on the beach with him instead of Franco, with those skimpy trunks and that swelling Sicilian tube-steak rising and rising.

He squirted a stream of lube he'd brought for just such a moment over his balls and stiff cock. Lifting one leg and pulling it back against his chest, he squirted more lube into his ass-crack. He pumped his cock with one hand and ran his other over his own round, smooth ass before he found his puckered hole and worked a pair of fingers up it.

Trying to keep his moans to a murmur while not shaking the rickety bed too much, he worked his cock and hole and imagined Vittorio's golden eyes staring down at him, his big calloused hands roaming over his body, and his no-doubt fat Sicilian dick driving in and out of his aching asshole.

Cum spurted so far from the head of his cock it actually hit his face. He licked it off his chin and fell asleep naked on top of his covers.

Over the following week, Paul split his time between swimming with Franco and lending Vittorio a hand at his seemingly endless chores around the vineyard.

If he had his choice, he would have spent every waking hour following Vittorio around like a puppy dog. There were many things to do, such as moving irrigation pipes, grubbing in the garden, weeding between the vines, fertilizing and checking the progress of the grapes. They also made their own wine, a modest operation, but demanding. Vittorio took him into the cellars where oak barrels filled with the Marsala wine they produced were quietly aging.

He explained how everything worked as they labored side-by-side, and Paul listened keenly enough. He wasn't that interested in wine or the processes behind its creation, but Vittorio's strong, soothing voice mesmerized him and truthfully, he would have listened to him say anything at all.

At night in his room, he jerked off. The feel of his own asshole throbbing around his buried fingers only increased a sense of growing desperation. The rickety bed and the whirring fan and his own groans muffled the sound of the door opening, and he didn't see the form hovering over him until it was right there.

In the near-darkness, he only saw tall amber flesh and the pale glimmer of white teeth smiling. His heart leaped, then crashed to earth as he recognized Franco and not the other he'd hoped for.

"*Scusi*, Paolo, but you are making so much noise tonight; I can hear you through the wall. Do you want some help with that?"

Franco was naked. His cock was as stiff as Paul's as he gripped the base and aimed it at the sprawled American. With a finger buried up his own asshole and a fist wrapped around his hard-on, he should have been embarrassed as hell. But, oddly, he wasn't. He and Franco had grown very comfortable with each other.

And he was horny, extremely horny. He was tempted, too. If not for his feelings about Vittorio, he would have gladly accepted Franco's offer. Foolishly hoping for something more than a friendly tumble in the sack, he refused.

"*Grazie*, Franco, but no," he murmured.

Franco nodded and murmured, "*Va bene*," but didn't retreat immediately. Instead, he began to pump his own fat cock as he stood beside the bed and stared down at Paul.

Paul grinned. He really did like Franco! There in the darkness, they jerked off together, not touching, or speaking, until first Paul blew, then Franco followed. With a gentle laugh, the Sicilian cousin melted away in camaraderie darkness.

That Sunday, they went to Mass at the nearby village. The medieval church boasted hard wooden pews, frescoes and statues of Saints. He hadn't been to mass for ages, abandoning the habit once he'd moved from home and gone to college. Not entirely comfortable, he turned to see Vittorio looking at him with those soft amber eyes. He winked, as if he understood whatever it was Paul was thinking, and he felt heat in the pit of his stomach, then his stirring dick. In church! Vittorio winked again and nodded. He had to work at controlling his own need to burst into hysterical laughter.

Truthfully, Paul was elated one moment and despondent the next. He told himself he was a fool to think Vittorio was going to fall in love with him, or even have sex with him. He told himself he should just be thankful for the generous friendship the older man offered him so freely. But, he was young and impatient and not at all accustomed to being so infatuated. Days more passed while Paul basked in the warmth of the Sicilian summer and the embracing acceptance of Vittorio's family. The time was passing too fast. The three weeks he'd planned to stay would be up, then what?

It was early morning just after he and Alberto, the youngest of Vittorio's sons, had come in from their regular jog. They had discovered through Franco's interpretation they shared an addiction to running. They didn't say more than a few words to each other, but it was comfortable, and the quiet camaraderie suited them both. This morning, though, Alberto was obviously in a bad mood and frowning more often than smiling. When they arrived back at the house, soaked in sweat, the young Sicilian ran into his father who was on his way out.

Alberto launched into a spirited diatribe that quickly escalated into shouting and lots of arm waving. Paul would have left them to their privacy, but Franco arrived with a pitcher of lemonade and stopped him as he poured out a big glass. He rolled his expressive brown eyes and grinned, as if nothing was out of the ordinary.

Paul had to hide his own grin. He'd experienced plenty of drama at home growing up, and he'd usually ignored it just like Franco. What surprised him about the argument was the way Vittorio handled it.

He listened, he answered calmly, he even attempted a few placating smiles and eventually placed a hand on his son's shoulder in a comforting gesture, but all to no avail. Alberto stormed off into the house, and Vittorio turned and headed for the vineyards.

Paul's own father or mother would have screamed back or even smacked one of their children who behaved like that. Vittorio's calmness shouldn't have surprised him by now; he'd witnessed it every day no matter the circumstances.

Inside, Franco announced they were all headed for Marsala for a day of shopping, and Paul was invited. He assumed Vittorio was staying behind, so he did, too. He found him down in a ravine between the rows of vines where a stone well squatted. He was busy repairing the hinges on the wooden lid.

"Paolo, *per favore*, forgive Alberto his outburst. He wants to take over more of the wine-making, but I don't think he is ready. His mother died when he was only five, so we have spoiled him a little and put up with his temper."

Paul's thoughts immediately strayed to the notion of why the Sicilian farmer hadn't remarried. But, he was brought back to the moment by Vittorio's next question.

"Why are you here, Paolo? Why not Roma or Venezia or Napoli?"

So much was going on in his head and his heart. Over the past two weeks he'd realized a lot of things. The most glaring, he'd abandoned his ancestry and his language, then here in this quiet vineyard among distant relatives who'd been so welcoming, he'd found a whisper of it, then now with Vittorio's words, a powerful punch to the gut.

Normally, he would have offered some blasé response off the top of his head. But now, for once in his life, he chose to be honest. Honest with himself.

"I don't like my job. I hate my job. It seems like our clients are getting screwed, we make money off fees and interest and advice, yet they're the ones who lose it when the stock market or the real estate market tanks. I get a good salary no matter what and even bonuses. It seems like there's just too much greed. Well, not just greed, but corruption, too."

"*Scusi*, but you have come to the wrong place if you are not in the mood for corruption. Sicilians invented corruption," Vittorio laughed and winked, then continued on. "The thing about corruption is that it stinks. And not just once. It keeps on stinking and stinking like dead fish on the seashore until an act of God finally washes it away in a violent storm."

He laughed and winked again at his attempt at wisdom. Paul flushed as the laughing farmer placed a hand on his shoulder and squeezed. He had no idea if Vittorio was being merely friendly or that hand meant more, a low-key kind of sexual advance. He was confused not only by Vittorio's generous and sincere affection, but by his own all-consuming lust for someone so much older.

"*Per favore*, Paolo, sit."

The hand guided him down to the well where he planted his butt on the closed wooden lid and placed his hands behind him, daring to stare up into the soft well of the older man's golden eyes.

"I can see you have much on your mind. And much to decide. I think you would like to make love, no?"

Paul's entire body felt like it was melting. Both the Sicilian farmer's large hands were on his bare shoulders, flesh to flesh. His big bare thighs pressed now against the insides of his own, spread wide as he sat atop the waist-high well.

"*Si, per favore, per favore*," he managed to gasp out.

"*Bravo. Bravo.*"

The hands held him as Vittorio's face descended, the full lips parted and then touched his.

The softness of that kiss did not soothe him, but inflamed him instead. A powerful shudder wracked his body, and he found himself opening wide and sucking on those lips, pulling in the broad tongue that easily obliged.

The fingers on his shoulders tightened their grip and that tongue roamed deeply. Neither had closed their eyes, so both hazel and amber orbs locked together in a silent exchange of growing excitement. Their mouths mashed as the hands that held him dropped to grip the bottom of his tank top and pull upwards. They broke the kiss briefly with shared gasps as the shirt was pulled over his head and then spread carefully behind him over the time-smoothed wood of the well's lid.

Paul understood why Vittorio did that, and raised his own knees obligingly as those capable hands found the waist of his khaki shorts and unbuttoned. Fingers hooked in the waistband of both shorts and underwear and pulled downwards.

His cock, which had stiffened into a curved pink stave, bobbed out in the air and slapped against his belly. Flushing and biting his lip, he was all too aware of Vittorio's eyes on him as his clothing was removed over his jogging shoes, his round butt lifted, and shorts and underwear draped beneath him so thoughtfully.

Neither said a word as the golden-eyed Sicilian removed his own shirt, then his shorts and underwear, all while standing between Paul's upraised thighs and staring down at him. Paul was acutely conscious of his own bare ass and twitching asshole, especially since he'd been bold enough to slip his hands behind his knees and lift them up and back, effectively offering that hole for whatever use Vittorio found for it.

The first sight of Vittorio's cock didn't disappoint. Very thick and dark, the hood slipped back to reveal a tapered head. Jutting out from his crotch half-hard, there was the promise of increased girth and length as it swelled right before Paul's mesmerized gaze.

The auburn-haired farmer smiled as he moved closer to place that big piece of meat down between Paul's spread legs, against his pale ass-crack and over his dangling balls and his own stiff cock.

"*Per favore*. Feel it," Vittorio murmured.

Paul, unable to speak at all and trembling wildly, did as he was told, which was exactly what he'd been dreaming of. He let go of his knees just as Vittorio gripped his ankles and placed them over his broad shoulders. His shaking hands dropped down to his crotch where that massive tube throbbed against him.

He moaned out loud. The cock he gripped immediately swelled and stiffened. The pulsing warmth flowed from cock into hands and upward through his body, melting him once again into trembling weakness.

As he massaged the stiffening cock, Vittorio slid his hands down from his ankles all along his calves, his knees, thighs and then up to his flat belly and lean chest. The big hands were calloused but surprisingly smooth as they explored so freely yet so gently.

Paul had grown tanned from all the time he'd spent in the Sicilian outdoors, but still he was more freckled and less dark than the big farmer that loomed over him. His stomach was rippled with muscle, which Vittorio stroked with his fingertips appreciatively before dropping down to stroke just as attentively along the sides of his raised ass, then back up slowly to the tightly-packed muscles of his smooth chest and strong shoulders.

Vittorio's gorgeous eyes followed his hands as they roamed up and down Paul's naked body. *"Bello, bello,"* he murmured repeatedly.

Paul was both elated and frightened. It was almost too good to be true. He wanted this so much he was terrified he would do or say something that would spoil it.

But the older Sicilian seemed to know just what to do. He leaned down and kissed Paul again. Tongue slid between his gasping lips as those big hands continued to roam everywhere, and his own hands gripped the fat tube of cock between their mashed bellies.

The feel of that powerful body heavy over his own finally stilled his trembling nerves. The gentle but deep probing of that exploring tongue and the soft fullness of those wet lips pressing against his soothed his deeper emotional fears.

This was where he'd dreamed of being. In Vittorio's arms.

The kiss was short, though, and as the auburn-haired farmer pulled up and away, he smiled and winked before his wet tongue descended to run under Paul's chin over his neck, then down to his chest, then over a nipple to tease lightly before moving to the other to flick there and lick.

Paul pressed up into that tongue with a gasp, his own hands still gripping the fat Sicilian tube pulsing so stiffly against his own aching cock. The tongue trailed downwards, over the firm muscles of his abdomen, then further to lightly dip into his belly-button, then further and all at once the cock in his hands slipped away as the olive-skinned farmer dropped into a squat and engulfed his rearing pink cock with wet lips and swabbing tongue.

Vittorio was sucking his cock!

It was amazing. The lips caressed the head, then slid downward to massage all along the shaft. The tongue tickled his piss-slit, then wriggled around over his shank. Vittorio took his time to bob up and down slowly and thoroughly, managing to take most of the length with a gurgle and smacking lips.

Paul's ankles had rested on the farmer's broad back, but now he seized the backs of his own knees and pulled them up and back again. Vittorio's big hands moved down from his belly and to the sides of his round ass, and now with the rising and opening of the young American's ass-crack, those hands slid into the parted valley and moved inexorably toward the pulsating hole.

They found it. As tongue twirled over his cock, fingers began to stroke the tight ring of his sphincter. He reared up into that mouth and those tantalizing fingers. Flushing all over, he was again momentarily frightened of doing the wrong thing, showing his eagerness too blatantly, revealing what a depraved, totally sex-starved, love-struck slut he imagined himself to be.

Vittorio's actions wiped away that fear as the mouth on his cock pulled off with a slurp and immediately descended to clamp over the snug lips of his asshole. They sucked at the hole, not the least bit gently, as plump tongue tickled and stabbed at the sensitive center.

If the big man was willing to suck and tongue his asshole, what could Paul possibly be afraid of? He relaxed into the slobbering hole-suck, pulling his knees farther up toward his chest and actually wriggling his pale round can into that teasing mouth.

The Sicilian alternated between eating his ass and sucking his cock, looking up now and then between the twin feasts to grin and wink, before diving back in for more. His hands were busy stroking wet hole or pumping wet cock at the same time, while Paul squirmed and groaned non-stop.

Vittorio finally rose and stood over him again, cock huge and throbbing at his waist.

"*Per favore*, run and fetch condoms and something to lubricate your asshole with. I am sure you have these things. I will wait."

Paul hesitated, unable to tear himself away from the perfect moment, and truthfully a little afraid if he moved it would all come to a crashing end. But, Vittorio slapped his ass playfully and pulled him up and to his feet.

"Naked?" Paul managed to ask.

"*Va bene*. No one is home. They have all gone to Marsala, even Anna."

Vittorio's golden eyes sparkled, and his grin was teasing. He had to laugh, and the Sicilian joined him as he again slapped Paul's bare ass and gently pushed him on his way.

He ran up the ravine through the vines and to the house, making sure he kept the slope between himself and the road down the hill. His bobbing cock and dangling balls slapped against his bare thighs. What a lark! Vittorio was turning out to be even more interesting than he'd imagined!

Upstairs in his room, he snatched up a bottle of lube and some condoms. Racing back the way he came, he flushed all over with the thrill of the naked romp and found himself giggling half-hysterically until he came to a breathless halt just before the well and the waiting Vittorio.

The older Sicilian sat on the well atop the blanket they'd created from their discarded clothing. A pair of olive trees offered dappled shade, darkening the deep bronze of Vittorio's naked flesh.

His muscular arms were behind him as he leaned back with spread thighs and rearing cock. He laughed out loud as he spotted Paul running toward him, balls and cock swinging.

"*Grazie, grazie.*"

Paul was momentarily flustered as he drank in the sight of the gorgeous Sicilian and once again found himself amazed at his good fortune. To counter that sudden nervousness, he did what he'd been wanting to ever since he heard Vittorio's first *ciao*.

He dropped into a squat between the Sicilian's sturdy thighs and engulfed his cock with a moaning slurp. More laughter was followed by those big hands coming down to slide over his lean back and down to his waist, then between the rounded globes of his clenched butt-cheeks.

As he sucked avariciously on that enormous boner, blunt fingers ran up and down his ass-crack to tickle, stroke and tap his pouting asshole. With the tall Sicilian leaning over him, his face was buried in his crotch, cock thrusting up past his tonsils. He snorted in the heady odor of cock, balls and crotch and allowed the pulsing head to slither into his tight gullet.

"*Grazie*, Paolo, but now it is time for me to fuck you."

He was pulled up to his feet, his mouth coming off cock with a moaning slurp. Dying to get that big Sicilian meat up his twitching asshole, he was quick to tear open one of the condoms he'd fetched and wrap it up as Vittorio grinned at him and winked.

"Now the lubricant, *per favore.*"

Paul squirted a big stream of the clear goo over the wrapped cock while giggling nervously. Vittorio moved, not in a rush, but with firm determination. He rose from where he was, physically lifted and turned Paul around then laid him on top of the well.

Raising his ankles and pushing them back, he aimed the lubed, wrapped head of his cock at the young American's pink hole. Looking down, those soft golden orbs were intent as they watched cock-head begin to push against the puckered entrance.

Paul watched Vittorio as the Sicilian gently but deftly began to feed his eager hole that slippery head. He shook all over, amazed and thrilled at the look of desire in those soft eyes. What more could he want?

But then, cock began to enter him. He groaned and wriggled his round white ass upwards toward the heated thickness stretching apart his snug ass-lips. His sphincter strained, quivered, then as he grunted and pushed upwards, finally gaped open.

Cock slipped past that defensive ring and into the pulsating interior beyond. Vittorio looked up into his eyes.

Paul had thought he was in love, but until this very moment he'd really had no idea what love was. As cock slid deeper into him, and those soft amber eyes gazed deep into his own hazel ones, he felt a profound change take place just as deep inside him.

He would never, ever be the same.

Vittorio fucked him. Half the giant cock probed him, then withdrew, then slid back in deeper this time. Again, deeper, and again even deeper. Paul grunted and wriggled and pushed up against the slow invasion, impaling himself impatiently while Vittorio grinned down at him and controlled the pace with his own steady thrust and withdrawal.

Paul's asshole and his cock were on fire. So was the rest of his body as the tall Sicilian's capable hands roamed all over it. His nipples were tweaked and tugged, his rippled abdomen stroked, his strong shoulders gripped and squeezed. The smooth cheeks of his ass were gently kneaded, then slapped playfully.

All the while, that enormous cock probed his gut. His ass-lips quickly surrendered, gaping open for that steady goring, but then clamping possessively over it whenever it began to withdraw.

In the midst of that maddeningly slow gut-plowing, Vittorio slid his hands behind Paul's back and lifted him. All at once, he was in the air, straddling the big Sicilian's hips and sitting on his massive cock.

They were face to face as Vittorio cradled him in his strong arms and fucked him. Paul bounced over the thrusting cock, now taking it right to the balls. They were both laughing until Vittorio clamped his mouth over Paul's and fucked him with his fat tongue.

All that cock was up his aching asshole, and he was loving it. But the big farmer had more in store for him. He turned Paul and placed him on the well again, this time in a squat facing away from him.

With his sneakers planted firmly under him, his hairless white ass hanging over the edge of the well, and his nicely-fucked hole gaping, cock once more slithered up into him. He let out a deep groan as all that hot meat slid home in one deep glide.

"Yes. *Si. Per favore*, Vittorio! Ohhhh! Fuck me."

Paul had been speechless for the most part until now. As Vittorio began to pump in and out of his ass with powerful thrusts, he squatted back over that hot fuck-tube and took it all the way. Lube squished and spurted, dripping down his naked thighs.

The tall farmer's hands were all over him as his big cock thrust up into his aching gut. His warm lips came down to kiss the back of Paul's neck and nuzzle his ears. Those hands ran over his ass, tugged on his balls, stroked his cock, ran up over his tensed abdomen and cupped his tight pecs. The calloused farmer hands possessed him as thoroughly as that cock owned his seething asshole.

In the midst of that pounding fuck, Paul finally managed to say aloud what he'd been thinking and feeling over the past several weeks. "Give it to me! *Si. Si.* Ohhhhhhhh! I want you to fuck me and fuck me! I love it! *Per favore, grazie!* I love your cock in me. *Per favore!* Ohhhhh! I love you."

It was the ultimate release. He's admitted his feelings, finally. It hit him all at once, a rush of relief and a rush of heat in his balls and up the stiff shank of his cock. As Vittorio's cock rammed into him relentlessly, he shot his load.

The orgasm was incredible. Vittorio continued to pump his fat cock in and out while licking his ear-lobe and tweaking his nipples and whispering in his ear. *"Bravo. Bravo. Si. Si."*

Another spurt of nut-cream was forced out of his cock with every deep thrust. It seemed he had a gallon of cum in him. He finally collapsed forward onto his face and chest, which only opened up his ass for a sudden crescendo of vigorous thrusts.

Vittorio was coming. Those powerful thrusts slammed against his sweat-soaked butt. The Sicilian cried out, then held his cock deep inside Paul and let loose.

His big arms surrounded the crouching American. His cock pulsed inside him. His hot breath beat against his ear as the big farmer gasped and moaned.

Paul wanted it to last forever. Truthfully, he was afraid of what came next. But, he shouldn't have been. After Vittorio finally caught his breath, he leaned in close and bit Paul's ear playfully before whispering in it.

"Scusi, Paul, but I could use a bookkeeper, and some of my neighbors, too. Would you be interested in helping out for a while? No corruption, just simple work if you wish to stay longer."

His heart skipped a beat. *"Si! Grazie.* Yes. *Per favore*, I'd love to stay longer."

"Bravo. And I would love for you to stay longer."

Vittorio gently pulled out, then turned Paul onto his back. Bending over him, he offered that beautiful easy smile. It warmed him all over, as did the kiss that followed.

As tongue gently explored his mouth, Paul banished the barrage of questions he knew eventually needed answering. Were they lovers now? Could he actually live here? What would Vittorio's family think? What would his own family think?

None of that mattered enough to spoil the moment. Hopefully none of that mattered enough to spoil his dreams.

Only time would tell.

DADDY'S DEER CAMP
By Logan Zachary

Being dressed like an orange construction cone wasn't the fashion statement I wanted to make, but in order to keep from being shot the opening weekend of deer hunting season, I complied. Needless to say, I wasn't allowed many choices that were currently public appropriate. Long underwear, red flannel shirts, and Levis were packed into my suitcase, so not only was that the right thing to pack for this trip, but also it was all I had.

This was my last trip to the cabin, and when the first pick-up truck pulled into the driveway, I held my Dad's urn. I had to make sure he was the first one into the cabin. He always was. I had called all of his old hunting buddies for one last opener, to see off Dad, and have one last chance to say goodbye to the cabin. It would go on the market Monday, when I got home.

Guy Lindstrom stepped out of his truck and waved.

"You're the first to arrive," I called.

Guy threw his backpack over his shoulder and picked up his gun case with the same hand. As he walked past my open trunk, he grabbed the case of beer and headed to the cabin's door. "Thanks for inviting me. After my dad died, I haven't been to the hunting camp since I went away to college."

"I'm not sure how many guys will come. Most of Dad's friends have moved, died, or have become rather sick."

"I know my brother Dave won't be here. He's off somewhere for his new job." Guy set the case of beer down by the refrigerator and motioned toward the bedrooms.

"Tim and Dale canceled, too, so pick whichever one you want. You know the rules, first come, first served."

"So your buddies aren't coming either? Then which one did you take?" he asked.

I smiled. "I took the adult one."

"Then I'll bunk in there, too." Guy took his gun case and set it on the table and walked into the bedroom with his backpack. "If that's okay?"

My mind flashed to many years ago ...

# # # # #

Dave, Tim and Dale bounced on the bed as they played cards. I sat in my long underwear as they wore only their briefs. I wasn't included in the game. I was only left to watch.

"Let's play poker."

"Strip poker."

"Truth or Dare."

I rolled my eyes. Why was I here? I know my dad expected this, but there must be another way to bond with him, his friends, and their sons.

My body was starting to change, and hair was starting to grow down there. I knew I was ahead of the other teachers' sons. Just what I wanted to show off, my new pubes and then sprout a woody to embarrass me to death.

"Let's do a snow job."

I cringed.

Tim, Dave, and Dale grabbed me and lifted me off the bed. I kicked and fought as they dragged and carried me to the cabin's door. The next thing I knew I was sitting in a deep snowbank. My bare feet struggled to get out of the cold before the boys locked me out. Sharp shards of ice cut my soles, and my exposed skin burned from the cold. I scrambled through the snow and pounded on the door.

As it swung open, "What the hell?" greeted me.

Guy stood in the threshold looking angry at me. After a few seconds, he realized, what had happened. "Those assholes," he said. "Come on and stand by the stove and warm up."

The snow fell off my long underwear and melted around my bare feet. My whole body shivered from the cold.

"Your long underwear is soaked. Take them off."

I went rigid. I didn't have any other underwear!

Guy walked over to the cabinet and pulled out a huge fluffy towel. He stepped in front of me and added. "You need to take those wet things off."

My face burned from embarrassment.

Guy wrapped the towel around me and looked over my head. "I won't peek."

I pulled the long sleeved shirt over my head and let it drop to the floor. Slowly, my numb hands found the waistband of my long johns. I pushed the wet waffle fabric down my slender legs. As my penis and balls swung free from them, I felt a woody start.

"Not now." What could I think of to stop this? Baseball, Dale, Dave and Tim, my dad, deer hunting, guns.

The wet underwear refused to slip over my feet. I kicked hard, trying to free myself.

Guy tried to help, but ended up dropping the towel.

I almost screamed like a girl, as the bedroom door burst open. I dropped to the floor and pulled the towel around my waist, covering my boner.

Guy stepped in front of me and pulled the towel around me and helped remove the wet underwear from my foot. After making sure I was covered, he stood up with my long johns and turned to the terrible three. "You guys are so mean. Do you want to go home?"

Tim kicked the floor. "We were just playing, goofing around."

"If you're going to pick on someone, pick on each other."

"Yes, Guy," Dave said to his older brother.

"Why don't you turn in? I've had enough of you guys for the night. Besides, you all better be sleeping when our dads get back." His voice demanded respect, and the terrible three turned back into the room, heads hanging low, and closed the door.

Guy turned to me. "You can bunk with me tonight. I'm in the one under your dad."

I thought I'd pass out.

He untwisted my long johns and hung them over one of the hooks above the wood stove. "They should dry pretty fast." He led me to the men's bedroom and pointed to his bunk. "I'll be right back." He left the room and went to the boy's bedroom.

I heard him through the wall. He yelled at them for teasing me and being such a bunch of jerks. A few minutes later, he returned with my backpack and pillow.

"Do you have a change of clothes in here?" he asked.

I shook my head.

"I was afraid of that." Guy shook his head. He noticed me shiver in the towel. "Why don't you crawl into bed?" He stepped to the edge of the mattress and pulled back the thick quilt.

I lifted my skinny legs into the bed and guided them under the covers.

Guy covered me and held out his hand.

I looked at him blankly.

"The towel."

My face burned hot.

"I'm sure it's damp and cold and will only tie you up into a big knot under there."

I removed the towel from my naked body and the coolness of the sheets descended over my body. I had a full blown erection now.

Guy took the towel and folded it over the headboard. "You look cold. Give me a second, and I'll jump in there, too. That will warm things up."

I closed my eyes. This couldn't be happening to me. This is what I dreamed of, and it was the one thing I should never want or desire. I wished the bed would swallow me whole, or I would die before he returned.

Maybe if I fell asleep before ...

Guy's heavy footsteps returned to the bed. He stood at the lower bunk and pulled his sweatshirt over his head. His T-shirt pulled up and revealed a furry belly. He unbuckled his belt and undid his jeans. He stepped out of his pants and hung them on the end of the bed. He slipped his socks off and gasped as his bare feet touched the floor. "Man, it's cold. I'm going to throw a few more logs in the stove, and I'll be right back."

I listened to his bare feet scurrying over the wood floor. Then, the kitchen stove's old metal door swung open on its rusty hinges. A few heavy thuds as the wood was placed inside, the metal door slammed, and his hurrying feet raced back to bed. Guy pulled back the covers as a cool draft washed over my body as he dove into bed.

His bare hairy leg brushed up against mine, sending shivers over my body.

"Are you still cold?" Guy asked.

My mouth refused to work. I felt him slid over to me. He pulled my body against his, spooning me to him. He wrapped his arms around me. "Better?"

OH MY GOD! I wanted to scream.

His hands rubbed my arms as he hugged me. "You'll warm up, soon."

One hand brushed the crest of my hip, a ticklish spot on me.

"Are you ticklish?"

"Cold," croaked out of my mouth.

"Hang on," Guy said, as he released me.

I felt him struggle behind me, and then I knew what he was doing. He was taking off his T-shirt!

I had seen his furry chest. My skin screamed for him to hold me again.

His embrace answered it.

I could feel the heat radiate off his body and soak into mine. The thick pelt of hair on his chest tickled my back. I snuggled closer, my bare butt pushed up against his pelvis. A warm hairy leg curled over mine and held me tight. I could feel a bulge stir between my cheeks.

Guy rubbed my arms and legs, warming me with his body.

I thought I'd burst into flames.

One hand wrapped around me and pulled me close. It wrapped around and rested on my chest.

My shivering had stopped.

"Warming up?" he asked.

I nodded.

"Good." His hand slipped down my chest and over my abs.

His arm came closer and closer to my …

Please touch it, don't touch it, please touch, don't … My erection reached out from my body under the covers, a heat seeking missile, looking for his hand, his caress.

His arm brushed against my tip, and I froze.

Guy stopped moving, too. "It's okay," he whispered into my ear. "Nothing to be ashamed of."

I couldn't move.

Guy gently rocked me. "It's okay."

I wanted to die.

Guy backed away and released me.

I felt him moving around behind me.

Don't leave. Don't leave. Don't leave. But I couldn't move. "I'm sorry," escaped from me.

Guy moved back and held me. His arms wrapped around me, and I felt him move back into place, but this time his underwear were gone. I could feel his furry balls and erection against my bare bottom. A thick pubic bush tickled me, but I snuggled closer.

His hand rested on my chest as our breathing fell into sync. He squeezed me to him and held me tight.

The thick covers and his body heat warmed me. I finally relaxed, and as I drifted off, I moved his hand down to my erection and fell asleep …

# # # # #

"What did you want to do about supper?" Guy asked, startling me out of my thoughts.

"I brought a bunch of steaks, but it's not looking like the old gang is coming." I bit my lower lip.

"Then we'll enjoy them and screw those guys."

After our steaks were gone and our bellies were full, I finally pushed back from the table and sighed.

"Great supper, you really know how to cook." Guy kicked back in his seat.

"You helped."

"I open a mean beer bottle and can set a fine table."

"Do you really enjoy hunting? I guess I never got it," I said. "It never was fun for me. What did you enjoy doing at deer camp?"

"I hunted because my Dad hunted. My favorite thing at deer camp was playing strip poker," Guy laughed. "I don't know why the boys enjoyed it so much. I always cheated, and they never knew."

"I think they thought they were real men playing an adult game."

"You never joined in, why not?"

"No one ever explained how to play and …"

Guy nodded. "You were always so much more mature than those three. You should've been in my grade and not theirs."

"You were so much older than we were," I said.

"Mom and Dad had Dave late in life. He was a surprise ten years after me, and he was always trying to keep up."

"I feel like I'm always trying to play catch up."

Guy stood up, cleared the table by slipping all the dishes into the sink, and returned with two more beers and a deck of cards. "It's time you learned to play poker."

"What?" I felt a stirring in my underwear. "I can't."

"We're the only two here, and I doubt anyone else is coming tonight. Besides, you wanted to learn poker, and I promise not to cheat."

"I don't …"

Guy ran to the door and locked it. He even slid the dead bolt and pulled all the curtains closed. "No one will see."

"But …"

"We can stop anytime you want, cross my heart." He sat back down, took a long swig on his beer and started shuffling the cards. "We start with five cards, and you try to have a better hand than I do. Three of a kind is better than two of a kind. Two kings are better than two fives and so on." He dealt out five cards to each of us and set the deck down.

Slowly, I picked up my cards. Two queens, a joker, a five and a two. "I have a joker."

"It's wild; it can be anything you want it to be. See, you're ahead already. So now, look at your cards and decide what you want to keep and what you want to throw away and maybe get better cards."

I took the five and the two and threw them onto the table face up.

"Don't let me see what you threw away," Guy said, reaching across the table and flipped them over. He quickly dealt two more cards and threw three of his away.

I looked at my two new cards and saw two aces.

"Now, you decide if you want to up the bet or fold, which means throw the cards away."

"How do I up the bet?"

"You must have a good hand. We could wager two articles of clothing instead of one."

"I didn't agree to strip poker."

"How else will you learn if you don't play? We could have a practice hand, if you want."

I looked at my cards, and I knew this was a good hand. Would my luck hold out? I sorted the cards again, three queens and two aces. That did seem like a hard hand to beat ...

"Okay, I'm in, but two articles of clothing this hand."

Guy looked at his cards and then back at me. He seemed unsure of what to do. Beginner's luck or a novice's play? Finally, he said, "Sure, two articles of clothing."

I knew he'd take his boots off, so by my count he had six articles of clothing on. I had on eight. "Deal."

"We've already dealt, so you say show those cards, or okay."

"Show me those cards."

He flipped over three kings and two jacks.

"DARN," I said as I threw my cards down.

"Let's see them," he said. He reached over and flipped them face up. "Wow! You beat me."

"How? I had only three queens, you have three kings."

He picked up the joker and added it to the aces. "You have three aces and two queens; that is better than mine." He pushed his chair back and pulled off one sock. "One," he said and tossed it on the table, and "two," smiled as he pulled of the other one. His bare feet hit the floor. "Brrr. The floor is cold."

I stood up and headed to the kitchen. "I'll throw a few more logs in the wood stove to heat things up." I wasn't having him back out so soon. The smell of wood smoke filled the room as I opened the wrought iron door and threw in a few more pieces.

Guy shuffled the cards and waited to deal as I sat back down. He took a sip of his beer and counted out five cards.

A ten, a two, a four, a joker, and an ace filled my hand. I kept the ten, joker, and ace, and threw the other two back.

Guy ran his fingers through his hair and looked at his hand. He gave me two and took one for himself.

Another ten and a two finished my hand.

"Did you want to fold or play?" he asked.

Two pairs seemed good, but they were low cards. "I'll play."

"You're not going to raise me are you?" His deep blue eyes gleamed with excitement.

Was he cheating? "I'll just play for one item this time."

Guy laid his cards down. "A pair of jacks."

"I have a pair of tens."

"Yeah, I win," he said.

"And a pair of twos."

He looked at me in disbelief. "You have two pair?"

I nodded.

Guy shrugged and pulled his sweatshirt over his head. He wore no T-shirt underneath. A furry chest appeared, big pecs with large nipples and a six-pack made darker with the coating of hair. There was some gray mixed in the pelt of hair, but it was thick and looked so soft.

"Good thing I have hair to keep me warm." He shuffled and dealt again. "Are you sure you haven't played before."

"Nope." I took a long drink on my beer, savoring Guy's naked torso. How I longed to run my fingers through his hair and hear the electric snap of static.

The next hand, Guy lost his jeans. "The cuffs were wet anyway," he said as he slipped them off. He hooked them by the stove to dry off. He wore a pair of white cotton briefs that hugged his ass. He had long hairy, muscular legs of a runner. His body didn't look his age at all. As he turned, the thin fabric showed a dark shadow underneath, where his hair filtered in. The pouch seemed to stretch over his package. His bare feet slapped the floor.

"Maybe we should play something else," he said.

I laughed. "You said no backing out."

"Easy for you to say with all your clothes on."

"One more hand," I said as I rubbed my hands together.

"Oh you think so." He dealt the cards, and things changed quickly. Then next thing I knew, I was sitting in my underwear, just as he was. "I think you're cheating, suckered me in and now ..."

Guy stopped shuffling and handed the deck to me. "You deal."

My hands fumbled as I picked up the cards. I didn't shuffle them as smoothly as he did, and I didn't have any flare as I counted out five.

He picked his cards up one by one as I dealt and smiled with each one. I put the deck down and picked up mine. I had four hearts and a two of spades.

Loser.

Guy threw down two and waited for me to give him the next cards.

I flipped them to him and dropped my two down. "And I'll take one," hoping my bluff would stop this game.

Guy's eyebrows shot up and waited.

I peeled the top card off the deck, just as the wood stove's door burst open. The wood shifted inside and sparks sprayed out. I dropped the cards, as did Guy, and we both padded to the kitchen. The spatula rested on the counter, and I used it to push the wood back inside.

Guy grabbed the oven mitts and patted the embers on the floor. The bigger ones he tossed back in.

Soon, all was safe, and I added a big chuck for the night.

"Well, that was exciting, but I'm beat, how about you?"

"I'm ready to hit the hay," Guy said. He grabbed a blanket and wrapped it over his shoulders. "I need to get rid of my beer and I'll be ready, how about you?"

My bladder instantly let me know it was full.

Guy raised his arm and wrapped the blanket around me. "This will keep us warm as we pee." His hairy body pressed against mine and warmth radiated off him.

"You're shivering," he said.

"I'm always cold."

"Hurry up and then we can jump into bed." Guy opened the cabin door and pulled me out onto the step. "I'm not going any further." He pulled back his side of the blanket and reached down to his underwear. A steaming stream of urine flowed out of him, the shadows hiding his dick.

"Hurry up, or I'll leave you out here, blanketless."

I pulled my half back and slipped my semi-aroused cock out of my briefs. I peed away from him, afraid he'd see my wood.

He waited as I finished and pulled the blanket around us. "Let's get inside."

We entered, and Guy removed the blanket and carried it to the bedroom.

"If you want your own room …" I started.

"I'll move out if you want me to," he said quickly.

"Nah, your stuff is already in there, stay if you want."

Guy nodded and entered the room. "Coming?"

"I'll get the lights out here, and then I'll be right in." My semi-wood turned into full wood as I turned off the lights. Entering the bedroom, I walked into Guy.

"I didn't know if you wanted the top or the bottom."

I laughed at the question.

"You really should have your dad's bed, and I'll take the lower bunk." He stepped back and let me slip under the comforter.

Guy stepped to the bed and his pelvis was just inches from my face. The thin cotton looked damp and almost see through. It took him a few seconds to jump up, and I enjoyed every millisecond. A wet spot formed in the thin cotton after he had peed, and the fabric outlined the mushroom head of his fat cock.

I licked my lips, as he landed on top of the upper bunk, Dad's bunk. A depression where his butt settled pressed into the soft mattress. I could see the indention of his body.

"Can you get the light?" he asked.

"Sure," croaked out of me. I sat up in the bed and reached through the posts and flipped off the switch. The room fell into darkness.

Our breathing slowed as we lay in the dark.

"Do you miss him?"

I didn't answer him. How could I? He was a bastard to me my entire life. He made me hunt and fish and play with all these teachers' sons that hated me; I'm sure they knew I was gay. That's why no one came.

"Are you alright?" Guy asked.

Before I could respond, he jumped down and knelt by my bed. His hand slipped under the covers and touched my arm. "Are you okay?"

All the hurt and pain and bottled up emotions broke free at that moment, and I cried.

Guy pulled back the covers and slipped in next to me. His arms wrapped around my body and held me close. "Let it all out, that's okay," he soothed.

His hands smoothed my hair and caressed my arm until my tears stopped.

I turned to face him as he wiped away my tears. His hands held my face, and slowly he pulled me closer and kissed me.

As his lips touched mine, fire blazed across my body. I wrapped my legs around him and pulled him close. My arousal grew and swelled, as it rubbed over him. My hip moved, and I felt his erection against mine.

Frantically, our hands peeled off our briefs, skin to skin, and cock to cock.

My fingers combed through his chest hair and his hands caressed my ass. Our pelvises ground into each other and our balls bounced off each other's. Our hair tickled and tangled together, as pre-cum oozed out of our dicks and slid down our shafts. The sensation grew as did the urgency.

His tongue entered my mouth and rubbed against mine. Our lips sucked on each others, trying to draw the other one in deeper.

My hands pulled his hairy butt closer, pressing him onto me. Our dicks slipped alongside each other, as more pre-cum flowed across our sensitive skin. The pleasure grew and grew as we rubbed faster and faster.

His hand grasped both dicks at the same time and held them together. As his shaft's length slid along mine, pre-cum continue to pour out of both of our cocks.

My heart pounded in my chest as my breathing came in rapid bursts.

Guy's hand clamped down, and I felt a hot, thick wet explosion cover me. My balls pulled up as my cock spasmed a second later, creaming his length. Wave after wave of bliss flowed over both us. We lay in each other's embrace as our bodies returned to normal.

Guy rolled over and away from me. He guided my cock to his butt and slid it up and down his crease.

My erection returned, and slowly, I entered him.

He pressed back against me and grabbed my butt, pulling me deeper into him. Our rhythm increased, and soon I was pistoning into him.

Another orgasm started in my balls and exploded out of my cock, filling him with white heat. Wave after wave of cum filled him.

As soon as my pleasure eased, he rolled me over and entered me. He didn't have to work very long as he shot his load deep into me. He collapsed on top of me and lay exhausted.

He pulled me closed as his body spooned mine.

And, I fell asleep in Guy's arms, cradled close. I slipped his hand on my cock and drifted off to sleep …

The next morning, Guy and I stepped outside into the brisk autumn and walked to the clearing. He held my hand as I carried Dad's ashes. "This was his favorite spot in the whole world."

"I can see why." Guy squeezed my hand. "And that's why he gave it to you. This place was special to him, and maybe he hoped, it would be special for you."

"It is now," I said as I kissed Guy. I knew I would keep the hunting camp.

I released Guy's hand, stepped back and opened the urn. I waited a few seconds as a breeze came, and I threw his ashes into the air.

Dad's ashes swirled in the wind and spread out into the forest, across the clearing.

"Thanks, Dad."

BROOKLYN BEARS
By Donald Webb

I've been entombed in my eighteen-wheeler all day, and all I want to do is drop the trailer at my destination and head for the nearest leather bar to look for a daddy. I'm horny. The only company I've had in weeks is the palm of my right hand.

I know I'm behind schedule, and the trucking company is probably closed for the day, but I hope someone will be available to let me into the compound. I'm wrong. The gates are padlocked. The only living thing in the compound is a growling German Shepherd who bares his fangs at me.

I can't unhitch the trailer and leave it blocking the entrance, and the street is too narrow to make a U-turn, so I shut it down and prepare for a long lonely night.

I climb down to the pavement and look around for a spot to take a leak.

Warehouses line the street. The only exception is a small electronic repair shop located directly across the street. A deck juts over the roof of the shop. A salt-and-pepper butch-looking bear reclines on a deckchair. His bare feet rest on the railing. He raises a beer can, saluting me.

"You think there'll be a problem if I park here overnight?" I say as I cross the street.

He stands up, leans over the railing to look down at me, and cocks one foot up to rest it on the lower railing. The breath catches in my throat as I stare up at him. All he's wearing is a baggy pair of white shorts. But what really stops me dead is that, from my vantage point, I can see up the wide leg of his shorts. His large uncut dick and low-swung nuts are clearly visible.

"No problem," he says. "Everyone's left for the day. They'll be back around six in the morning."

"You think I can use your toilet? My bladder's bursting."

"Stairs are round side of building."

I climb the stairs to the second-floor. He's waiting at the door for me. As I pass him, I'm nearly overcome by the masculine aroma emanating from his huge body. He points to the bathroom, and then goes back out onto the deck.

"Feel better?" he asks when I join him.

"Sure does."

"You thirsty?" he asks.

I nod.

"Bruno," he says, offering me his hand.

"Jason," I say.

He unfolds a deckchair for me. I'm soon slurping down an ice-cold brew.

I want to put the make on him, but the gold band around his left ring finger dampens my enthusiasm.

"You live alone?" I ask.

"Nah ... if you look close you'll see the ball-and-chain. The boss is visiting the old country. Won't be back for a month – thank the Pope."

"You don't miss her?" I say.

"Yeah, like a wisdom tooth. Wasn't getting any, anyways ... says she's not into sex no more."

"You not lonely stuck out here?"

"Nah ... but it's nice to have company." Then after a brief pause, "You hot? You wanna borrow some shorts?"

"I have some in the truck."

"Go get 'em. You might as well get comfortable."

I fetch my overnight bag from the truck and change into a pair of silk running shorts. I leave my chest bare, so he can get a look at me. I'm disappointed when he doesn't even glance at me. I settle down in the chair and prepare to spend time with a straight bear.

What a waste!

He bends one of his legs, rests a massive thigh against the armrest, and props a foot on the railing. I'd had numerous glimpses of his huge cock and bull-sized balls, but now the whole enchilada is on display. He might as well have been naked. His soft uncut cock looks to be a good eight inches, so I can imagine how huge it must get when fully hard. I change position so he can't see my hard-on.

Does this guy know how absolutely desirable he is? If he wasn't straight, I'd be on my knees sucking his toes.

He reclines and scratches his sweaty mat of gray chest hair.

I'd love to run my fingers through it, if only he'd ask.

He takes a toilet break. When he comes back outside, and puts the family jewels back on display, I can see his dick has hardened up some and his thick skin has slightly retracted. I'm mesmerized when a drop of piss dribbles out of the big hole in his dick-head.

What would he say if I leaned over and licked it?

His voice breaks the spell I'm in. "You gonna be stuck here all night," he's saying. "You might as well stay up here ... it'll be too hot in the truck."

"You sure I won't be in the way?"

"Like I says, it's nice having company." Then after a brief pause, "I'm starving. You wanna Pizza?"

"Sounds good to me."

Bruno gets on the phone and orders Pizza. We're still guzzling beers when the Pizza boy arrives. I'm surprised when he comes in without knocking and marches out onto the deck with two large Pizzas in his hands.

"Hey, Dino," Bruno says. "How's it hanging?" Then turning to me, he adds, "This guy works with my old lady. He drops in every day, on her orders, to make sure I got no pussy stashed in here."

Dino's giving me the eye when he drops into a chair and opens the Pizza boxes. He's obviously trying to figure out who I am. He looks to be about eighteen. His white T-shirt is stretched tight over his muscular chest and arms. His faded jeans are skintight and do little to hide the huge bulge at his crotch. When the Pizzas are finished, I go into the bathroom to empty my bladder. I can hear him quizzing Bruno about me as my piss gushes into the toilet.

"I'm going for some more beer," Bruno shouts.

I'm washing my hands when Dino comes into the bathroom. He squeezes by me and unzips his jeans. I watch in the mirror as he pulls out his thick sausage, slips his foreskin back, and then empties his bladder. As he milks the last drops of piss from his lengthening dick, I look up at his face and see him staring back at me.

I hold my breath. Normally I'm not into kids – I prefer bears, but I'm so horny I have to have him. Bruno's got me all juiced up.

He comes up behind me, pushes his basket up against my butt, and wraps his arms around my torso. We both watch in the mirror as his fingers run over my chest then slip down my hard abdomen to my shorts. He pulls my shorts down to expose my completely stiff boner, and then cups my nuts in one hand while gently masturbating my shaft with the other. His stiff rod pumps between my moist butt cheeks.

His tongue traces down my spine as he sinks to his knees. His hands press my upper body onto the vanity, and I can feel his hot breath on my hole when he spreads my cheeks apart.

"Oh yes," he says. "Nice and hairy, just how I like it."

He buries his face between my ass-mounds and chews on my crater. I spread my butt for him, wanting to feel his tongue in my hole. His thumbs dig into my channel, opening me up, then he slaps my cheeks as he voraciously chews my hole.

I want him in me. It's been a while, and my hole's craving dick.

"Quick, fuck me," I say, "before Bruno comes back."

I watch in the mirror as he comes to his feet. His face is wet with saliva and ass juice. He pulls a safe out of his pocket and rolls it over the plum-shaped head and down the shaft of his enormous rammer. He places the head at my dilated orifice, and then with one push, he's balls deep in my inner core, stretching my sphincter to its max.

I wiggle my ass when he starts to pound my channel. He pulls the big fucker out of my hole, slaps my butt with it, and then long poles me again and again.

The sound of Bruno's truck in the driveway brings me back to reality.

Dino speeds up. Battering my rear-end like a machine. In and out, in and out, he goes, practically lifting me off my feet with his youthful exuberance.

I can feel his dick throbbing when he ejaculates. He quickly withdraws, flushes the condom, dries his glistening dick on a hand towel, pulls up his jeans, and dashes out of the bathroom.

I raise my shorts and join him on the deck. Just in time, too, because Bruno's coming through the door.

"Hope you guys behaved while I was gone?" Bruno says with a laugh.

If you only knew, I think, as ass-juice oozes from my well-fucked hole.

Dino's cellphone beeps. "Aw, fuck," he says when he reads the message. He jumps up from the chair. "Gotta run, guys."

"Don't fuck too much pussy tonight, Dino," Bruno shouts over the railing when Dino appears below. "Don't forget you gotta work tomorrow."

Dino waves, jumps into his car, and takes off.

"I like to kid with him," Bruno says, "but I know he's gay. I saw the way he was giving you the eye. Hope it didn't freak you out?"

I shake my head, but I'm thinking I should've got his number.

We have a couple more beers, and it's past ten, when Bruno suggests we hit the sack. I'm still not sure what the sleeping arrangements are, so I'm ecstatic when he leads me into the only bedroom.

"I sleep on this side," he says, pointing to the left side, "there should be room for the both of us."

He dowses the light.

"I hope you're cool with this," he says, "but I sleep in the raw."

"Me, too," I answer as I quickly strip.

"Fuck, I'm drunk," he says falling onto the bed. "I probably won't remember nothing about tonight."

Where've I heard that line before?

The streetlights illuminate his sweaty body. He's rubbing his hairy chest and lazily scratching his big nuts. My cock immediately hardens up as I watch the erotic display. There's only about an inch separating our bodies because his big bear physique takes up more than half of the double bed. I can feel the heat emanating from his body and can detect his funky male aroma.

"Fuck, I'm horny tonight," he says. "I'll never get to sleep with this woody. Will it freak you if I jerk-off, or should I do it in the bathroom?"

"No, I have the same problem. I'll join you."

We're both stroking our cocks, like adolescent boys at a circle jerk, when he says, "Whenever the old lady's out of town, Dino hangs around here, hinting that what I need is a good blowjob, but I could never let him do me ... he's like family."

"You ever get a blowjob?" I ask.

"No, never did get one. I used to ask the old lady, but she wouldn't do it."

He spits in his hand and uses both hands to stroke his long shaft. "Did you ... ah ... ever make it with a guy?" he asks.

Here we go.

"Yeah, there's nothing like getting blown by guys. They really know how to do it."

He keeps stroking, and stroking, and I'm dying to get my mouth on him.

"What about you? You ever fuck around with a guy?" I ask.

"No, but – just between us guys – I've always wondered about it. Just never had the opportunity, I guess."

"You want to see what it feels like?" I say.

"Why, you wanna do me?"

I place my hand on his shaft.

He grabs my hand to stop me, but I keep stroking.

"Oh, fuck, man, we shouldn't be doing this."

"Relax, no one's gonna know." I say, as I run my hand up and down his slick shaft.

He releases my hand and covers his eyes with his forearm, as though trying to block out the image of another man playing with his dick. I quickly turn onto my side and hold his cock upright. I nibble on his pliant foreskin for a while then slip my tongue between the thick skin and the crown of his dick. It's nice and tasty.

He lets out a long sigh.

I take hold of his big nuts then slowly sink his throbbing dick into my throat, peeling back his foreskin as I descend. By the time his shaft is buried to the hilt, he's groaning and thrashing around on the bed. I move between his legs and continue to deep-throat him, anxious to make his first blowjob one he'll always remember. My asshole twitches as I suck his cock, reminding me that I, too, have needs.

I pull some safes and lube out of my bag. He's watching me when I roll one down his thick shaft. It's a tight fit, and there's plenty of skin still exposed when I reach the end of the sheath. I lubricate my hole, straddle his hips, engulf his shaft with my insatiable chute, and sink to his hips. His dick head is way up inside me, deeper than one's ever been before.

"Oh fuck, you're so tight ... and hot. Doesn't it hurt?"

"Does it look like I'm in agony?" I say, as I milk him with my inner muscles.

He grabs my waist, bends his knees, and pistons his joint in and out of me, slamming his dick-head against my g-spot. I grab my leaking cock and jerk-off in time to his thrusts. My ass-ring involuntarily clamps down tightly when I blast, bringing him to an immediate climax.

"I'm coming, I'm coming," he howls, as his juice explodes in my inner core.

I grab hold of his nuts and milk the cum out of his shaft with my ass muscles, then I gently ease him out of my well-fucked chute. I peel the safe off his dick and go into the bathroom to cleanup. What a load. He's been storing it up for a while. I take a washcloth back to the bed to clean his body.

The next morning, I slip out of the bed and go for a piss. I'm walking back to the bedroom thinking about him, when the outside door opens. I stand rooted to the spot in shock, not knowing what to expect.

Dino steps inside.

"Morning, Jason," he whispers in my ear. "I had a wet dream thinking about your hot body last night."

He runs his hands over my back and ass-cheeks and fingers my hole. His hot breath sends tingles down my spine when he whispers in my ear, "Did you have him last night?"

I nod.

He tiptoes across the room, pulling me with him, and we both stand at the bedroom door staring at Bruno. He's lying on his back with his legs spread apart, his huge hard-on begging for attention.

"Fuck he's huge," Dino whispers. "Did you let him fuck you with that big thing?"

I nod.

"Fuck I'd like it up my ass, too, but I don't think I can take such a big one."

My mind's working overtime. "You want me to open you up?"

He doesn't think about it. "Oh, fuck. Yes."

"Go into the bathroom," I say.

I sneak into the bedroom and collect a safe and lube. Dino's naked and bending over the vanity when I enter the bathroom.

I sheath up, spread lube over his hole, and finger his chute. He opens up for me. I slip two fingers into him and twirl them around. When he's nice and dilated, I stick him with my rod. He lets out a long groan when I hit bottom.

I place my hand over his mouth. "Quiet, boy," I say. "You'll wake daddy up."

I fuck him for a few minutes, until he's totally relaxed, then I withdraw and say, "You're ready for daddy."

Bruno's still spread out on his back with his arm across his eyes. I straddle him, with my back toward his face, roll a safe down his throbbing dick, and cover it with lube.

Dino's standing in the doorway, fingering his hole.

I place my finger over my lips and beckon him. His dick swings back and forth as he climbs on the bed. He places one foot on either side of Bruno and lowers himself. I hold Bruno's dick upright and guide it into Dino's chute. Dino's mouth opens in a silent scream when he sinks down the massive shaft.

I lean over and suck his dick.

Bruno's stirring. He groans and thrashes around, but we've got him pinned.

I move out of the way.

His eyes open wide. "Oh, fuck, Dino," he says. "What're you doing?"

A car horn sounds. I jump up and look out the window. The compound gates are open.

I quickly dress. Dino is bouncing on Bruno when I exit the room.

I'll be back next week. Hopefully, Bruno will forgive me because I need a fulltime daddy.

SUGAR DADDY
By Rawiya

"Baby, where did you put the extra towels?"

Smiling, upon hearing my man's voice, "In the closet," I replied.

"Okay, but maybe we should start putting everything away, so we can find things, yes?" The sounds of his footsteps were behind me, I knew he was close. Within seconds, I felt that strong hand on my shoulder, gripping it, then the hot breath on my earlobe.

I grinned, not turning around because his hardened flesh was grazing my buttocks, his hands encircling my waist, a soft purr escaped my lips. "Well, I wanted to finish putting it all away, but I recall a certain man wanted to have fun last night as opposed to unpacking."

"Aye … yes … indeed my love. This man required the warmth between your thighs. I could not allow you to continue working when I could be enjoying that spot down below." He kissed the side of my neck; the shivers went down my spine.

"Mmhm … do you want to enjoy it some more," I asked before finally turning around to look into the deep brown orbs of my hot man, well not quite … yet.

Sighing, taking my lips into his, "Yes, but is it not time for young Matthew to go to class?"

Pouting, I drew up my lips, caressing the grey hairs of his goatee. "Yes, it is, but I thought maybe you would give me a reason to cut today especially since we just moved into this place."

Again, he gave me a peck, "Ahem, no, remember, I gave you the conditions of us moving in here would be that you would not miss school, yes. You need your education. That … my good man always comes before everything."

"Yes, Daddy … we can't break the rules just once?" I placed light nips along his jaw, causing his breaths to turn to pants. Slowly, I massaged the bulge in his trousers as I went further down his neckline. "Please, baby … once, yeah?"

He cleared his throat while bringing me into him, making me feel his erection on the crotch of my jeans. "Matthew, you are irresistible, the only problem with allowing you to break the rules is that you will want to do … mmhmmm …" he stopped mid sentence when I began unbuttoning his silk shirt, exposing his chocolate skin. I wanted my sugar daddy, now; forget about class, I was passing with honors anyway.

# # # # #

"Goddamit, Matthew, I wish you would get your own man and stop looking at mine," Devon said when we left multimedia class. My good friend Devon Hunter was dating the resident hot teacher, Professor Edgar Vincent. All the girls were crazy about him; it's too bad that they didn't know he had a desire for ass of the male variety instead of the female.

Rolling my eyes, I shrugged, "Sorry, it's hard not to gawk at him; he's really good looking. It's too bad he saw you first before me."

Devon put his hand on my chest, lightly shoving me, "What the hell is that supposed to mean? It doesn't matter anyway; he ain't into white boys anyhow …"

"His loss," I replied as we walked to our lockers that were side by side.

Devon chuckled, and then muttered, "Bitch …"

Smiling, I retorted, "You love me though …"

"Yep," he winked, turning the combo lock.

This conversation was normal between me, Matthew Davidson and my good friend, Devon Peartley. We had known each other since grade school and were now attending the Chelsea College of Art and Design in the midst of our second year of the Graphic Design Communications course; both of us aspiring art directors, who desired to work in either television or movies. We had been close seemingly forever, like brothers. We'd only screwed around once after being drunk at a party after graduating from middle school. The reason why? When you become that insanely tight with someone, where you know every stinking thing about one another, you really don't want to complicate things by having sex. Moreover, Devon was not really attracted to white men; he preferred those of his own kind or Hispanic. I liked that as well, but of the older variety.

So, even though I had given Professor Vincent more than a nod, I really wasn't all that interested truthfully; I only did it to piss off Devon.

"Devon, I want a man. I'm tired of being alone." I pouted, leaning against the door.

"So get one, and keep away from Doc Vincent." He closed the door, glaring at me.

"I don't want your Professor, Devon. You know I am into older black men." I slid my Blackberry out of my pocket, looking at the screen.

"Yeah, and my doc is an older bloke ..."

"Uh huh, but not old enough for me..."

Devon's eyes widened, "What? You mean you're looking for an elder, a senior citizen ..."

"Fuck you, you tosser, hell no; I'm searching for," I paused glancing upwards, moving my hands. "A man that is established, in his late forties, early fifties, with intelligence, strength ..."

"A libido?"

Rolling my eyes, "Yes, most definitely. Someone that will take care of me, stimulate my mind and my groin, you know?"

Devon sighed, "Uh huh. A sugar daddy …"

"Yes, but a brown sugar daddy … really dark chocolate, sweet to the core, but rugged, rough …"

"Mmm, sounds like a tall order. Just where do you think you will find one of those?" Devon put his hand against the wall.

Drawing up my lips, "Not sure … the personals?"

Devon burst out into laughter, "What? Are you kidding me? Those are only for losers, not anyone like you … c'mon you can do better that, mate." He hit my arm making me wince.

Wryly smiling, I rubbed my arm. "Okay, then how about one of those dating sites?"

"Again … boo …" He put a thumb down.

"Well what, fucker? I mean, damn. I'm just tired of going home and whacking off every night ya' know? I need someone in my life. Man must not live on choking the chicken alone …"

"True, well chap, just not sure. I know we can do better than the ads or any dating sites online. Besides all the men on those are married on the DL, and you don't want that …"

"How do you know that's not what I want?"

"C'mon Matt, you don't want to share the man you like with some bitch … please. You are fine enough to get your own."

"Not what I want, Devon. The black men that I want to date are not the ones I desire. I want my man to take care of me in every way possible. My only hope might be to get with a man who's on the low, with a wife and grown kids. Maybe I just might make him switch fences," I winked.

"No ... no, no ..." Devon said as we began walking to our next class. "That situation is just asking for trouble. You don't need that. I mean your parents already can't live with the fact that you're gay. Now, just how would you be able to explain to them that you are seeing someone that's married?"

As we trotted down the corridor to Communications Room 105, I pondered over what my best friend was saying. Truthfully, I did not give a flying rat's ass what my folks thought. I wanted my brown sugar daddy; that was all that concerned me.

# # # # #

"Ohhh ... Antwon ... God's ... ooh ..." I cried, as he slipped his hardened muscle into my not so tight space. I loved the way he felt going inside me; I was always satisfied. My long legs were around his waist, binding him to me; ankles tickling the small of his back, nails digging into his cocoa skin.

"Matthew," he growled before burying himself into my neck, nibbling on my pale flesh, his hands tangling in my brownish red locks. He ordered that I do not cut my hair, and like the good little boy I am, I obeyed.

Contrary to what he was trying to say about breaking rules and doing so repeatedly, I convinced him that missing one day was not going to be a large issue. Besides, Devon could get my homework for me. I was already on the Dean's list, and the term was close to ending. All that mattered to me was being in our new flat that he'd just purchased, so he could come see me whenever he wanted. He was also preparing for what would be a messy situation. In a few days, he was letting his wife know that he was leaving her for me; the kid that he invited back to his house as part of the father/son mentoring program. A cover up to get me into his house that he might end up relinquishing because of a messy divorce that was to come.

This, all because daddy wanted a little cream to go along with his dark chocolate; I was the milk he needed to complete him. My sugar daddy could not deny that feeling anymore; despite how hard he tried to fight it.

# # # # #

After school one day, Devon came over to my place as he usually does when he didn't follow Professor Hottie home. I had told him that I saw an ad on GayMatch.com of a man who wished to talk with someone of Black or Hispanic variety that I had been in conversation with for about a week. Now, the man who had the screen name, dlovr69, wanted to see a picture. I really liked this guy; he seemed so sweet. Our chats that started innocently as we talked about my school, his work as an attorney, his wife, my single life would end with me wiping myself on my T-shirts or whatever cloths I had nearby after we cybered. God, I wanted him so badly, and now this could all be gone in seconds when he found out I was not what he asked for.

We put down our bags, then, went straight for the computer to check my email. I had told him that I needed to get a friend to take my photo because I did not have any that were recent. When I switched it on before clicking on the IE icon, there was a message from him with an attachment.

Devon raised an eyebrow, "Uh oh, the moment of truth. I hope Mister wonderful has teeth and he's not in a walker."

"Piss off ..." I said since I had informed him that my 'buddy' says he's fifty-six. Taking a deep breath, I closed my eyes and opened the message.

"Ooohhh shit ..." I heard Devon say, "Fuck, no way, that is not him ... no fucking way ..."

Hoping that it was a good reaction, I lifted my lids, gazing upon one of the most beautiful individuals I had ever lay eyes on. "Fuck ..." I muttered glancing at a man, dressed in a suit, a baldhead, a grey goatee, nearly perfect skin; not at all muscular, but definitely no stranger to the gym. "Shit ... the perfect hue of brown, too. Dark chocolate ... fuck me ..."

"Uh uh ... this has got to be a mistake. He is not this fine. What picture did he steal?" Devon said, shaking his head.

Still staring, I wanted to know the same. He was not pretty; I did not like my men that way. I preferred ruggedly handsome, sort of edgy. Dlover69 fit the bill to a tee, if this were really him. "I dunno, mate. I mean, I'm not sure what to believe. Though, I have been very dishonest with him while we have been talking. I did not tell him that I was white, I told him I was a middle class black kid from Liverpool."

Devon shrugged, "Hmph, figures. You would borrow my info just so you can get further with this bloke." He paused, before nudging me to the left. "You know, you should just let me have a go with him since you told my story and all …"

"No way, you got your prince, remember?" I pushed back, tapping the refresh button on the on the task bar.

Devon laughed, "Yeah, well what now? He wants to see a picture … what'cha …"

"Wait; hold on, here is another email from him." I hit the mouse twice with my index; the text appeared …

"Choco88

"Hey, instead of me seeing a pic, why don't we just meet for coffee if you are free? How about tomorrow after you get out of class? I have not stopped thinking of you since the last time we cybered. My name is Antwon btw, how are you? Reply back quickly …"

Upon seeing that, my eyes widened. "Shit … what now?" He wants to meet? Devon, what do I do?" I put my hand on my chin, leaning back in the chair.

He looked over, "Let me go …" he grinned.

"Fuck you, I am not! I gotta think of something …"

"Matthew, you should not have done this, you had to think that he would want to hook up sooner or later. Especially after having cyber sex …"

I swallowed hard, shaking my head, "No, no, I really didn't. He only mentioned that he wanted to chat and well, I was feeling lonely that night and ... we just started talking. Gods Devon ... I just dunno. I really want to meet him ..."

"Then you have to tell him the truth. That's all I can guess. Maybe he will relent, a bit, when he sees the fine man that he has been talking to, huh. Don't fret man, but really, I think you should just go on and tell him that you are not the man that he asked for and brace yourself because if he's not into young white boys then you'll lose him. Thank God you haven't been talking for that long, at least there are not many emotions involved here." Devon gripped my shoulder attempting to comfort me.

Once I again, I opened the message with Antwon's picture. From what he had told me, everything about him was exactly what I had been looking for. The ruggedly handsome man, dark, sweet, seemingly kind, intelligent, established, and financially stable. My sugar daddy was right in front of me, staring me down, and because of my dishonesty, he might slip through my fingers.

# # # # #

"Matthew ... damn, yes ..." Antwon whispered as he pounded me into the mattress. We had made this day off special with him using his silk tie to bind my hands together, above my head while he pummeled my ass, making me lose focus along with the hard plastic that he pushed in along with himself, since he knew I got off on double penetration.

"Oh, fuck, Antwon," I yelled, wanting to caress his baldhead. The sweat from his brow dripped on my lips. Hungrily, I devoured it before dragging my tongue against his sideburns. "Mmmhh baby, I'm gonna come ... I wanna come ..."

"Yes, Matthew. Come for me, yes," he spoke softly in his African tone that made my toes curl. I loved his accent, one of the many things I enjoyed about my sugar daddy and now, it would only be a matter of time that Mrs. Bantu would be part of his past.

Thank God one of his strong points was forgiveness.

# # # # #

That following day after seeing his note, Devon and I met him in the Gladsbury Park not too far away from school. I had told him that I was bringing a friend not only because I was nervous, but because I thought it would relieve some of the tension that would go along with our conversation. I had mentioned to him that I had not been honest about my appearance. When he questioned what I meant, I told him simply, "You'll see …"

As Devon and I looked at our watches seemingly at the same time, we spotted a man walking towards us with a bouquet of flowers. He was dressed in what looked to be a suit from Oswald Boateng, both me and my friend were well aware of these because we loved them but we could not afford them. His brown head shone in the sun; he donned a pair of designer shades that looked to be either Gucci or Sean John.

"Oh," I gasped, "he is every bit as advertised, just look at him." The man that called himself Antwon came closer; there was a huge lump in my throat. He smiled when he saw Devon right in front of me.

Devon was grinning back. "Are you sure you don't want to just let me have him, damn he is … wow …"

"Fuck off, man …" I mouthed, since Antwon was now less than ten feet away.

With a Cheshire cat expression, "Gentlemen, which of one of you is Matthew?"

Both of us took a deep breath, "Ahem, I am …" I said stepping forward hoping that Antwon would not react negatively.

Antwon raised an eyebrow, "Really? You are not what you said on the profile then … you are not exactly black …"

I bit my lip, nodding, "No, I am not, but … well … that day I was so lonely and your ad, it was just so interesting. Then we started chatting, and you seemed to be exactly what I wanted. I really did not think we would meet and then boom, all of a sudden that changed. I'm sorry, Antwon, I am very sorry for misleading you. I did have a lovely conversation though; I apologize for not being what you asked for. Maybe we can still chat at least, yeah?"

Antwon shook his head, looking down. "Well, I must say, this is a bit of a shock, but I really do like chatting with you. Who is this with you, your friend?" He tilted his head forward, giving him an eye after removing his glasses.

Devon stepped forward. "Yes, this is Devon. His information is actually the things I shared with you, even though we did both grow up in Liverpool." I paused, I was about to do something bitchy, but I did not care. "He is taken though, maybe I can help you find what you are looking for. I might have some …" Devon glared at me, nudging my side.

"Matthew stop, please, no; I really want to get to know you. You might not be black or Hispanic. Truthfully, I only asked that because I did not think that anyone of Caucasian variety would be interested in an old African man like myself." He continued to grin, and he handed me the three roses. "Let's go have coffee …" He put out his arm, inviting me to take it. I did just that, slipping my free hand through the empty space as we walked, with Devon tagging alongside. What a relief that was to know that Antwon actually wanted to get to know me; I might just get my sugar daddy after all.

# # # # #

"Damn … Matthew … ughh …" he cried out, his body crashing against mine when he had tossed the plastic cock aside. Nothing was better than his chocolate dipstick inside of me; I never desired anything more than that.

"Ohh baby … ooh Antwannnn …" I yelled, my wrists hurting from the tie, but I no longer cared about the discomfort. The liquids of my desire shot out of my cock, coating his stomach and mine.

"Yes …" he breathed, engulfing my lips, biting the bottom while his precious seed filled me to the brim. My head was spinning; I lost complete control every time we had sex.

"Fuck, yes ... 'twon ... Gods I love you ... I love you more than anything else in this world."

"As do I my little cuppa cream; can't wait to fully move in with you."

After hearing that, I wrapped my bound arms around his neck, gazing into his chocolate drops. I kissed him, devouring his mouth fully while forcing my tongue deep inside languishing in the tastes of the Italian roast coffee he'd had with breakfast and the Cuban cigar he'd just smoked before we hit the sheets. "Damn baby ..." I smiled, repeating my act, running my fingers along his bare noggin.

The rules had been broken, all of them. Not just the ones he had made but seemingly any of the unspoken others that had existed. A young Caucasian man, dating an older black one, which just does not happen.

And, to think that he only asked for similar ilk because he thought that no one like me would be interested. Another myth dispelled. If only Antwon Bantu would have been in the cards a lot sooner, then my heartache would have never existed. Now that I had my brown sugar daddy by my side, nothing could be as sweet.

UNCLE CARLOS (*TIO CARLOS*)
By Jesse Monteagudo

Uncle Carlos was not really my uncle. In fact, I don't think he had any nephews or nieces, or any sons or daughters for that matter. He was a *guajiro*, a small farmer who lived his life near the town of Revuelta in the province of Las Villas, in central Cuba. Born when Cuba was still a Spanish colony, Uncle Carlos did not have much of an education, nor did he need one. Growing up on the farm, he knew all that he needed to know to make a living. At the time I went to live with him, just before the Revolution began, Carlos was a sixty-year-old widower, having lost his wife many years before.

Though he did not have much to brag about as far as money or education or children were concerned, Uncle Carlos Suarez was regarded by his neighbors as the local patriarch. Throughout the years, he contributed to the local community by giving to local charities and by hiring a series of young men to work on his farm, young men who would grow up, move out, and become important figures in Cuba's political, economic and social life. Even when they moved on, these young men would remember their time working for "Tio Carlos" as a high point of their lives.

One of those young men was my dad, who as a young man worked for Carlos Suarez before he moved to Havana to start a career and raise a family. When Dad moved to the big city, he promised Uncle Carlos that he would send his oldest son down to work for him, as soon as that son turned eighteen. It was now the summer of 1958; I was the oldest son, and I had just turned eighteen. Though the impending Revolution was shaking Havana to the core, the village of Revuelta was still quiet and peaceful. Having just graduated from secondary school, I had two lazy months on my hands before I planned to enroll in the University of Havana. Having a son around the house with nothing to do was not an ideal situation as far as Dad was concerned. The way he saw it, it was better for him and me to send me away, far from the big city, to spend the summer working for his old friend. It was a decision that I was not happy about.

"Why do I have to go out into the country, to work for an old man I have never met before?"

"Because he will keep you out of trouble and make a man out of you. There is a lot of shit going on around here, and I want to keep you as far away from it for as long as I can. Carlos Suarez did a lot for me when I was your age, and I'm sure he will do a lot for you if you just go along with what he says."

The very next morning, Dad took me to the bus station and put me on a bus headed for Revuelta. As the bus rolled down Cuba's main highway, I looked out the window and wondered who Uncle Carlos Suarez was and what he looked like. My dad had an old photo of Carlos on his desk: a black-and-white shot of a middle-aged farmer dressed in his best *guayabera* shirt. That photo was taken just before Dad left Revuelta; more than twenty-five years ago. Anything could happen in twenty-five years, especially to a dude who works outdoors, day after day, from dawn to dusk. All I knew was what my Dad told me and what I knew about Revuelta – that it was a small, sleepy town in the heart of Cuba.

The summer sun shone brightly the next morning when the bus finally arrived in Revuelta's town square, a typical central Cuban small town square surrounded by shops and an old Spanish church that even then was only frequented by old women and small children. As I stepped off the bus with my suitcase in hand, the local townspeople gathered around the bus, to greet family members back home from Havana and to receive packages and parcels sent over from the big city. Standing out in the crowd was Uncle Carlos Suarez.

"Welcome to Revuelta!" Carlos said, in a booming bass that would soon become familiar. You could not hide Carlos Suarez, not even in a crowd. He was six feet tall, a half a foot taller than I and unusually tall for a Cuban. His wrinkled, sun-worn face, framed by thinning white hair and a thin white mustache, was ruggedly attractive, with a firm nose and sharp, black eyes that shone with great intensity.

Carlos wore a white, short-sleeve *guayabera* over a pair of trousers and work shoes. On his head, a straw sombrero protected him from the hot summer sun. He was clearly a man to reckon with, but his bright smile soon put me at ease.

"You must be Paco Perez. Your Dad told me you were coming," he said, as we shook hands. "He sent me a photo of you, so I'd know what you look like. You are just what I expected of you."

"Thank you, *Señor* Suarez. I am happy to be here," not sure that I was.

"Please call me Uncle Carlos or, better yet, plain old Carlos. That is what your dad and everyone else around here calls me. And, you are just in time. My boy Luis is leaving this afternoon, and there's a lot of work to do, more than I can do on my own."

"I will do what I can, though I've never worked on a farm."

"You are going to be just fine. But first, we have to get you out of your clothes."

"Excuse me?"

"And put you into some work clothes. Save those fancy duds for your trip back to Havana. By the way, can you drive a truck?" he added, pointing at an old truck that was parked on a side street.

"I think so."

"I'm glad to hear that. The first thing you will do is drive over to the farm, change your clothes, and go back to town to buy some supplies. I would do that now, but I have to rush back to the farm to see Luis before he leaves. Can you do that?"

"Sure."

"Good. You just take it easy tonight, and tomorrow you'll get to work."

"What will I be doing?"

"Help me out on the farm, harvest the crops and raise the animals and get the place ready for the hurricane season. It is hard work, but you'll get in shape and learn a thing or two about farm life. As you see, I am doing pretty good for a guy my age," he smiled, flexing a well-defined muscle. "I can't afford to pay you, but I will feed you and clothe you and give you a bed to sleep every night. I will even teach you how to play the guitar, if you want to learn."

"What do folks do around here?"

"Not much. Sometimes, some of the boys and I get together in town to drink rum and Coke and play music, and you are welcome to join us. Sometimes a band or singer will drop by, and then we have a dance that goes on til dawn. Beny More was here last year," he added, referring to Cuba's greatest singer. "There is also a church in the town square where you can hear mass on Sundays if you want to do so. But I never go. In fact, I haven't been to church since Aunt Juana died," he said, referring to his long-gone wife.

We climbed into the truck. "Things don't change much around here," Carlos said, as he drove us out of Revuelta. Though the truck had a few years on it, it drove at a brisk speed, stopping only to allow a procession of Cuban crabs to cross the road. Soon the town gave way to the suburbs, which in turn gave way to the countryside. It was all so quiet and peaceful, in comparison to Havana's hustle and bustle. Carlos Suarez's farm was five kilometers outside of the town of Revuelta. Though it could not compete with the opulent plantations of Cuba's sugar and tobacco barons, it was large enough to make him the main landowner in the township of Revuelta. A young and handsome mulatto, a couple of years older than I, was waiting for us when we arrived.

"Paco, this is Luis," Carlos said to me, as Luis and I shook hands. "Luis is twenty years old, and he's been working for me since he turned eighteen. He is now leaving us to join the Army. It is a strange time to join the Army, with revolution in the air."

"You always worry about me, Uncle Carlos," Luis laughed. "But I will be just fine." This was the changing of the guard; Luis was leaving just as I was arriving. The only thing that stayed the same was

Carlos Suarez, his truck and his farm. But Luis meant a lot to Carlos, and for a moment, I thought Carlos was going to lose his composure. But this was a fleeting mood, and soon Carlos was to the business at hand.

"This is no time for small talk," Carlos said. "Just give me a few minutes, and we will settle some matters before you leave," he told Luis. "And as for you," he added, referring to me, "we need to go over to the house and change your clothes." As Luis and I said our goodbyes, Carlos led me into his modest house, a small country homestead. "I need to get out of this *guayabera* myself, before it gets all sweaty." As the two of us removed our shirts, I could not help but admire Uncle's muscular torso, the fruit of a lifetime of hard work. Thick white hair covered his masculine chest and shoulders. One of his powerful arms was scarred, the product of an early farm accident.

"I was charged by an angry bull," Carlos said, as if he read my mind. "But I got off better than the bull," he laughed, as he flexed his muscles. "This comes from fifty years of hard labor. But you are in good shape, too, for a big city boy."

"I play a lot of baseball," I said, referring to Cuba's national sport.

"I play baseball, too, when I'm not working. You will be playing for the local team in no time! But enough of that. Here is a list of items for you to buy in town and plenty of pesos to pay for them. And if anyone asks who you are, you tell them that you are Carlos Suarez's new boy. Luis and I will be finished by the time you get back."

As Carlos and Luis conferred outside the house, I took my suitcase and went into my room. There were two bedrooms in Carlos's home: a master bedroom where Carlos slept and a smaller bedroom that was used by Luis but which would now be mine. Not being one to waste time, I dropped my suitcase on the bed and hurried out to the truck to make my errands before the sun set.

A shopping spree in Revuelta was nothing to write about. The town merchants seemed eager to do business with me, having heard about Carlos Suarez's new *muchacho*. Though Carlos expected me to be away for a couple of hours, it only took me seventy minutes to buy all the items on the list and drive them back to the farm. The farm was quiet when I arrived, with not a soul in sight. Leaving the purchases in the truck, I walked around the farm, calling out for Carlos or Luis as I walked around. Suddenly, I heard a low moaning noise coming from a nearby shed. As I looked inside the shed, I saw Luis, naked from the waist down, crouched on all fours as Carlos repeatedly thrust his hard cock deep inside Luis's firm round ass. Having grown up in Havana, I associated men-loving-men with effeminate artists or tourists. I never expected to see two small-town machos to be doing the deed. I ran back into the house, but not before Carlos, looking up, saw me run away. Back in the house, I sat on my bed, wondering what to do next, when Carlos walked in.

"Luis just left. He's spending the night with his family before leaving for the Army barracks tomorrow morning," Carlos said, as he sat down on a chair next to the bed. "I did not expect you to be back so soon. I wanted to have some time alone with Luis, to say our goodbyes before he left."

"That is quite a goodbye you gave him! What would my Dad say if he knew that the great Carlos Suarez was queer?"

Carlos looked as if he was going to punch me. "I am not queer! Queers are effeminate artists and tourists. I am as much of a macho as any man who's ever lived here in Revuelta! I ought to give you a good whipping for even thinking such a thing!"

"But, Luis?"

"Luis can beat the crap out of you, and he probably would, if he was here right now. He is a great worker and a great fighter, and he will be a great soldier. He will not be the first one to take it up the ass," he said. "But, most importantly, he knows how to treat his elders with respect, which is more than I can say about you." he added, as he picked up and lit a nearby cigar. "Now apologize."

"What if I don't?"

"Then I will whip your ass and send you back to Havana! And don't even think about telling your dad that you saw me fuck ass. I will just tell him that you are a liar and a thief, who makes up crap about me to hide the fact that I fired your butt. And don't try to fight me. I'm bigger than you are and stronger."

He was right. "I am sorry, Carlos, I did not mean to call you names. But I never expected to see a man like you doing what I saw you doing, fucking another dude's ass."

"Apology accepted," Carlos said, as he puffed on his cigar. "I should have told you as soon as you came in. Things are not the same here as they are in Havana. There you have men and you have queers. Here in Revuelta we only have men; men who fuck women most of the time but who sometimes fuck men. That does not make us less of a man. And you have to admit that Luis has a gorgeous ass," he smiled.

"He sure does." Young mulattos have the most tempting butts on the planet and are often the stars of Havana's male bordellos. Carlos was surely not the first man who has enjoyed Luis's firm round *culo*. "Was he your first?"

Carlos shook his head: "When my beloved wife Juana died, I was still a young man. As much as I tried, I could not love another woman the way that I loved her. Then one day Lazaro came to work for me. He was eighteen years old, black and beautiful, with an ass that would make Luis's butt seem plain by comparison. I fell in love with him, the feeling became mutual, and before long we were lovers. Our love lasted for over a year, until the day came when Lazaro left me to join the Merchant Marines. I was heartbroken."

"From that time on there was a pattern in my life. I would hire one young man after another to work on the farm, hoping to find a new Lazaro. At the beginning, it was just a work relationship, and it often remained that way. But sometimes our relationships became sexual; and they remained so as long as we stayed together. Most of those young men went on to have wives, children and careers, though I am happy to say that they often think back fondly at the time that we spent together."

"My dad worked for you. Was he one of your lovers?"

"God, no! Taking it up the ass was the last thing your dad could ever think of, even back then. He'd certainly would not be sending his son down here if he thought his beloved Uncle Carlos was going to fuck him in the butt."

"What did the boys' families think?"

"They never knew, as far as I could tell. And in case you wonder, it was never a case of a lecherous old man forcing himself upon an innocent boy. All of the boys who worked for me, even your dad, were over eighteen and knew a thing or two about sex with other boys, girls or even farm animals. And while some of the boys were so beautiful that I wanted to jump on them the moment that I met them, I always let then make the first move, and they often did."

"I guess things are different around here. And, I have a lot to learn. Can we start over?"

"Of course we can," Carlos said, as we shook hands. "But now we have a lot of work to do. Are you ready for some hard work?"

"I am ready."

"Good. Let's get going!" And so we did. For the next several days, Uncle Carlos and I worked from dawn to dusk, feeding the livestock, raising the crops, and getting the farm ready for the hurricanes. It was hard work, but it was also productive work. And, every day I learned more about farm work and about life in general. Working for Carlos Suarez was like taking a master course in the school of life, taught by an experienced professor. And every day that I worked for Carlos, I felt a closer bond to this older man, whose strength and wisdom and energy made me forget that he was sixty years old. Working without our shirts in the hot sun, we were drawn to each other's muscular, masculine bodies, and it was only a matter of time before the inevitable happened.

"Let's take a shower, Paco," Carlos said, after a hard day's work. "We need to wash off the dirt and the sweat." We ran to the house, throwing off our clothes on the floor as we dove under the showers. Now completely nude, we playfully rubbed soap on each other's bodies, washing away the grime. Though this was not the first time that Carlos and I stood naked together, it was the first time that I allowed myself to check out his muscular body in its entirety, especially his dark, thick, uncut cock and his low-hanging balls. Our dicks got fully erect as we moved closer to each other, craving each other. We were two men hot for each other; and the fact that one of us was eighteen and the other one was sixty made no difference. Without a word, we took hold of each other's hard cocks, pushing back each other's dark foreskins as we playfully stroked each other.

"You like my cock, don't you Paco?" Carlos said, as he kissed me passionately. In spite of his age, Uncle Carlos was very virile, and his cock stayed as hard as mine. This was my first time with a man; and I wanted it to last. As the shower continued to pour water upon us, Carlos and I continued to explore each other's bodies.

"Suck my dick, Paco," Carlos begged, as he pushed me down on my knees. "I know you want to. *Mamame la pinga!*" Though I never sucked a cock before, I knew what I wanted and how to get it. Now on my knees, I licked Carlos's hard cock-head with my tongue. I then took his massive *pinga* inside my mouth, taking the full eight inches down throat. Carlos sighed with pleasure as I sucked on his peter, giving oral pleasure to this powerful, sensitive macho. After I worked on Carlos's cock for a while, I began to suck on his balls, taking each low-hanging ball in my mouth and driving my lover wild with desire.

"Stop, Paco, you are getting me close," Carlos said, as he pulled me up to my feet, greeting me with a kiss. As Uncle and I kissed, his calloused hands took hold of my firm round buns. "You have a beautiful ass, Paco! Please give me your ass! I want to fuck you and make you feel good! You'll like it, I promise you!" As he spoke, Carlos's strong hands pulled my buns apart, allowing him to slip a finger inside my virgin asshole. As Carlos's finger probed inside me, I instinctively spread my legs apart, allowing him to slip another finger inside my rectum. Now deep inside me, my lover's fingers began to massage my tender prostate, giving me a unique pleasure that I've never experienced before. For the first time in my life, a man entered my ass, and I enjoyed every minute of it.

"You like it?"

"Yes, Papi, I do. But I want more than your fingers inside me. I want you to fuck me, the way you fucked Luis and all those other boys." While his fingers continued to possess my tender hole, Carlos turned off the showers and led me into his bedroom. As we both fell upon the bed, Carlos took his fingers out of my bum, replacing them with his now-lubricated cock. With my back to the bed and my legs in the air, I grew tense as my ass got ready to receive the object of my desire.

"Relax, Paco, it's going to be all right," Carlos said, as he thrust his prick inside my virgin *culo*. I shuddered with pain as Carlos's *pinga* went inside me, pain that soon became pleasure as Carlos fucked me with all his might. I moaned with pleasure as Carlos continued his savage fuck, holding me tight as he took my ass, again and again.

"You are a beautiful boy, Paco," Carlos moaned, as he continued to fill my asshole with his potent *pinga* while holding me with his powerful arms. "And soon you'll be a beautiful, masculine man." All of my life, I was never close to my dad or to any other man. And here was this sixty-year-old macho, as strong as he was sensitive, loving me the way that no other man has ever done, or ever will again. We were two sex-hungry men, transcending the boundaries of age to enjoy that most primal act, male fucking male. Thanks to Uncle Carlos, I learned that a man could be strong and macho and still enjoy the pleasure of another strong macho's cock up his ass. As Carlos reached the point of no return, he took hold of my hard cock, stroking it and giving me some of the same pleasure that he himself was getting.

"I am coming, lover!" Carlos shouted, as he shot his cum deep inside my asshole. "Take my cum!" As Carlos came and came, he grabbed my cock with his calloused hand, bringing me to an orgasm as powerful as his own. I screamed with pleasure as my cum flew all over my lover's hairy chest, just as he fell on top of me. Completely spent, the two of us held on to each other, sealing our union with a kiss.

"Welcome home, Paco," Carlos said, as we shared a post-orgasm kiss.

The summer of 1958 was the high point of my life. I was Carlos Suarez's worker by day and his lover by night. Alas, summer ended much too soon; and the time came when I had to return to Havana. Soon after that, the Revolution came, and Carlos Suarez was one of its first victims, dying of a bullet wound as he tried to defend his small farm from revolutionaries. And while I have had many lovers since then, none of them would ever take the place of my Uncle Carlos – the wise, wonderful, powerful, strong, mature man who taught me about love and sex and farming and so much more. I will never forget him.

THE GUY DOWN THE HALL
By Milton Stern

I really dreaded moving out to a complex in the burbs, but after my upstairs neighbor shot her husband and missed sending a bullet through her floor and into my apartment, my friends convinced me it was time.

So, here I was in one of those secure buildings with 500 neighbors. That is 500 people who walk by you without smiling, who look at you strangely when you say hello, and who turn up their noses when they see your dog, even though it is a pet-friendly building. I always lived in bad neighborhoods, where people say hello because if you don't know your neighbors, you won't know whether someone is a gang member, mugger or a rapist. It is not that I was too poor to move; I was just too comfortable, paying a low rent and making excuses.

After a few weeks, I made up my mind that no one was going to say hello and that was just how it is with this "station of society" as Hyacinth Bucket would say on *Keeping Up Appearances*. I came back from walking my dog, who was in her twilight years, when the fire alarm went off. I never lived in a building with an alarm, so I scooped up my dog (she had gone deaf and partially blind by then, so in order to evacuate, it was better that I carry her), and we made our way to the stairs. I had moved to the top floor for obvious reasons (bullets tend to go down rather than up). Outside it was raining, and all I was wearing at the time was an undershirt and shorts. After fifteen minutes, we were given the all clear and made our way upstairs. The whole way, no one said a word. They didn't even comment about my dog and why I was carrying her.

Once on our floor, I put Lucille down, and we walked back to my apartment. As we reached my door, my neighbor from around the corner came around and said, "Hey, I see we had another false alarm."

I was surprised for two reasons. One, he said something to me, and two, he was wearing a sleeveless shirt and boxers. What a sight. He was a little over six feet, maybe a drop over two hundred pounds, with dark hair and eyes and the most fit build I had ever seen, or could see from what was exposed. He was also half my age at around twenty-five.

I had picked up Lucille at that point to keep her from running into him, being partially blind and all, and that made my bicep bulge. I should let you know that I am over six feet myself and close to two-hundred-sixty pounds and a professional trainer and competitive bodybuilder. Approaching fifty, when not in competition, I carry an extra inch or two around the waist, and that is all I will admit.

"False alarm?"

"Yeah, the burger joint downstairs tends to set off alarms all the time. My name's Matt, by the way."

"Nice to meet you," I said as I extended my right hand and shook his. I also put Lucille back down on the floor. "This is Lucille; she's pretty old, deaf and partially blind; that's why I picked her up, so she wouldn't bang into you." And then I shut up, realizing I was giving more information than was necessary and probably because this was the first conversation I had with anyone since I moved in.

"And, your name?" he asked.

"Oh, yeah. I'm Martin."

At that point he started staring at my arms, and my shirt was still wet from the rain, so his eyes glanced over my pecs as well. "Hey, my fiancé and I are throwing a little party tomorrow night around seven. Come on over. We're in five-eighteen."

"Sounds good," I answered and watched as he turned and went back to his apartment. I also hoped he never wore more than a T-shirt and boxers in the future.

As it turned out, I answered too quickly, since I already had plans the next night with a couple of friends to have dinner. So, the next afternoon, I bought a bottle of wine and knocked on five-eighteen.

Matt answered the door, dressed similarly to the night before.

"Hey, Martin, what's up?"

I handed him the wine and said, "I answered too quickly. I have plans tonight, and I didn't want to blow you guys off and just not show up. Here, this is a thank you for the invitation."

"You didn't have to do that," he said in protest.

"I insist. My mother raised me right," I answered. "Can I ask you a question?"

"Sure."

"Do you own pants?" I asked with a grin.

He laughed, and I heard a woman's voice in the background, "I'm so glad you said that." She appeared from another room, and was she gorgeous and a little thing about half his size. "I'm Gina. Thank you for the wine. I'm sorry you can't make it. He promised to wear pants tonight."

We laughed, and I said my goodbyes.

It was a few weeks before I saw him again. I go to the gym very early and am usually out the door around a quarter to five in the morning. I ran into him one morning as he was headed to his gym, and we exchanged pleasantries, and this became an occasional occurrence. Although beautiful to behold, I made up my mind after meeting his fiancé that he was off limits, and I was never into "flipping" guys anyway. I am too old to go around blowing straight guys, besides I never saw the thrill in that. I never said it out loud, but anyone can figure out I am a big fag from the rainbow Mezuzah on my door frame to the rainbow Star of David tattoo on my shoulder to the parade of flaming queens, who are my friends, who would drop by for dinner.

Besides a fifty-year-old personal trainer/competitive bodybuilder is a dead giveaway.

One morning as I headed out my door to the gym, I saw a shirtless body walk by and noticed it was Matt. He was wearing very short, gray running shorts that were not unlike the ones President Clinton would wear early in his administration. I yelled at his back, "It is freezing outside. I just came back from walking Lucille."

He stopped and turned around, and I saw his bare torso for the first time. He didn't shave and had the perfect amount of dark hair and that theory about him having the most fit body I ever saw was confirmed. I immediately thought that if this guy has a big dick there is no God.

"They say it's seventy outside." He smiled that beautiful smile as I said this.

I walked up to him and got a better look and thanked myself for putting on a tight jock that morning. (I said I was not into flipping straight guys, but that didn't mean he couldn't turn me on.)

We walked over to the elevator and stepped in.

He hit the L and asked if I had an early client.

"No, just working out this morning," I answered.

"Cool, we should work out together sometime," he said.

And then, my odd sense of humor took over when I asked, "Can I pull one of your nipples?"

He looked right at me, smiled and said, "I wish you would."

And, I did. And he leaned in and planted his mouth on mine while simultaneously hitting the red button, stopping the elevator between floors. His tongue was down my throat before I could protest, and I decided not to protest and felt up that perfect body.

I finally came up for air and with a gasp asked, "What about your fiancé?"

"We're both bi," he said and proceeded to remove my shirt and pull down my shorts.

In the time it took for me to fully comprehend what he said, my jock was around my ankles, and my dick was in his mouth. He had pulled his shorts down and was stroking his cock while working mine, and I figured we didn't have a lot of time, and he figured we didn't have a lot of time, and he sucked me for points, and knew I would blow any minute, and I tried to get him off my dick, so I could get at his, but he was insistent, and I just shot my load, and he swallowed every drop while jerking his and shooting between my legs and hitting the wall of the elevator. It all happened so fast, that I was still comprehending what happened when he stood up, pulled up his shorts, and I retrieved my shirt, jock and shorts, and he hit the button, and we stepped out of the elevator.

"Have a good run," I said as he took off.

A few weeks later, his fiancé went to visit her parents, and he came over, and we did it again. This time, however, we took our time. He has since married Gina, and their wedding was beautiful. And on occasion, he stops by for a little pre-run workout.

THE WINDOW ESTIMATE
By Milton Stern

I hate being an apartment manager, and I only agreed to do it because my landlords promised me a fifty percent reduction in the rent for the four years they would be in Brazil. The worst part is that I have to listen to the constant complaining from the fat redneck, her drunk asshole of a husband and her future serial killer, slut daughter upstairs. I just wish the daughter would get it over with and kill them already, so I can clean up the mess and rent the place out to a couple of hotties. But, until then, I have to be the responsible one and that includes getting estimates for work that I would rather let go in the hopes the cast from Cops upstairs will leave in frustration.

Most of the time, these estimates are for things they have broken, and I know that the constant yelling and banging that goes on is the reason the frame of the large bay window in their master bedroom was cracked causing the glass to fall down into the wall, leaving a four-inch gap on the top.

I took my sweet time getting an estimate, but when the rain seeped in causing water to leak into my apartment, it became my personal problem, so I called a couple of window companies. I figured I would punish the landlords as well for sticking me with these assholes and get an estimate for all the windows.

Two salesmen had been here already, but they were so slick, I threw away their estimates before the door closed behind them.

On the day the third and final guy was to arrive, I pretty much didn't care anymore. I decided to work from home that day, so it was amazing I even bothered to shower, although I only wore a pair of gym shorts (actually cut-off sweat pants) and a wife-beater. I was totally engrossed in work when I heard a knock at the door.

I opened the door and standing there was what looked to be a teenager, wearing a loose fitting All-Weather Window Company polo shirt. He gave me the taillights to headlights three-second once over I tend to get from guys who see me for the first time, which doesn't even faze me anymore.

You see, I am an ex-professional football player (not that anyone remembers – third string center), and I am six-foot even, weighing in at around two-hundred-sixty pounds. At thirty-five, I still work out as if I am being paid to, and I won't deny I ever took a needle in the ass. We'll leave it at that. Now, I work as a bookkeeper for a nondescript company in a nondescript cubicle located in a nondescript building. I am one of the lucky few to have actually gotten paid to be a professional football player, but after almost five years on the bench, I got bored. I was told I was too nice, not aggressive enough, but the coach liked me, so I held onto my job.

Now, the kid in front of me may have played some sports. He had that college jock, too many frat parties body. You know the type – broad shoulders, decent arms, and remnants of the 'freshman forty' still around the middle. If they are straight, the paunch is there for life, and if they are gay, well, they wouldn't have taken on the freshman-forty in the first place. No gay boy in his twenties would allow such a thing to happen to him. This kid was definitely straight, which was fine with me as I don't like them young. I like them older, much older. I like being fucked silly by a big musclebear with gray hair. If this kid had a twelve-inch dick, I couldn't have cared less.

"Mr. Kennedy?"

I let him in, and he introduced himself as Allan. I showed him all the windows upstairs and downstairs in all the apartments. Of course, the redneck had to butt in and say what she wanted in a window, but I shut her up immediately and continued to follow Allan from wall to wall while he measured and wrote on his legal pad.

When we were done, we returned to my apartment, and I had to ask him his age.

"I'm twenty-three. I couldn't find a job in my field, so I took this sales job, which has made my college education a waste … can I ask you a question, a personal question?"

I said sure.

"I can see you work out …"

He could see I work out. He was brilliant. My arms relaxed are eighteen inches around. My pecs are so huge, I can't see my feet, and he can see I work out.

"I've been trying to lose this gut since I graduated, and nothing I do works. Should I do more cardio?"

"You should quit drinking so much beer," I said and raised my eyebrows. I may let a quack doc shoot what is probably horse piss into my ass to get huge and ripped, but I never drank or did drugs. Yeah, I know, what I do is just as bad. Whatever. You'd fuck me if you had a chance, especially if you saw my rock hard and huge bubble-butt.

"Yeah, I guess you're right."

"So, how long before I get an estimate?" I asked.

"Oh, I can have one for you this afternoon. I'll email it to you."

And with that, he was gone.

I went back to work and took a mid-day break to go to the gym because I have body dysmorphia or manorexia or some other psychological shit because I think I'm fat or skinny and have deep emotional issues. Please. I know what I look like. I look like a fucking freak, but I like the freak look, and the old musclebear dads I let fuck me like it, too. Don't assume you know guys like me.

After I returned from the gym, I was mixing myself a protein shake when there was a knock at the door. I was back in my cut-off sweat shorts but not wearing a shirt anymore. I opened the door, and it was frat-boy window guy.

"I decided to hand deliver the estimate," he said as he handed me the envelope. "I can explain it to you if you like?"

I gave him my best you think I am a dunder-headed muscleboy with the IQ of a baboon look.

"Oh, I didn't mean it like that ... uh, I mean I like to explain why we may be higher than most anyone else," Allan recovered.

"I may look mean, but it takes a whole hell of a lot to offend me or piss me off ... believe me, kid, I haven't lost my temper in years," I said with a smile as I motioned him inside.

What, you say? A juiced-up freak who hasn't had a roid induced hissy fit? See, you read too much. I have never been a hot head. That is why I sucked as a professional football player. I'm too easy going. The only side effect I ever got from the juice was shrunken balls, but I can still come a gallon of spunk.

I offered Allan a protein shake, and he accepted. As we sat there drinking our whey concoctions, he explained all the window crap, and I pretended to listen, but I couldn't get over how he was avoiding looking at me. I was shirtless, pumped from the gym and sitting no more than two feet away from him. Although I had showered at the gym, I hadn't bothered putting on deodorant, so I had a light musk about me, which some guys like.

When he finally looked up, I could tell he was enthralled by my pumped pecs and my nipples, which I pulled on constantly. They stick out a good inch even now.

"You want to touch them?" I asked.

His eyes bulged.

"Look, it won't make you gay. Straight guys always want to touch my muscles to see what they feel like. Are they hard, soft, will they vibrate?" I said with a chuckle and a smile.

"Sure," he said as he slowly reached over to kind of poke a finger at my bicep.

I flexed it for him, and he then caressed it a bit before taking his hand away. So, I was wrong about him. He was a big ole fag. I grabbed his hand and put it on my pec while I made it bounce.

"Damn, they are hard as a rock," he said.

I was not turned on by this. He just wasn't my type. Yeah, I know, get over it.

"Now, about this estimate. What can we do to get you to come down by at least ten percent?" I may have been pissed at the landlords, but I was still a tightwad at heart, and I wasn't going for the obvious scene you are expecting here.

"Become my personal trainer," he said.

I sat back and looked at him. He had potential and a good frame. And that gut he complained about wasn't really that bad, just a little soft.

"Take off your shirt," I said.

He stood up and without hesitation removed his shirt. His shoulders were broad, and his biceps a nice size, too. However, his chest was a surprise as it was huge, which made me make a mental note to suggest he wear a tighter company shirt, and it was covered with hair, curly blond hair that trailed down to his pants.

"You'll have to shave that," I said pointing to his chest.

"Really?" he said as he ran his hand seductively down his torso.

"But not until after you bend me over this table and fuck my brains out. The condoms and lube are in the drawer behind you. If you want me to train you, you better be ready to do what I say at the drop of a hat," I said without stopping to take a breath. Then I stood, dropped my cut-off sweat shorts revealing my hard five-inch dick. Yeah, I know, everyone in these stories is hung like a horse. Well, I'm a bottom, and I may not have a lot of dick to play with, but I certainly have enough muscle to make up for it. Besides, little dicks get hard, stay hard, and shoot nice creamy loads. So, get over it.

I also know that I said he wasn't my type. But, I wanted that estimate lowered, and my hole filled at the same time. He was there; I was horny; do the math.

I then bent over the table, while he fumbled around with his pants.

"Hurry up, I don't get this horny often, just grease it up and plug me," I said over my shoulder.

I then felt the cold lube dribbling down my crack. He sort of rubbed it all around, and I could tell he was nervous. I then heard the condom wrapper being opened; he cursed himself while he tried to roll it on. I clearly had him flustered.

"Are these the largest ones you have?" he asked.

I turned around and saw what looked to be a good ten thick inches of circumcised dick sticking straight out at me. There you go – a horse-hung top in a porno story. Are you happy now?

"Look in the back of the drawer. They must have slid back. There should be some extra-hungs or whatever they call them," I said as I marveled at his heat-seeking moisture missile, which is a friend's nickname for huge cocks.

"Found them," he said with delight.

"Good, slip one on and fuck my brains out," I said as I again bent over the table. "And, don't bother eating me out or fingering me, just stick that barbell up my chute … I hate foreplay."

He did just that. All the way in, no apologies, no hesitation, no finesse, no bullshit, and I loved it.

"Now, reach around and pull my nipples as hard as you can while you fuck me."

And, he did just that. He reached around and pulled my big nipples, no apologies, no hesitation, no finesse, no bullshit, and I loved it.

He practically pounded my huge muscular ass over the moon (excuse the pun) and pulled my nipples another inch. I was in heaven. He was having a pretty good time, too. Or, he was good at faking it because he kept telling me what a hot ass I had and what a sexy motherfucker I was. And at one point, he started nibbling on the back of my neck, and that did it.

I cried out as I came. I wasn't even touching myself since I was using my hands to hold onto the edge of the table while he pounded me for points. And, right after I came, he filled that extra large rubber with his own load and yelled out loud what a "man slut" I was, and amazingly, I came again – hands free.

When he recovered, he apologized for calling me a man slut and gave me ten percent off on the windows in addition to another ten percent for the hot fuck.

I never told him, but calling me a man slut was the best part of the fuck.

The windows look great. And Allan? He is a muscle freak now, too.

I love being me.

FOOTBALL DADDIES
By Milton Stern

Dan and Bobby had played football together for close to thirty years, from peewee, through high school and finally on the same pro team and always on the offensive line. When Dan decided before he turned forty-two that it was time to retire, Bobby came to the same conclusion within minutes. He couldn't imagine playing the game without his best friend around, especially since they had been lovers for the past fifteen years. But, they didn't know what to do in retirement? A lot of football players went into the restaurant business or lent their names to other service industry venues, but Dan and Bobby had no interest in that. Their decision became easier when they heard of a gym that was up for sale in their hometown because the owner had died and his kids had no intention of running it.

They flew down to Elkhart, North Carolina, a small town most maps ignore, and made an offer on the old place. The heirs were more than happy to unload the business and accepted their price without hesitation. Dan and Bobby paid cash and found themselves in the gym business.

Once they found a place to rent until they decided where to live permanently, they began the work of renovating what would become the D&B Fitness Factory. This was one of those old-time gyms with benches, free weights, no machines to speak of, and only a couple of stationary bikes serving as cardio equipment. There were mirrors on all the walls and an open shower room that could accommodate eight people at a time.

The work began with getting rid of all the old equipment, so they donated it to an organization that sends fitness gear to developing countries. They ordered all new benches, rubber coated plates, a few basic machines and a couple of treadmills and arc trainers. Their goal was to keep the gym as 'old-school' as possible. They figured if they tried to go fancy, they would not be able to compete with the 'pretty boy' club in the next town.

Elkhart may have been a small town, but football was huge there. Dan and Bobby weren't the only former residents to go pro. Many of their former teammates bought property near the coast, which was only a thirty minute drive from where they were, and once they opened for business, the D&B Fitness Factory filled up every day with quite a few muscle daddies.

Dan and Bobby were all too happy to offer a gym their fellow gray hairs could enjoy. Dan stood over six feet and weighed over 250 pounds of solid muscle with a fifty-inch chest, nineteen-inch arms and maintaining a thirty-six-inch waist, all covered in salt and pepper fur from his head to his feet. Bobby was smooth, but no less impressive with a shaved head to match. He stood barely five-ten, weighed almost 225 pounds, but had just as much muscle as Dan with an even broader chest and bigger biceps, but he carried a few inches around his belly. He had one of those tight bellies that many a boy finds sexy. Dan loved Bobby's belly and would come on it every chance he could get. They were both also hung very nicely and circumcised with big round balls, making for a beautiful sight in the bedroom.

The gym was doing very well as they had tapped into a market that the mega-gyms were ignoring. It also helped that they did not require that their members wear shirts, only proper footwear and shorts as long as they cleaned off the equipment after each use. Dan and Bobby did this mostly for their own entertainment since they both enjoyed watching big men get all sweaty and pumped. Even with the lenient rules, the place was kept immaculate, especially the shower room, which was no small feat considering some of the action rumored to be occurring in there especially before the 10:00 pm closing time.

Dan and Bobby had not engaged in any of the antics but had witnessed a few while they were working. They had hired a college senior, who was getting a degree as a physical therapist, to work the evening hours, so they could have a life outside the business, and he was a very hard worker. Miles was also an offensive lineman in high school, who decided not to play college ball for reasons he never explained, so Bobby and Dan took a special liking to him. At twenty-two years old, Miles was already as big as many of the pros, standing at over six-foot-four and over 260 pounds with a solid frame holding a fifty-two-inch chest and twenty-inch arms. He was not only big and muscular, but he was devastatingly handsome as well with dark features, curly black hair and covered in just a touch of curly black fur. When he smiled, men and women melted regardless of their sexual inclinations.

Dan joked that he didn't care how competent he was; Miles had the job the second he applied. What made him even more appealing was his lack of attitude or ego. Miles was a damn hard worker and kept the gym spotless and in order. He never engaged in 'activities,' nor did he do anything inappropriate. He was quiet and respectful with a pleasant demeanor. He only made one request. Miles wanted to be able to work out after the gym closed for the evening since this would not interfere with his studies. Dan and Bobby suspected Miles was a bit of a loner, for he never received personal calls, was seen texting or had any buddies come by the gym to visit. They wanted to invite him over for dinner, but somehow never got around to it. What they did learn was that his parents died when he was very young and that he was raised by his grandmother, who recently died. He had no other family and lived in the apartment where he was raised.

Dan and Bobby would usually work out mid-day when the gym was the least busy, but this became a hassle as the business of running a business takes more time than people realize, so they decided to try working out at 4:00 am before they opened. This lasted only a couple of days because getting up at 3:00 am was nearly impossible, too. That was when Dan suggested they follow Miles's lead and work out after hours. This would work since they hired Bobby's nephew to open for them during the week, and they could come in around 7:00 am. Bobby's nephew was competent but not worth the trouble of describing since he spent most of his time at work surfing the net and texting his girlfriend. He was just there to occupy space until Dan and Bobby came in. Miles left the place in such order that there was nothing to do in the mornings, and Bobby told Miles that he knew his nephew was useless, but he needed him for those two hours, so he and Dan could get some rest. Miles never complained. And, Dan and Bobby would keep the place in order while they worked and tended to the business as well.

Around 10:30 pm, Dan and Bobby showed up on the first night they decided to try their new workout schedule. The gym was closed, and the blinds were drawn indicating it was closed, but they could see Miles's shadow as he worked out inside. They told Miles they would be coming in to work out, so that he wouldn't be startled when the door opened.

Dan and Bobby walked in just as Miles lay down on a bench to perform dumbbell presses with 110-pound weights. They both stopped in their tracks at the sight before them. Wearing nothing but a pair of black 2xist briefs that did little to hide his candy and a pair of New Balance cross trainers, he was pushing the weights up, and his chest was glistening and pumped.

He finished his set and sat up on the bench. "Hey, when you didn't show up at closing, I decided to get comfortable. I'll go get my shorts," Miles said as he greeted them.

"Don't … ," Dan almost shouted.

" … worry about us," Bobby interrupted. "Stay comfortable."

"Are you sure?" Miles asked as he stood up, revealing his body to them for the first time.

"I didn't realize how hot it gets in here with the AC off. Why didn't you reprogram it to stay on for an hour after closing?" Bobby asked.

"I didn't think I had the authority," Miles the ever-dutiful employee responded. "Besides, I prefer it warm when I work out."

Dan and Bobby walked toward the locker room to put away their gym bags, and Miles dropped to the floor to do a set of push-ups. They each glanced at his perfect, big and muscular butt as it went up and down.

In the locker room, Dan took off his shirt as Bobby did the same. "Should we strip down as well?" Dan whispered.

"I might pop wood," Bobby said with a smile. "But, what the hell?!?"

They each stripped down, Dan to a pair of white Calvin Klein briefs, and Bobby to a pair of black trunk briefs of the same brand. They exited the locker room and joined Miles in the gym. Miles went about his chest work out as if everything was normal, and Dan and Bobby did the same while they worked legs.

Occasionally, they would smile at each other, but Miles was very serious about his workouts, as were Dan and Bobby, and after the initial excitement of being half naked with the college senior wore off, all were grunting and sweating their asses off.

Miles was attempting to do a set of incline dumbbell presses with 100-pound weights, but was struggling to lift them into position to begin his set. Dan noticed this and offered to help him.

"Thanks, maybe I should begin with these. I can never lift them up this far into my workout," Miles said as Dan walked over. Bobby followed.

"Lie back; Bobby and I'll hand them to you."

"I'll give you a spot, once you get started," Bobby added.

Miles lay back, and Dan and Bobby on either side of him lifted up the dumbbells and waited until Miles was holding them firmly. Bobby then positioned himself behind Miles to spot him. He managed five reps before he needed assistance, and Bobby helped him with two more.

Once he was done with the set, Miles thanked them, but Bobby remained crouched behind the bench. Dan looked at him, and Bobby motioned downward with his eyes, for he was sporting a hard-on that could not be hidden.

"Let us know when you are ready for another set," Dan said and winked at Bobby.

Miles lay down on the bench again, and was ready in thirty seconds. The kid really did an intense workout.

They helped him get a grip on the dumbbells again, and Bobby hoped Miles didn't see the bulge in his trunk briefs.

Miles did this set and another, and at that point, Bobby's underwear was soaked with precum. He quickly went to the locker room to fetch another pair he hoped he remembered to put in his gym bag. There was a pair, and by the time he had removed the soaked pair and wiped off his dick, he was no longer as hard, but still a little firm. He changed into a matching pair of black trunk briefs, which was a relief, for he would have to explain the change in wardrobe.

He exited the locker room and the sight he saw was about to ruin another pair of underwear. Dan was doing a set of squats, and Miles was spotting him from behind. Bobby stood there awestruck at the sight before him, and his dick was now out of control, hard as a rock and leaking like a faucet. When Dan struggled for a few more reps, Miles leaned in closely to help. Two reps later, the set was done.

Miles stepped back, and Dan stepped away from the rack, and he was now sporting a rager equal to Bobby's. He looked over at Bobby, who looked over at Miles, who looked at both of them and smiled.

"I get hard when I work out, too," Miles said. And when they looked down, they noticed his underwear was beginning to stretch quite a bit. He then dropped down and did another set of push-ups, while Dan and Bobby watched.

Dan looked at Bobby and shrugged, and Bobby shrugged back. Miles then finished his set and declared his workout was done, and he was going to take a shower. Meanwhile, the bulge in his briefs was bigger than before and the head of his dick was sticking out of the waistband. Miles walked past Bobby and into the locker room. Within seconds, the sound of a shower being turned on was heard, and Bobby turned to follow him.

"Are we done working out?" Dan asked as he followed Bobby.

Bobby never answered. He stepped out of his newly precummed briefs and into the shower room where Miles was using the middle-most showerhead. Dan followed suit. Bobby chose the shower to the right of Miles and Dan decided to occupy the one on the left. They watched as Miles soaped himself up and were mesmerized by his pumped, heavily muscled and lathered body and his enormous circumcised cock that stood out and up. Dan and Bobby's not quite as big, but big enough dicks were just as hard.

Dan soaped himself up waiting for Bobby to take the lead if anything were going to happen. And, take the lead Bobby did. He lathered up his hand, reached down, and began stroking Miles's dick, and he was met with no resistance. Dan then leaned in and kissed Bobby full on the mouth, and their tongues wrestled as Miles reached down and stroked both their cocks. Within seconds, Bobby was ready to pop, so he grabbed Miles's hand to stop the momentum, but Miles proved to be quite strong. That strength was all it took, and Bobby was shouting and shooting a load all over Miles's hand and leg.

Not even a second after that, Dan added to the spunk on Miles and shouted his pleasure as well. The hands of a physical therapist were obviously magic. Dan planted his mouth back on Miles and Bobby continued to stroke the enormous cock until it shot a load all over the shower wall – a load so impressive that Dan and Bobby almost applauded.

Once he caught his breath, Miles declared, "I've never touched a man before. I have wanted to do that with you guys since the day you hired me."

"You never touched a man?" Bobby asked with surprise.

"Where did you learn to stroke like that?" Dan asked.

"I guess from playing with myself," Miles said as he resumed soaping himself up.

Bobby stopped him, and Dan joined Bobby as they lathered up Miles, taking turns kissing him and stroking him until he shot another load – this time on the shower floor.

# # # # #

Dan and Bobby soon found a 19th Century home that suited them perfectly and settle in nicely. Miles graduated from college and landed a job at a local hospital as a physical therapist.

Does Miles still work at the gym part-time? You bet he does, and he still works out in his underwear after closing every night along with Dan and Bobby. But now, they sometimes shower at the gym or the three of them go home afterward to shower, where they live in a polyamorous relationship that has 'worked out' quite well.

Teammates for life!

THE ONE
GIVING THE ORDERS
By Milton Stern

Another scorcher on Paris Island, South Carolina, and Master Sergeant Masters was ready to call it a day. Seven weeks into boot camp with the latest flock of recruits was taking its toll on Masters, and he swore after week eleven, once they were done with him and off to infantry training, he would retire. Twenty-five years he had spent in the Marines, and he was damn proud of his service to his country. Although he never saw combat, he had trained by last count over 11,000 recruits – the majority of whom arrived as long-haired pussies and left as jar-headed fighting machines.

His once deep resonating voice had matured to a prematurely raspy quality due to years of yelling orders and berating the greens.

After marching his boys into the barracks, he handed over control to Master Sergeant Earl, completed some paperwork, hopped into his Dodge pick-up, and drove to his home in Beaufort. He had chosen to live off base a few years before when he spotted the little house while out for some R&R one weekend. There was a for sale sign on it, and once he had contacted the real estate agent and taken a tour, he knew it was the home he always wanted. Having always lived modestly, driving an almost thirty-year-old truck at the time and always living on base, he was able to pay cash for the house with a little to spare to fix it up. His favorite feature was the basement. Basements were rare in these parts being so close to the coast, but this house was over 100 years old.

Masters pulled up to the house, parked his truck around back, and hopped out. He inspected his garden, then he stretched his arms and let out a roar. Barking orders all day had taken its toll, and at forty-six, he was getting seriously tired of always being in charge. Masters looked down at the garden and noticed some weeds popping up, so he started pulling them out. The sun was baking, so he pulled off his olive-green T-shirt, revealing his hairy, muscular torso. All he had on were his fatigues and boots. At six-feet even and over 225 pounds, Masters was a solid mountain of muscle. Prominent veins, which could be seen over the matt of salt and pepper hair on his arms, popped from his forearms up across his biceps right over his deltoids. His chest was two solid mounds of pectoral muscle covered in the same salt and pepper hair, which didn't conceal his large protruding nipples – nipples one just wanted to suck and chew on for hours. And, Masters wouldn't have minded that as they were hot-wired right to his gigantic dick.

He continued pulling the weeds and was working his way across the garden, when he heard a vehicle pull up in front of his house. He then heard a door open and shut, then another.

"What have we here?" came a voice at the foot of the garden.

Masters looked up and saw two men, both wearing fatigues and boots and no shirts standing there in his backyard looking at him. He recognized both of them. The man who had spoken was Private First Class Boneman, who finished boot camp a little over a year ago. Boneman was around five-foot-ten 170 pounds with light blond hair covering his young, muscular body, a handsome face with blue eyes and a blond high-and-tight haircut. Standing next to him was his boot camp buddy, Private First Class Firestone, who was considerably shorter than Boneman, but weighed the same, displaying a thickly muscled frame. The little man had dark features, smooth skin and hauntingly black eyes. One could tell immediately he was not the brightest guy, but sexy nonetheless.

"I think it's our favorite drill instructor, Master Sergeant Masters," Firestone answered.

Masters stared at the two boys, expressionless. He didn't know why they were here, nor did he care. Once the boys were done with boot camp, he was done with them.

"So, growing pretty flowers, Sarge?" Boneman asked as he walked toward Masters with Firestone beside him.

"What do you boys want?" Masters said as he stood up.

Instantly, Boneman lunged toward him while Firestone grabbed his arms and pinned them behind his back. Boneman held a hand at Masters' throat while he grabbed the top of his fatigues with the other hand.

"We're here to have a little fun with our favorite drill instructor," Boneman said as he spit in the sergeant's face.

Masters just stared him down.

Firestone removed his military-issue belt and tied Masters' wrists behind his back, and Boneman grabbed the older man's dog tags and led him into the house. They entered through the back door into the kitchen, where Boneman opened the first door he saw, which turned out to be a broom closet. He opened a second door, which opened to a staircase leading to the basement. After feeling inside the wall for a light switch and turning it on, he continued to lead Masters by the dog tags while Firestone held onto his bound wrists and pushed him from behind as they descended the stairs into the dimly lit basement.

"Woo hoo, lookey here," Boneman said as he scanned the room.

There was a sling hanging down in the middle of the room, off to one side was a wall with permanently attached restraints, a weight bench was situated in one corner, and in the opposite corner was a claw-type bathtub. Interestingly, hanging over the bath tub were chains with wrist restraints attached at the ends. Various brushes, hoses and other odds and ends were sitting on a table next to the tub.

"Get him into the tub!" Boneman barked at Firestone, who did as he was told. Masters tried to resist, but the little muscleman was still able to steer him over and into the tub. Boneman reached up and pulled down the two chains, removed the belt that Firestone had used, while the little man held onto the sergeant's wrists. Boneman grabbed one of his wrists, brought it in front of him, and restrained it on the chain then he did the same with the other. He then pulled the chains up, so Masters' hands were above his head.

Boneman looked him in the eyes, and when he did, Masters spit in his face. Boneman wiped the spit from his face then punched

Masters in the gut, which to the young man's surprise was like a brick wall. The feel of the older man's rock- hard abs against his fist sent a shockwave to Boneman's crotch, and he punched him again. Three more punches, and his dick was drooling. Masters only grunted with each punch, being no stranger to pain.

"Get his boots and pants off!" Boneman ordered the little man.

Firestone did as he was told, and when Masters tried to resist, Boneman punched him again.

Masters was now standing in the tub only wearing his olive green boxers, which Boneman wasted no time ripping off him.

"Hey Firestone, look at that?" Boneman said as he scanned the big naked man in front of him. "What do you think, eight, nine, maybe even ten?" he continued while pointing to the older man's dick, which was flaccid but hanging a good seven thick inches nonetheless.

"Those hairy balls are as big as apples," Firestone chimed in. "Pretty impressive for a girl with a flower garden."

Boneman chuckled at the little muscleman's joke then he ran his hand down Masters' body, feeling the salt and pepper hair and then grabbing his nuts, which barely fit in his hand. Masters' dick started to grow with Boneman's handling of his sack.

"Clean him out," Boneman said to Firestone, while still holding the sergeant by the short hairs.

"With what?" Firestone asked dumbly.

Boneman reluctantly let go of the balls and grabbed the hose that was attached to the faucet. It was a chrome hose with a narrow spray attachment at the end, shaped too much like an enema.

"With this … I'll loosen the chains, so he can be on all fours in the tub," Boneman said as he handed the hose to Firestone.

Boneman loosened the chains and guided Masters down, so he was now on all fours with his big, hairy, muscular ass in the air. The sight of the sergeant's hairy hole up in the air was almost enough to make Boneman cream his fatigues, and one look at Firestone's pants confirmed that he also appreciated the view.

Boneman turned the tap on lukewarm, and Firestone inserted the hose into the sergeant's hairy hole, and the drill instructor didn't even flinch, for he didn't want them to have the pleasure of knowing how much they were humiliating him.

"Fill him up. I want him clean before I go in there," Boneman said with a smile.

"The hell you will!" Masters protested, speaking for the first time since entering the basement.

Boneman leaned down, cupped Masters' chin and said, "Did I ask you to speak? You aren't in charge here. I am. Maybe it's time you learned to take orders rather than give them. You got that, you miserable motherfucker?"

"Yes, Sir," the sergeant mumbled.

"I didn't hear you, pussy!" Boneman barked.

"Sir, Yes, Sir!" Masters bellowed as his bowels were filled with the warm water.

Firestone removed the hose, and Boneman told him to push. As the water sprayed from his aching hole, it was not as clear as Boneman would have preferred.

"Do it again, and keep doing it until it's clean enough to drink," Boneman told Firestone.

And, again, Firestone inserted the hose. After five times with the hose and evacuating on command, the water was crystal clear, and Firestone used the hose to spray the excess water down the drain.

"Now, we'll get him all cleaned up ... the same way he used to order us to clean up that stinky recruit with a scrub brush ... what was his name?" Boneman asked.

Firestone answered, "Robert Taylor."

"Yeah."

Boneman removed the enema attachment from the hose and attached a garden sprayer, while Firestone removed his own boots, pants and boxers, then put his boots back on, revealing his own hefty meat, which was secured with a leather cock ring, making his full balls swell.

"I don't want to get wet … man I got to take a piss," Fireman said, while handling his prick.

"Take a piss then, just be sure you aim for his face," Boneman said as he removed his own clothes.

Firestone then positioned himself in front of the sergeant and released a healthy stream of his urine all over Masters' face and hair, while the sergeant just closed his eyes. Boneman noticed how the older man opened his mouth slightly to taste the nasty stream and chuckled at what a pig the man was. Boneman then put his boots back on, and marveled that Firestone was still pissing, when he decided to join in and released a healthy stream from his own thick meat, which was supported with a chrome cock ring, all over Masters' face and hair. When they were done emptying their bladders and shook the last drops on the older man, Boneman turned on the hose and sprayed down the drill instructor starting with his hair and working his way back to his well worked over hole. He then handed the hose to Firestone, while he pulled the chains bringing the man to a standing position again.

When the two young men looked down, they saw that the sergeant's dick was standing at half-mast and a good ten inches in front of him.

"I knew it would get huge," Boneman said to Firestone, who whistled. "Now scrub him down."

Firestone sprayed the water into a bucket that was next to the tub, filled it with the liquid soap that was on the table, grabbed the scrub brush, and dipped it into the sudsy water. He then started with Masters' head, which was a reach for the shorter of the two men, and worked his way down Masters' entire body until he was covered in suds and clean enough for inspection. Boneman then rinsed the suds off with quite a hard setting on the sprayer, yet Masters refused to acknowledge even the slightest pain or humiliation.

"He's a tough old fart," Boneman said as he turned off the faucet.

"A hot one, too," Firestone said. But, Boneman gave him an angry look for saying anything positive about the older man.

"Let's get him over to the sling," Boneman ordered as he undid the restraints on Masters' wrists. "And if you try anything, you'll be sorry, old man," he said as he looked Masters in the eye, and again Masters spit in his face. Boneman immediately followed with another punch to his stomach. He then punched him two more times, and his own dick reacted at the feeling of the sergeant's rock-hard abs against his fist.

With the position of authority firmly established, they marched Masters over to the sling, lifted him into it, and secured his wrists and ankles, so he was on his back with his powerful legs spread. Surprisingly, the drill instructor's cock got even harder once he was restrained, and almost reached its full eleven by seven inches, when Boneman clamped two clothespins on Masters' large hot-wired nipples. Boneman grabbed the huge dick, gave it a good squeeze, and said, "Too bad you're such a bottom pussy, motherfucker."

Firestone's thick seven-inch cock was standing straight up at this point as he awaited his next order, and Boneman's eight inches were almost at full staff, too.

"Bring me that tin container over there," Boneman ordered as he pointed to the table of supplies. "And that black rubber glove, too."

Masters' eyes popped open.

Boneman looked right at him, and said, "I want to see if my fist'll fit up this big hairy hole of yours. Think you can take it, old man?"

Masters didn't answer, but gave him a look that practically said, "I'll kill you when this is all over with."

Firestone brought over the tin container and the black rubber glove and stood there watching as Boneman picked up the glove, then discarded it, and then opened up the container, scooping a handful of white grease into his right hand. He then slathered it liberally over his hand before he aimed for the sergeant's hole. He dispensed with pleasantries and decided to begin with two fingers, and the sergeant grunted for the first time, acknowledging the intrusion.

"What do you want me to do?" Firestone asked dumbly.

"How about you keep him quiet."

"How?"

"Stick that thick cock of yours in his mouth … that should shut him up," Boneman suggested.

Firestone then positioned himself at Masters' head and grabbed his face, opened the older man's mouth and stuffed his stiff rod clear down to the hilt. He then fucked the sergeant's face with long, slow strokes, enjoying the warm feeling.

"Careful he doesn't bite the head off. If he tries, just punch him in the face," Boneman told his buddy.

Boneman then inserted a third finger, and Masters' dick twitched, and his groan was muffled, but he didn't clamp down on the thick meat he was sucking. Firestone kept up his rhythm as Boneman inserted another finger, making it four total. Again, Masters groaned, and Firestone's eyes rolled up. Boneman noticed Firestone's expression and barked, "Don't come yet, dumb ass, I'm just getting started."

Boneman rolled his four fingers around, loosening up the hairy muscular hole, and slowly introduced his thumb. With that, Masters muffled a scream or was it a yell, and with Firestone's cock now resting in his mouth rather than pumping as he was trying to hold off, one couldn't tell. But, Boneman was not done. He then slowly worked his fist into the ass of his former drill instructor, and with a slow but steady motion, worked it all the way in, past his wrist and almost halfway up his forearm. Boneman's cock released a long stream of precum that dangled to the floor; Firestone's eyes lit up at the sight of his buddy's arm up Masters' asshole; and Masters' eyes rolled up as his dick started to swell then twitch rapidly.

Firestone lost it first as the sight before him and the mouth on his hot cock was too much for the horny little muscleman. His cock shot a hefty load into the sergeant's mouth that the older man eagerly swallowed without missing a drop. And, that was enough to send Masters over the edge as the fist up his ass, the clothespins on his nipples, and the sweet load in his mouth made his eleven-inch cock twitch violently until he came clear up to his neck without even touching himself.

There was a lot of panting as Firestone removed his cock from Masters' mouth, and Boneman was the only one who still had full balls.

"Damn, did I give anyone permission to come!" Boneman yelled.

"Fuck you, prick," Masters said.

With that Boneman removed his fist from the sergeant's ass, walked over to the side of the sling, and punched him repeatedly in the stomach, which wasn't easy considering Masters was still in a supine position. Again, the rock hard abs against his fist turned Boneman on, and as he felt the load work its way out of his balls and up the length of his cock, he grabbed it and aimed for Masters' face, releasing a load that was heftier than the two released by the other men.

"Now, who's the prick, motherfucker?" Boneman said as he shook the last of his spunk out of his still-raging cock and onto the older man's mouth.

Masters just looked at him and smiled. Boneman let out a little grin also, and Firestone couldn't control himself any longer, saying, "Fuck, that was hot."

"Damn, if you don't stop breaking scene, Firestone, I am gonna stick my whole foot up your ass!" Boneman said, almost seriously.

"Promise?" Firestone asked with a smile.

# # # # #

After cleaning up, the three men were sitting in Masters' living room drinking a few beers and finishing one of the three pizzas they ordered. They were all wearing nothing but their boxers, and the pizza delivery guy had given them a curious look, but seeing the muscles on the three men, decided not to say anything, just collect his money and leave.

"So, how long to retirement?" Boneman asked.

"Four weeks," Masters answered as he took a swig of his beer.

"We'll be in Afghanistan by then," Firestone said with a sorrowful look.

Masters looked at the two young men he had trained not too long ago, and he felt a heaviness in his heart at the thought of them going off to war, but he was not one to get sentimental, at least not outwardly. He also silently prayed they would be OK and be able to see him again when they returned.

"Man have I got to take a piss," Masters announced as he stood up.

Firestone looked at him, then at Boneman, and got up from the couch and walked to the bathroom. Masters followed him, and Boneman did the same. When they arrived in the bathroom, Firestone was in the tub, naked and leaning on the wall.

Without saying a word, Masters dropped his boxers, whipped out his monster meat and aimed for the little muscleman, covering him with his hot stream. Boneman, positioned himself beside the sergeant, dropped his own boxers, put his arm around Masters' waist and added to Firestone's golden shower. Boneman then looked up at the sergeant, who then looked down at him and planted his mouth on the young jarhead's, driving his tongue inside and enjoying the taste of beer and pizza while they continued spraying their buddy, who by now was stroking his cock at the sight before him and the feeling of warm piss all over him.

WHO'S THE DADDY?
By Milton Stern

Wayne left work his usual time and drove home not thinking about much of anything. Lately, he had been in a funk. He didn't know why. His career was going great. He was in a happy loving relationship with a hot man twenty years his junior, and although he was fifty-five years old, he had the body of a man in his twenties. Wayne was over six-feet tall with 200 pounds of silver-fur covered muscle and a tight bubble-butt that would be the envy and desire of any man at any age. But, even with all he had going for him, he sighed as he pulled into the driveway.

He opened the front door and looked down to see his thirty-five-year-old partner, Marty, on all fours in the living room wearing nothing but a dog collar, a leash and a leather cock ring. Wayne looked at him and gave a faint smile. Normally, he would be up for some puppy play, but he couldn't muster the energy to train his dog today.

Wayne walked past the living room into the kitchen and opened the refrigerator. Marty stood up and followed him. Marty was four inches taller and had twenty-five more pounds of muscle than Wayne, and the cock ring only added to the allure of his long, thick cock and heavy balls. He had dark features and jet black hair, and his body was smooth with just a touch of black hair in between his mountainous pecs that trailed down to his thick black pubic hair. He kept his huge balls shaved smooth, and Wayne kept Marty's crack shaved smooth as well, for he preferred it that way.

"Don't you want to play with me?" Marty asked as he licked Wayne's neck.

Wayne shrugged away. "I'm sorry, Babe, another time. I'm just not in the mood right now." He closed the refrigerator door after grabbing a beer, looked at Marty and grabbed the younger man's balls. "It's not you. It could never be you."

Marty's cock responded as it always did to Wayne's touch, but he knew that this was not the time to push his partner – or beg. Wayne released his balls and turned to look out the kitchen window while drinking his beer.

They had been together for over ten years, and each knew the other better than the back of his own hand. They knew when the other was not in the mood, and neither would push or whine just to play, probably because they played almost all the time and rarely were not in the mood. And, play they did – from puppy play to water sports, fisting, light bondage, heavy bondage, ball torture – you name it. But, no matter how they played, Wayne was always the dominant one, and Marty the submissive, and they took to their roles with relish.

Marty turned from the kitchen and went upstairs to change. A less secure partner would be hurt by the rejection, but Marty knew Wayne was in a funk. The problem was this funk seemed to last longer than usual as they had not played in over a week – an eternity for them. He went into the bedroom, took off the collar and cock ring and put on a pair of sweatpants. Wayne entered the bedroom as Marty was tying the drawstring. He walked up to him, put his hand on the back of his head and kissed him long and hard. Again, Marty's cock responded. Wayne released his lips from Marty and looked down at the hefty bulge.

"God, you're a sexy motherfucker," he said to Marty with a smile.

Marty smiled back at him and said, "Why don't you go out tonight? Maybe you need to get some fresh air. I'll be all right. I have some more work to do anyway." Marty was a writer of gay erotica, and he worked from home and often into the night, so it was not unusual for him to suggest Wayne go out on his own.

"You sure?"

"Yeah … besides you seem a little distracted lately. Why don't you go to The Falcon. I hear the fleet is in town," Marty said with a grin.

Wayne agreed. He stripped off his business clothes, and although it had been a decade, Marty still got a thrill looking at his silver-fur covered muscular lover as he walked to the shower. He thought about joining him but decided it was best to leave Wayne alone.

Within an hour, Wayne was on his way to The Falcon, and Marty was tapping away at his computer.

The Falcon was the town's oldest leather bar, and on some nights, Wayne and Marty could swear there were still patrons there from opening night. However, The Falcon's location was advantageous as it was located near the Norfolk Naval Station, and when the fleet was in, it was hopping with hunky sailors looking for a good time.

Upon Marty's suggestion, Wayne dressed low key this evening and was wearing jeans, a black leather belt, a black T-shirt, and black motorcycle boots. He also decided to go commando, but that didn't stop him from putting on a leather studded cock-ring that Marty had recently bought for him. He entered The Falcon, nodded at a few familiar faces and seated himself at the bar. No sooner had he ordered a beer, when a hunky blond, who was obviously a sailor, sat next to him. Having served in the Navy, Wayne could spot a sailor from a mile away. Marty had also served in the Navy and was still a sailor when he met Wayne.

"What's your rate?" Wayne asked knowing that the word 'rank' did not apply to Navy enlisted men.

"Senior Chief Petty Officer," the blond responded in an equally hunky voice. "You must have served."

"Twenty years … Master Chief Petty Officer," Wayne responded.

"I guess that makes you the Daddy," the hunk said as he swigged his beer.

Wayne smiled but did not respond.

"So, Master Chief Petty Officer, what are you looking for tonight?"

Wayne took a good long look at the hunk. He was thickly muscled, not unlike Marty, but with piercing blue eyes rather than Marty's green eyes. He had to be no older than thirty.

"What's your name, sailor?"

"Adam, and yours, Daddy?"

"Wayne," he told him while his eyes trailed down to the large basket that strained the crotch of his jeans. Adam was wearing a white T-shirt that hid little of his physique, and Wayne liked what he saw, but again, he just wasn't in the mood. "I have a partner ... we have an understanding ... but I'm just not in the mood to play Daddy tonight ... I hope you understand."

Adam looked right at Wayne, put his hand on Wayne's crotch and said, "Good. Because I'm not in the mood to play boy." He gave Wayne a squeeze, released him and looked up at the TV screen, which was showing some reality nonsense no one cared to watch.

Wayne took a swig of his beer, and suddenly he was intrigued. He had never played submissive. He never had to. His hair had gone prematurely gray, and for as long as he was into the scene, he gladly played the Daddy. Being with Marty was easy because as big as Marty was, he loved being the boy. This was a huge turn-on when they first met as Wayne never dated anyone taller than he, especially someone who was also more muscular, and finding a muscleboy who enjoyed taking orders was a treat indeed. They were also madly in love with each other, but they always had an understanding. They knew men were pigs and monogamy was near impossible. The only rule was they had to give total disclosure – and all the details. Marty loved hearing the details, often including them in his writing or just jacking off while listening to Wayne recount his escapades.

Funny thing was Wayne, who was twenty years older, played way more than Marty did. He once questioned him about this, feeling guilty for always engaging in extracurricular activities. Marty said that as a submissive he oftentimes found it hard to trust people, so he preferred to be careful as the scenes he enjoyed opened someone up to serious injuries if one got carried away. He also assured Wayne that he was totally cool with Wayne playing around, joking that he only had a few good years left. Wayne ended up taking Marty over his knee and spanking him for that comment and ended up with his muscleboy's spunk all over his leg as a result. Then Wayne handcuffed Marty and fucked him doggy-style on the floor as punishment for not feeding his spunk to his Daddy. Marty was sure to let Wayne know when he was about to blow, and Wayne flipped him over and slapped Marty's balls while swallowing his load, and his boy was in heaven.

Wayne looked over at Adam and thought about the proposition. He could not remember the last time someone offered to dominate him. Did anyone ever offer? He thought back but could not recall.

"You got a place?" Wayne asked, surprised at his quickness to respond.

"I got a friend with a basement set-up ... you interested?" Adam said, looking over at Wayne.

Wayne finished his beer, set the bottle on the bar, spun to face Adam and said, "If you got the balls, yeah, I'm interested."

Adam gulped down the rest of his beer, got up from his stool and headed out the bar.

Once outside, he grabbed Wayne's ass and said, "My friend's place is a short drive, you got a car?"

Wayne agreed to drive, and they drove over to Granby Street to his friend's house. Upon pulling into the driveway, Wayne started to get a little nervous. He thought about how Marty said he needed to be careful as a submissive and not all guys could be trusted. Although Adam was a bit shorter than Wayne, he was packed with muscle. Wayne also thought about 'Don't Ask, Don't Tell' and wondered if this guy would kill him when all was said and done to protect his career.

"Listen, I'm not sure ..." Wayne began.

"Hey, I know," Adam interrupted. "Look, I'm not out to hurt you, just have a good time. We'll even set some ground rules if you like."

"OK," Wayne answered. "No bareback, no blood, no scat, and no drugs."

"That's cool. I gotta stay safe if I want to keep my job."

"Nothing that will leave a mark, or at least a permanent one, as I have to go to work on Monday," Wayne said with a smile.

"Totally cool," Adam agreed. He then exited the car, and Wayne did the same.

Wayne stopped Adam before they reached the door, grabbed his arm and said, "And, I don't bottom. I don't get fisted and nothing gets shoved up there."

Adam looked at Wayne's ass and shook his head, "Too bad … but I guess that's cool, too."

They entered the house, and Adam took off his shirt right after closing the front door. Wayne took a look at Adam's body, and his breath was taken away. The Senior Chief Petty Officer had the body of a god, covered in light blond hair, and he thought that this guy would be perfect for Marty, who liked that type. He reached over to grab a pec, but Adam grabbed his wrist and said, "I didn't say you could touch me."

"Yes, Sir," Wayne answered as he followed him into the kitchen.

"You want something to drink?"

Thinking he better keep his wits about him, Wayne asked for water. Adam pulled two bottles of water out of the fridge and handed one to Wayne.

"My friend is out to sea, so he said I could use his place whenever I am in town and on leave," he told Wayne.

He then put his bottle down and reached for Wayne's shirt. Wayne didn't resist as Adam pulled his shirt over his head. He obviously liked what he saw and roughly felt Wayne's muscles. He then reached for Wayne's belt, but stopped.

"Take off your boots, boy."

Wayne did as he was ordered.

"Now the jeans."

Wayne again obeyed. He was now naked except for the leather studded cock-ring, and his dick was getting hard and almost to its full thick nine inches. Adam grabbed his dick and said, "Nothing like a boy with a big dick ... you need to piss?"

"Yes, Sir."

"The bathroom's right over there," Adam said as he pointed across the hall. "Leave the door open."

Wayne did as he was told. His dick went down slightly as he started to piss, and just as his stream started, Adam walked in and watched him piss. Wayne looked over, and Adam was now naked with the exception of a brass cock-ring that encased one of the thickest cocks he had ever seen. Wayne figured hard it was probably seven inches and at least seven or even eight around also. Wayne finished pissing and shook his cock, and as he went to step out, Adam stopped him.

"Grab mine, I gotta go."

Wayne wrapped his hand around the Senior Chief Petty Officer's cock and pointed it at the bowl. Adam let go with a strong stream of piss that would make a garden hose jealous, and the feeling of holding that thick rod while it drained caused Wayne's cock to rise up to full attention. When Adam was done, he shook his cock for him, and it started getting hard from the attention.

"Don't move," Adam said as he exited the bathroom.

He returned seconds later with a collar and a leash. He snapped the collar around Wayne's neck and led him out of the bathroom down the hall and downstairs to the basement.

The basement was not the dungeon Wayne expected. There was a bed, a dresser and not much else. It was dimly lit and smelled a bit musty. Adam led Wayne over to the bed and ordered him to lie down on his back. He then took the leash and secured it to the wall on a hook behind the bed. Adam then reached under the bed and grabbed a rubber restraint and secured Wayne's left wrist, walked around and did the same with the right wrist. Adam admired the sight before him then secured Wayne's ankles the same way he secured his wrists.

Wayne was alternating between being turned on and being nervous. Adam sensed this and walked over to the head of the bed, bent down and kissed Wayne hard on the mouth wrestling his tongue with Wayne's.

"Don't worry, boy. Daddy's gonna take good care of you," he said as he released his mouth then he ran his fingers through Wayne's hair.

Wayne's dick started to get hard again as he watched Adam walk over to the dresser and admired how the sailor's muscular butt flexed as he bent down to open the bottom drawer.

Adam turned around holding two nipple clamps and a candle. He walked over to Wayne and scanned his body before putting the nipple clamps on him. Wayne moaned when the clamps were applied, and his cock let out a stream of precum, which did not go unnoticed.

"Whatta ya know, you little pig, leaking like a faucet," Adam said with a smile.

Adam then located a lighter on the dresser and lit the candle. He walked over to Wayne holding the lit candle about twelve inches above Wayne's chest. Wayne felt assured at that moment because an expert knew to hold the candle to allow the wax to cool a bit on its way down and not leave a scar. For the first time, Wayne truly relaxed in Adam's presence.

Wayne flinched when the first drop landed on his chest, and his dick twitched and leaked some more. Adam worked the wax down his torso, and with each drop, Wayne leaked. By the time, Adam reached his balls (he skipped his dick), there was enough precum to fill a bucket. Wayne was in ecstasy as his nipples were pinched hard by the clamps and the hot wax landed on his big smooth balls. He also knew that if Adam kept that up, he was going to come, and somehow Adam also sensed this. He stopped dripping wax on Wayne and blew out the candle.

Adam walked back over to the bed and twisted one of the nipple clamps causing Wayne to half moan, half scream, then he squeezed the other one getting the same reaction. Without saying a word, Adam climbed on top of Wayne and straddled his face, facing away from him, dropping his huge nuts toward his mouth and his ass toward his nose.

"Lick my balls, boy."

Wayne went to town on those furry balls. He slathered them and rolled them in his mouth and tried to get both in his mouth at once. This was not easy considering he was restrained and collared. Adam's muscular legs did a good job of holding him up, so he did not crush Wayne's face, but this was not easy as Wayne was an oral expert, and Adam's cock was leaking almost as much as Wayne's. Adam then scooted forward.

"Lick my hot hole, boy."

And, Wayne did as he was told. He did his best to get his tongue between those muscular cheeks and licked the blond fur-covered hole, almost coming just from the feeling of having this musclehunk squatting over his face.

Adam never experienced anything like Wayne's technique, and the sight of Wayne's huge leaking cock was making him want more. He let Wayne get him really wet then he hopped off the bed.

"Good boy."

Wayne's tongue was sore, but in a good way.

Adam walked over to the dresser again and opened the top drawer and pulled out a bottle of Gun Oil, a packet of condoms and a ball gag.

Wayne started to protest, but Adam was quick to place the ball gag over his mouth. Now, Wayne was starting to get scared again, but Adam leaned down, ran his fingers through his hair and said, "Relax, boy. I know the rules." Then he grabbed Wayne's still raging dick. "And you better not lose this hard-on, boy."

Adam opened the condom packet with his teeth and rolled it onto Wayne's dick. He then pumped some of the Gun Oil into his palm, rubbed some on Wayne's cock and then lubed his ass with his own fingers.

"Now, boy, if you fuck Daddy really good, I'll have a nice treat for you."

Adam again straddled Wayne, but facing him this time, and with one fell swoop impaled himself on Wayne's thick nine inches. He then grabbed the nipple clamps and rode that hard cock while twisting on those clamps. Wayne bucked up as best he could while the blond musclehunk sailor gave his own quads a good workout riding him up and down. Adam's thick cock grew even thicker with each thrust, and the head was swollen and purple and smacking against his belly. Wayne felt his own cock growing in length as he felt sensations he had not felt in a long time.

"Come on, boy, fuck me good!" Adam ordered.

With the ball gag, he was finding it hard to respond, but his eyes said it all.

Adam stopped twisting the clamps and flexed his biceps for Wayne and licked them admiring himself in the process while continuing to squat up and down on the large cock that impaled his hot hole. He then ran his hands over his pecs and gave Wayne quite a muscle show, flexing and feeling and licking himself.

'How does he know how much flexing turns me on?' Wayne thought. 'If he doesn't stop, I'm going to shoot!'

Adam continued to flex and squat until his dick was so hard it hurt. He reached down while still riding Wayne and removed the ball gag. Then, he pulled off Wayne's dick, moved forward and shoved his aching cock into Wayne's mouth, and his extra-thick cock shot a huge load into his mouth and down his throat. Wayne swallowed every delicious drop. All this action was too much for him, and he shot a huge load of his own into the condom that was still on his dick.

Adam stepped off the bed and looked down at the cum-filled rubber, and out of breath, but laughing, he said, "You fucking cum pig."

Wayne said nothing as he tried to catch his breath and continued to taste the semen from the sailor.

Adam then undid the restraints and the collar, and Wayne thanked him.

"You may wanna shower before you go home," Adam said.

Wayne took him up on his offer and once cleaned up and dressed was ready to leave, totally satisfied.

"Thank you, Sir. That was just what I needed," Wayne said as he shook Adam's hand.

"Well, it is what Marty said you wanted," Adam said with a wink.

"That little shit," Wayne responded shaking his head.

"Hey he ain't so little, and be nice to him. There aren't too many partners who would do what he did for you," Adam admonished.

Wayne knew Adam was right and knew at that moment he loved Marty more than anything.

"Tell me then. Did you ever bottom for Marty?" Wayne asked.

"With a cock like his? Of course. Don't you?" Adam asked as if the answer were obvious.

Wayne didn't answer. He gave Adam his number and suggested a three-way sometime, which Adam eagerly agreed would be fun.

Wayne arrived home an hour later to find Marty had already gone to bed. He stripped off his clothes and crawled into bed with his lover. Marty moaned as Wayne spooned him and grabbed his Daddy's hand, pulling it to his chest.

"Did you have a good time, Daddy?" he asked sleepily.

"If you fuck me, boy, I'll tell you all about it," Wayne growled.

Marty's eyes popped open, for he wasn't sure he heard what he thought he heard.

Wayne then pulled Marty on top of him, wrapped his legs around his boy's waist and begged him to drive his huge cock into him. Marty immediately grabbed some lube from the nightstand, greased up Wayne's asshole and rammed his huge hard cock all the way into his Daddy before he changed his mind.

In ten years, he had never fucked Wayne, and he was not about to miss this opportunity. Wayne didn't protest Marty's rough treatment and no-holds-barred fucking, actually getting totally turned on and rock-hard from the way his boy wasted no time impaling him. Marty leaned in and kissed him roughly and told him how much he loved him, while Wayne reciprocated, and Marty gave his Daddy the ride of a lifetime, practically fucking him into the next building. Wayne loved every minute of it as his muscleboy pounded his virgin hole with all his super strength, feeling those huge balls slap against his ass while Marty's muscular body glistened with sweat from the workout.

It was a total muscle fuck.

And, all the neighbors heard for hours that night was "Fuck me, boy! Come on, you can fuck Daddy harder than that!" along with the grunts and heavy breathing of a muscleboy giving his Daddy the ride of a lifetime.

Anchors aweigh!

About the Authors

DERRICK DELLA GIORGIA was born in Italy and currently lives between Manhattan and Rome. His work has been published in several anthologies and literary magazines. www.derrickdellagiorgia.com.

DIESEL KING is the proud poppa of his first short story collection, *A Good Time in the Hood*. As he completes his first and second novels, he is constantly adding to his publishing credits with STARbooks Press.

DONALD WEBB was born in South Africa and currently lives in Victoria, BC. His work has been published in several magazines. He is currently seeking an agent for a completed 74,000 word mystery novel. andon402@shaw.ca.

HL CHAMPA has been published in numerous anthologies. www.heidichampa.blogspot.com.

Published in dozens of gay erotic anthologies, **JAY STARRE** pumps out fiction from his home in Vancouver, Canada. His steamy gay historical novels were also published by STARbooks Press.

JESSE MONTEAGUDO is a freelance writer who lives in South Florida with his partner of over twenty-five years. Monteagudo's column, "Jesse's Journal," appears regularly in *South Florida Gay News*, *GayToday.com*, and *Bilerico.com*. This is Jesse's twenty-sixth contribution to a STARbooks Press anthology.

KALE NAYLOR is an Atlanta, Ga. based writer whose work has appeared in a number of gay erotic publications. An All-American frat boy, many of Naylor's stories are based on his real life misadventures. That is, the stories that won't get him in trouble with law enforcement are the only ones he's admitting to. www.kalenaylor.wordpress.com; www.kalenaylor.tumblr.com.

LANDON DIXON's writing credits include numerous stories in STARbooks Press anthologies.

LOGAN ZACHARY (loganzachary2002@yahoo.com) is an author of mysteries, short stories, and over forty erotica stories, living in Minneapolis with his partner, Paul, and his dog, Ripley, who runs the house. www.loganzacharydicklit.com.

MARK JAMES is a writer of gay erotica with several published short stories. www.asstr.org/~Shadowlands.

MILTON STERN is an author of biographies, novels, screenplays, and dozens of short stories, living in Maryland with Esmeralda, his rescue beagle. www.miltonstern.com.

R.W. CLINGER lives between Pittsburgh and Tarpon Springs, Florida. His fiction has appeared in various gay magazines and story compilations. STARbooks Press has published his novels.

RAWIYA is a happily married mother of two, who has had six short works accepted for publication. www.rawiyaserotica.blogspot.com.

ROB ROSEN, author of two novels, has been published to date in more than 100 anthologies. www.therobrosen.com.

About the Editor

ERIC SUMMERS resides in West Palm Beach, Fla. This is his fourteenth anthology for STARbooks Press. He is between the Daddy and Troll stages of his life.

BUTCH MEN PLAY HARDER!

BUTCH DIXON

g any underwear. "Excuse me," I said, having a hard time lookin

ed by that bulge in his crotch, "but don't I know you?" "Maybe,"

of t   bout a m

Ray   God, you

er?   in?" he a

'Lik   s stronge

ody   e on Gree

he l   s I ever sa

to t   any ideas

ing   e same

oul   ery long

rac   ne swell.

with   e in store

go c   behind s

ee u   in publi

" he   vent to th

cy.   grabbed

d. I

rac   t, so firn

t, ha

h my   bing dic

ng, I   n cock, b

ound of unzipping filled the small space. I don't know who's han

t before I knew it, I had his rod in my hand, and mine was in his.

do?" he asked, his tone challenging. I knew exactly, and sank to

9 781934 187906